THE LEAST OF THESE

Every life has value.

Mitchell S K

Also by Mitchell S. Karnes

Water Grave

An Abbey Rhodes Mystery
Volume 2

THE LEAST
OF THESE

MITCHELL S. KARNES

WordCrafts Press

The Least of These is a work of fiction. The author has endeavored to be as accurate as possible with regard to the times and places in which the events of this novel are set. Still, this is a novel, and all references to persons, places, and events are fictitious or are used fictitiously.

Scripture quotations taken from the (NASB®) New American Standard Bible®, Copyright © 1960, 1971, 1977, 1995, 2020 by The Lockman Foundation. Used by permission. All rights reserved. lockman.org

Scripture quotations marked (ESV) are from the ESV® Bible (The Holy Bible, English Standard Version®), copyright © 2001 by Crossway Bibles, a publishing ministry of Good News Publishers. Used by permission. All rights reserved.

To Room in the Inn,
Nashville Rescue Mission,
the Salvation Army,
and others who work with
Nashville's homeless population.
Thank you for showing us that every life has value.

"And the King will answer them, 'Truly, I say to you, as you did it to one of the least of these my brothers, you did it to Me.'"

~Matthew 25:40 (ESV)

Chapter One

Thursday, March 20, 5:45 AM—Davidson Street, Nashville

Death doesn't keep a schedule. Dispatch called at four-thirty this morning announcing another homicide in Nashville. Unfortunately, I was on my morning run and left my phone at the apartment. Once I saw the message, I showered, dressed, and added a touch of makeup. When I arrived at the crime scene in the warehouse district of Davidson Street, the officer directed me past the gate and to the right of a gravel split. It was a materials recycling lot approximately six hundred fifty feet wide and about five hundred feet deep from the streetside fence to the Cumberland River. It gave the owner access to the river, the railroad, and the street. They could move everything in and out by any of the three methods.

I stepped cautiously, avoiding puddles of water from last night's rain. I looked up and couldn't believe my eyes as I passed a second pile of scrap metal. It wasn't the dead body. I was getting used to seeing that. After all, what is a homicide without a dead body? There, amongst the gravel, dirt, scrap metal, loading trucks, and heavy machinery, sat a brand-new Bentley Continental GT. It was a stunning topaz blue, the newest color, and had to be worth at least a quarter of a million new—a sharp contrast to the rest of the scene. I caught myself gawking at its beauty, even with the visible blood and bullet holes throughout the front seats and the crushed right and rear panels. Parts of the bumper were loose on the ground. Someone had made three-inch deep ruts in the gravel, trying to back the Bentley out of the recycling lot in a hurry. The driver crashed through the plastic orange barrier, lodging the Bentley onto the pile of steel and scrap metal. If this hadn't been a crime scene, I might have cried over the loss of a priceless car.

Sam whistled. It was his way of saying, "Hurry up." I flashed my credentials as I ducked under the police tape. "Detective Abbey Rhodes, Homicide." The young officer waved me on, and I joined Sam. It was much colder than I remembered when I was running earlier. Of course, then I was wearing sweats and generating my own heat. My dress pants were thin and offered no defense against the cold, damp air.

Sam looked old—older than usual. "Well, Detective Tidwell, you certainly got an early start today," I said with a smile. Beneath it, my teeth were chattering.

"Nice of you to finally join us." He was in a sour mood.

That's my line. Punctuality was not one of Sam's strong suits—neither was his choice of clothing. If I didn't know better, I would venture that he was in his late sixties, not his fifties. Plain suits and winged-tip shoes went out before he started wearing them. Thankfully, some things like his skinny ties were making a comeback—no thanks to Sam. He was staring at his watch, hidden beneath his crime scene gloves. Anyway, I always beat him to the crime scene and the office. Not today.

Sam handed me a cup with my name written on it. "Iced Caramel Macchiato."

My favorite. "You remembered. That's so sweet." I took the cup from his hand. He'd been trying hard to be nice to me lately. No more looking at me like he just saw the ghost of his daughter, Molly. No more snide rookie remarks. No more tricks or traps. No old cop, new cop, just...

"Young people don't even know what real coffee is, Abbey." And there it was—the *young people* comment. I couldn't help the fact that I was twenty-five and looked fifteen. Sam took a sip of his drink to emphasize his point. "Coffee…black…hot." I watched the steam roll out of his mouth as he said a long, drawn-out, "Ahhh."

I was freezing. I needed to get Sam back on track and focus on the case so we could get on to the warmth of our Homicide offices. I said offices, but they were nothing more than a bunch of cubicles all jammed together. Sam and I shared one. "How did they find the crime scene? This is not something you see driving by." I turned and tried to see any visible line from the car to the street. There was none.

"On a 911 call," Sam said. "One of the drivers came in early to take his load to Chattanooga."

I glanced down at the body lying at Sam's feet. White male in his early twenties with curly brown hair and eyes frozen in fright or surprise, with a fatal wound in his neck and two in the chest. He wore faded blue jeans, a rugby shirt, and a leather jacket. The young man lay in a dark red patch of blood that had soaked into the gravel road. He held a small Ruger .380 in his right hand. I examined the car, approximately thirty feet north of the body. "That's a high-money Bentley." Both the driver and passenger side doors were open. I couldn't see inside from my current vantage point. As I walked past it on my way to his body, I noted that the interior was riddled with bullet holes and blood splatter. The car was set at an angle, the highest point being the right end of the trunk.

I walked over to examine the Bentley more closely. The driver's seat was soaked with blood. Without leaning in and grabbing it, I determined the pistol lying on the passenger floorboard to be a 44 Glock. I donned my Mylar gloves to preserve the integrity of our crime scene. "What do we have so far?" I asked, turning back to Sam, who was studying the body of the victim.

"Three GSWs, two to the chest and one to the neck. All kill shots." He pointed to the car. "It looks like he stopped the car-jacking, but at the cost of his life."

"Not dressed like a Bentley owner, and he's so young."

3

"Coming from you, that's something." There it was again—the jab at my youthful looks, which was how I like to put it instead of what I heard some men say. Sam winked. He could tell he was getting under my skin a bit. He pointed to the street just beyond the open passenger door. "Looks like the carjacker was hit multiple times. Blood trail leads out the passenger side, up the scrap heap of metal, and down the other side. Then, it heads northeast but stops at the edge of Davidson Street. There's a pretty good trail of blood in the gravel and pavement."

"An accomplice probably picked him up," I said as I counted the holes in the seats, dash, and passenger door panel. I walked over to Sam and the body. "Any ID?"

Sam held up the vic's wallet and phone. "The key fob is still in the console." Sam tossed the wallet to me and looked at his notes. "Dean Swain, twenty-two. According to the zip, he lives in the Buckhead section of Atlanta. Serious money."

I opened the wallet and looked at the ID to confirm what Sam told me. "That's either the owner at your feet or a young man who took the wrong turn during a joy ride." I turned my attention back to the Bentley. I carefully climbed on the pile. It wasn't easy. The scraps had sharp edges. Once around the open passenger side door, I opened the glove box. "Car's registered to Dean A. Swain. Our dead man is the owner. Wonder what he was doing here of all places? It's not the kind of place you would imagine seeing this kind of a car. Any sign of drugs?" That's the only reason I could find for this car being in the salvage lot.

"Not so far. The officers secured the sight at four-o-eight and interviewed the truck driver. One of them took photos of the scene. Officer Chen just finished the sketch, complete with accurate measurements. I haven't been here long myself. So far, no casings have been discovered."

"My guess is he either used a revolver, or he stopped to pick up his empties."

Sam looked up at me. "What about the car?"

4

"It's totaled."

"No kidding?" Sam asked sarcastically. I tested the solidity of the car's placement upon the plastic barrier and heap of metal before I leaned into the floorboard. I did my best not to compromise the crime scene or jeopardize the evidence. "We got casings here." I could see the brass. One lay on the console between the front seats, just two inches away from the key fob. The other two lay below the brake pedal. I reached under the driver and passenger seats. Nothing else. "Three forty-fours here." After examining the Glock, I added. "That's exactly how many are missing from the magazine."

"All three hit. Not an amateur. I'll wager he has to be an experienced shooter to score three kill shots while being shot at. I couldn't do that."

"Expert shooter; terrible driver." I didn't mean it to be funny, but Sam laughed.

He examined the bullet wounds in the boy's throat and chest. "I'd say the holes match a forty-four." Sam scratched his salt-and-pepper beard with his clean hand. Deep lines formed on his forehead. It was his *something doesn't fit* look. "We need to begin by focusing on the shooter. We have solid evidence for him. The rest we'll have to piece together."

I grabbed my knife and dug out one of the slugs lodged in the passenger door. "Nine-millimeter."

"You sure?" he asked with doubt in his voice.

"Positive." I dropped it in an evidence bag and dug another slug from the far-right edge of the dash. Same. "He was trying to back out while being shot at. The only way forward would have gone through Dean, who was holding a gun. There's no way Dean made these shots from his angle." I returned to Sam, glad to be out of the scrap pile. I sipped my drink and put my other hand in my coat pocket. "It's cold out here, especially this close to the river." In times like this, I wished I could drink my coffee like Sam did—hot and black. My iced Macchiato just made me cold on the inside too.

"It's the first day of spring, Abbey. Be thankful." He started whistling a bright song. He knew his peppy optimism aggravated me on days like this.

"It doesn't feel like spring." I jogged in place to create some body heat. Last night's rain brought in another cold front. "I should have dressed better but was rushing out the door." When I arrived at my army base in Grafenwoehr, Germany, everyone laughed at me, the little girl from Central America. The slightest cold front came in, and I would wear multiple layers under my heavy coat. I'd come from balmy Guatemala, after all. But I adjusted to the cooler climate of Germany a year into my service and didn't mind it. Then it happened all over again when I moved to Nashville, Tennessee, and I grew accustomed, once again, to the warm seasons of the south. Now, I was at the mercy of changing seasons. I felt the slightest downward dip in the thermometer, and I cringed. I was getting soft. Jumping up and down to warm up encouraged sniggering from the patrol officers. I didn't care. It warmed my body and made me feel better.

I glanced over the lot, which had small puddles of water. "What time did it rain yesterday?"

"Between eight and nine. It was short, but it came in pretty heavy." He stopped what he was doing and looked up. "What are you thinking, Abbey?"

"We're lucky. I can tell you this happened after nine o'clock. Dean Swain's clothes are dry. That tells us any footprints we find were made after the rain. Do we have a time of death?"

"Not yet. I'll get a preliminary time when the ME gets here. What do you think about the scene?"

I examined the footprints in the granules of the gravel. The rim around each impression was almost as precise as the plasters we made of crime scenes. There was a clear picture of last night's event. I could easily make out Dean's path from the car toward the river. The prints stopped abruptly twenty feet past where his body lay now. "Look here, Sam. I can see where Dean stopped and turned back."

"Meaning?" Sam asked. I'm sure he had his own theory by now. He probably wanted to hear mine. He was always encouraging me to grow in my observations.

"Well," I began in a whisper, almost as if I was talking to myself. "On the surface, Dean was dumb enough to leave his keys in his very expensive car. So he either trusted his passenger or thought he was alone. When he heard the car start, he stopped and ran back to see what had happened. He knew his key fob was still in the vehicle. When Dean came back this way, the driver panicked and shoved it in reverse while his door was still open. He hit the barrier with enough force to run it over and get stuck on top of the metal. He didn't go forward because Dean had his gun. In a panic, he floored it and spun out on the wet surface. Before he knew it, he'd wrecked the car and was hopelessly stuck on the debris."

"Where did the driver come from?" Sam asked, forcing me to fill in details off the top of my head. "Someone must have followed the Bentley here and taken advantage of its missing driver, who, for some reason, was walking toward the river. Then, when Dean ran toward the car, we had a shootout, and both parties were hit multiple times." Sam nodded. "Make sense to you, Sam?" I asked, hoping he was getting the same vibe.

"Not really. But that's what we're supposed to think." It was music to my ears. Sam had come a long way since the Ripley case when he wanted to jump at the first opportunity to close the deal and move on. Now, he was back to his old self, looking beneath the surface and searching for all the clues.

"Sam, don't you think this is odd?" He glanced up and smiled. I was still getting used to calling him by his first name. We'd grown close in my year and a half in Homicide. "Two major things are wrong with this scene. First, if you were shot in the chest and the neck, could you hold on to your gun?" He shook his head. I bent over and picked up the gun in Dean Swain's hand. "A three-eighty. Wrong caliber." I showed Sam the slugs in the bag. Ejecting the magazine from the Ruger, I pressed down on the top bullet. It didn't budge. I checked the chamber, and it was still empty. I smelled the barrel. All I could detect was cleaning oil. "All the bullet holes in the car tell me the shots came from behind the driver's door. Dean is nearly thirty feet to the front. Whoever staged this scene was either in a hurry or didn't know what he was doing."

"That—or he thinks we're stupid, which adds a different animal into the mix." Sam studied Dean's hand. "When CSI gets here, have them swab his hand. I bet they don't find any powder residue on it."

"Smell it. The gun is clean. It's not been fired for some time."

Sam took the gun from me and smelled it. He nodded and flipped it over. "Serial numbers are still in place. We'll run a search for the owner. Probably stolen."

I noticed a bulge in Dean Swain's ankle, bent over, and pulled up his right pant leg. "Ankle holster. Small enough to fit a three-eighty." Swain's wounds matched the forty-four, but the slugs I pulled out of the car were nine-millimeter. Dean didn't shoot the carjacker, at least not with this gun. "There had to be another shooter, Sam. It fits the evidence so far. But I'm confused. If he was defending Swain, the shots would be justified. So, why leave the scene? Why not report it?"

"That's a good question. I've been wondering that myself. He probably panicked. Or maybe he has a record. Maybe the gun's not registered. Or maybe he ran after the shooter. Whatever the reason, he left."

"What about a security guard?" I asked.

"I already checked. They laughed and said, 'Not to watch scrap metal.'"

I examined the prints around Dean's body. I knelt behind his body and looked at the Bentley. Holding out my hands like I was shooting a gun, I tried to line up the shots. The open driver's door blocked my line of sight. "Not possible to hit anything but the exterior of the driver's door from here. I looked down and noticed another set of footprints led to Dean's body and away to the back of the lot. They disappeared when they reached the blacktop drive.

From Dean's body, I took a step to my right, another and another, and finally a fourth. In that position, I could see clearly into the car. "The first shots came from this angle or even further to my right. I still can't see the front of the passenger door or dash."

"Assuming the shots occurred after the car hit the barrier," Sam said.

I knelt. The ground was harder here and didn't display good prints. I had to search in a wide arc to find the trail. "Sam, the prints start here," I said from the rear of a semi-trailer sixty feet from the Bentley. I searched the trailer's exterior and found a lone nine-millimeter casing stuck in the treads. "I got something." Sam came to my side and bagged the evidence. I looked back at the body. Dean bled out where he lay. The gravel absorbed almost all of the blood, making a perfect marker for later.

"Do you see any blood over where you are?" Sam asked.

I glanced around. "No, but there were only three casings in the car, and Dean was hit exactly three times. The other shooter must have surprised the car thief. He obviously hit him. The seats are soaked, and the trail leads out the far side to the street." I examined the ground around the trailer. "We have some good shoeprints here if we want to make plasters."

"No other casings. How many shots were fired at the driver of the car?" Sam asked.

"At least five that I could find. That doesn't include any stray bullets or direct hits still lodged in the carjacker's body."

"Someone cleaned up the scene and tried to make it look like Dean fired back. Why would they do that?"

"But Dean didn't get a shot off," I insisted.

"No. He didn't. But the shooter wants us to think he did. For some reason, he wants to keep himself anonymous—free of the investigation."

"If he really wanted us to think it was just Dean and the car-jacker, why not take the time to fire off several rounds from Dean's gun first? And why not take the time to line up the body with the shots taken?" This was an amateur job of staging a scene. This wasn't a trained killer, or he'd know better. Any shooter worth his salt would know the differences between a three-eighty, a nine-millimeter, and a forty-four. "Who would have shot the driver and tried to hide the fact that he was here?"

"I don't know, Abbey, but I have a more puzzling question. Where's the carjacker now? We know he's wounded and lost a lot of blood. Assuming someone picked him up at the street, based on the blood trail, where would they have gone?"

"To get emergency help," I said. "He'd have to get help quickly, or he would bleed out, too."

"That's right. If he lost that much blood, he was in dire need of immediate medical attention."

I paused and thought for a moment. The first and most obvious answer would be a hospital. They had the equipment and the staff to handle gunshot wounds successfully. Secondary sources of healing and possible surgery would be a veterinarian hospital or clinic, a dental surgeon's facility, or an urgent clinic. "I know we need to follow the clues to the carjacker's identity, Sam, but I also want to know who shot him. Who else was here last night?"

"That's the million-dollar question, Abbey," Sam said, pausing to sip his coffee. He held the cup in both hands to absorb its heat. Then, he sipped from it again. "We have a crime to solve, Abbey. It's what we do best."

"Okay, Sam. Let's do our due diligence here, find every available clue, study every aspect of the scene, and then we can run scenarios back at Homicide where it's warm." A gust of wind blew my hair over my face. I set my cup on the ground, pulled my hair back into a ponytail, and secured it with a black hairband that I kept on my wrist. I turned back to Sam. "When will the ME's office get here?"

"They're running a little later than usual. They'll get here when they get here. Don't worry about it."

"Any witnesses? Anyone see or hear anything unusual last night?"

"None and no cameras in sight."

"Someone had to hear this many shots," I said. The lot was too close to Broadway and its outside activities for no one to hear gunshots.

"What's your gut telling you, kid?" he asked.

There it was again, the *kid* comment. I didn't know if that made it worse for me or for him. If I were a kid, that would make him an old man. *Focus, Abbey.* "Well, at first glance, it looks like a random carjacking that went wrong. Not only did he damage the car and lodge it on the barrier, he was shot several times before he could escape. Of course, you know I don't go with first glances. This car would be big money to anyone willing to steal it. Why is it back in the middle of this lot, and who was waiting to find it?"

He smiled. "Go on."

"Also, the timing is too convenient. We have some rich kid out here in the middle of the night two weeks before the council votes on a development plan for the East Bank Project. My gut says he's tied to the project in some way. We have to dig into Dean's background and see why he chose this lot for a stroll last night. Any way you slice it, there's more here than meets the eye."

"Well, then, let's get at it," Sam said. "I'm cold."

"It's spring. Remember?" I noticed something fall from Sam's beard as he laughed. I bent over and picked it up. "Hey, you didn't say you brought chocolate donuts. Where are they?"

"Who told you?" Sam asked, looking quickly at the officer to his right. The officer put his hands up in the air as if to say, "Don't look at me." Sam had a guilty look, and he couldn't hide it. "Honestly, I meant to give you one, but I ate them both. I couldn't help myself."

I leaned forward and brushed the remaining pieces of a chocolate donut from his beard. "Let's just hope our carjacker and shooter are as careless and obvious as you." I laughed and punched him lightly in the shoulder.

We meticulously analyzed the crime scene, photographing tire and shoe impressions and measuring the different strides of the steps. I photographed most of the site myself, even though I knew an officer had already done so. I also mapped out the area specific to the crime scene and bagged everything inside the car. There were two partially smoked cigars. Sam bagged those as well. We walked around the lot several times to ensure we didn't miss anything else.

Sam said, "We need to get a list of workers on the lot from the end of the rain to the time of death and rule out their shoe prints."

"Sam, they ought to make great casts of all the prints." The rain hardened the concrete powder, which made its own mold. "I hope they can make casts of the various-sized shoeprints. It could tell us how many people had been in the lot since last night's rain."

"We'll see." He shouted to an officer at the site, "Make sure they get casts of each print marked. And don't forget to list the location for each."

The ME's office arrived and signed the paperwork to take possession of the body. They gave an approximate time of death between twelve and two. A few minutes later, the CSI team began their site work. We returned to our cars and made plans to sort through the evidence back at Homicide. My body was almost numb from the cold. Just as I was getting in, a gust of wind knocked the empty cup from my hand and blew it to the far side of the lot. Sam said to let it go, but I hated to litter, even if it was in a scrap yard lot like this. The cup rolled here and there. I must have looked like an idiot chasing the cup around like a cat chases a light on the floor. Another gust of wind finally lodged it beside the fence separating the parking lot from the Cumberland River.

I ran to get it and noticed a flash of light from the opposite bank. The sunrise reflected off someone's binoculars. A man in fatigues was watching me. *Maybe he was watching the events of last night, too.* "Sam, come here!" Just as I called out, the man dashed into the brush.

Chapter Two

I rode with Sam as we hopped on the interstate and crossed to the other side of the river. We followed the split to the right and took the first exit. Backtracking on the road parallel to the river, we passed what looked like an old school or possibly a church and took a left. Three old campers were parked on the left of the road. As we passed them and headed down the winding road, I noticed several camping tents at the top of a small bluff. Just below that, between the bluff and the road, trash was scattered across the side of the hill: mattresses, bags, furniture, and debris. Sam continued down the road and drove across the railroad tracks toward the riverbank. He pulled inside a fenced-in gravel parking lot that held an abandoned loading dock for the railroad running to its south and pulled up to a chain link fence separating the lot from the river.

From the car, I could see several box-shaped lodgings covered with blue tarps, which served as makeshift lodgings for the homeless along this side of the river. It was a long but narrow camp that stretched two hundred feet along the bank of the Cumberland River. As expected, the ground was full of trash in all directions, although it was not as prevalent as the two camps on the above road. About three hundred feet to our right, the land rose into a small hill that plateaued beneath the interstates above. I could see four small two-man tents scattered about the pillars supporting the interstate, making a fourth camp. The concrete pillars were approximately fifty-five feet in length and five feet wide. The tents were set up on the river side of the pillar. That portion was on federal property, but the homeless were a minor nuisance. The government didn't bother enforcing the law there. If it did, its agents would have to address the relocation of the camp's inhabitants. Easier to ignore them.

I had mixed feelings about these people, having been homeless myself. On one hand, they were at the mercy of others. It was nearly impossible to get a job without a home address, not that they could afford a home in this economy. On the other hand, I'd learned that where there was a will, there was a way. Sure, you might have to compromise your standards—do things you might not be proud of—but you could make it. You could rise above the need to beg and live at the mercy of others. In my opinion, homelessness was a choice and, in some cases, the opportunity to shake off the shackles of society's rules and restrictions. In other cases, a single mistake threw away a different, more prosperous life. It threatened to bring back horrible memories.

"Are you coming?"

I nodded and got out of the car. We walked toward the fence to our west. "I saw him about sixty yards that way," I said. "He was wearing army fatigues and had binoculars in his hand."

"Keep a hand on your Sig, Abbey. They're a little paranoid of strangers, especially cops. Even though we're dressed in plain clothes, they can tell." Sam had his right hand on his Glock. He hated the idea of shooting anyone, so he must have been scared.

Unfortunately, I knew how the homeless population felt. When I was kicked out in my mid-teens, I was terrified. I was hyper-vigilant, a term I learned to savor as an MP in the Army based in Germany. As a child, vigilance was not a positive experience. It was exhausting and filled me with anxiety, but it was a matter of survival.

Trying to lighten the mood, I teased Sam, "Scared?"

"Cautious and realistic." He tried to convince me he wasn't afraid, but Sam's voice betrayed his serious nature and anxiety. "Just keep a watchful eye."

14

"Always." *Ever Vigilant!* Being on high alert didn't faze me, but the thought of being watched triggered haunting memories. I fought the images that were threatening to overtake me once again—experiences of helplessness and vulnerability—times of complete and utter isolation. Unlike whistling in the dark, which was a vain attempt to ease your fears, listening to Sam's voice calmed, soothed, and kept me focused on the task at hand. I prayed he would continue uttering his advice and assure me he had my back. In times like these, I didn't mind Sam being fatherly to me, as long as he didn't demean me or my ability as a detective. I was probably more capable of protecting him than he was of me.

As we slipped through an opening in the fence leading to the river, I scanned the brush in all directions. Orienting myself by the opposite bank, I said, "I saw him at the river's edge right over there."

"Gotcha." Sam glanced to our right and whispered, "We've got movement just beyond the campfire."

I nodded. I'd spotted them the moment we breached the fence. Thankfully, the shrubs were only beginning to leaf, which helped us keep an eye on the three men moving our way from the main river camp. A tall, wiry man in a dingy blue jacket carried a small hatchet. Another held a machete. They flanked a more petite man in the middle. Luckily, the bare branches also helped us scan for the man in fatigues. "Sam, over there." He stood still, watching us again. He put his right hand to his cheek and mumbled something before scrambling back into the woods toward the city's heart. The thicker trunks made a better cover for him. We followed him as far as we could but lost him as he doubled back on the railroad tracks. "Where did he go?" I asked.

Sam was huffing and puffing. He finally stepped on the tracks. With his hands on his knees, Sam looked back and forth. "I don't see him."

I wanted to continue the search, but I let Sam catch his breath. Sam was terribly out of shape. A man in his fifties, Sam despised exercise, and it showed. The man was fast and light on his feet. I was sure he knew these woods better than we did. Even if I left Sam here, I didn't know which direction to look for him. He was probably watching us from his hiding place. "Let's head back. No use wasting our time trying to catch him now."

We followed the tracks in silence until we hit the road where we entered. The only sound was Sam's heavy breathing. I'm sure they could hear it down in the camp. We followed the gravel road as it twisted back to the loading dock. The more I thought about it, the more certain I was that this man had seen something in the scrapyard last night. He seemed to have a keen sense of awareness and noticed us immediately. He was toying with us. We entered the gate and headed to Sam's car. "Isn't that Susan Ripley's car?" he asked.

"Where?"

"Over there next to the woods."

A blue Honda Odyssey with a bumper sticker that read, Follow me to Living Water Church. What was she doing here? "That's Susan's car, all right." I ran to it. "It's empty." My eyes darted left and right, scanning the various *homes* in the camp. My vigilance went into overdrive. Didn't she know how dangerous this place was? I slipped through the break in the fence again. The tall, slender man grabbed his machete. This time, I headed straight for the group of men standing next to the fire. "What did you do with her?" They ignored me. I pulled out my Sig and shouted, "Hey! I'm talking to you."

Susan climbed out of a small green tent. "Abbey, put that down!"

I wanted to hug her and hit her at the same time. "What do you think you're doing, Susan?"

"Put the gun away first, and then I'll explain." She looked over my shoulder. "You too, Sam."

We holstered our guns but kept our hands at the ready. I glared at the smaller man in the middle; he was grinning ear to ear. I could sense an arrogance about him. He was flanked by the men with the hatchet and machete and acted like he was king of the river. "You think it's funny?"

16

"What are you going to do? Shoot me? You're in my home now, Sweety," he said.

Sweety? I wanted to slap the grin right off his face. He didn't look much older than me. I despised that southern attitude where people younger than I was would call me *sweety*, whether it be a waitress at a diner, a clerk at a gas station, or some woman in the drive thru. What a condescending word. I'm sure they didn't mean it that way, but he did. I had to restrain myself.

"Who do you think you are?" I snapped. I flashed my badge. "I'm Detective Abbey Rhodes, Nashville Homicide."

"Well, Abbey Rhodes, I'm the mayor of this little city." He looked up and down my body, either sizing me up as an enemy or scoping me out as a woman. It unsettled my nerves. He was intentionally rude and condescending. He was pushing one of my biggest pet peeves—disrespect.

Susan reached out and put a hand on my left shoulder. She'd become an expert at reading my emotions over the last fifteen months. It was like she could read my thoughts as well.

"Easy, Abbey."

I frowned at her, then turned back to him. I could play his game if that's what he wanted. I said, "No, sir. You're on Davidson County land…" I put my hand back on the handle of my Sig. "What's your name?"

"Damien Jones. This is public land. If you're here to try and scare us off, you've got another think coming. We don't scare so easily."

As much as I wanted to kick him into the Cumberland, that's not why we were there. Sam stepped to my right. I saw his hand on his gun as well. "We're not here to dispute your right to assemble here."

"Sure," Damien said before he spit at our feet. "You're all alike. Act tough until someone with equal power pushes back."

"Equal power?" I scoffed at him. I'd take my gun over their hatchet and machete any day.

17

Sam took a step forward. "Abbey, why don't you talk with Susan while Damien and I have a little chat."

Susan tugged me into the little tent. "*Shhh.* You're embarrassing yourself."

"Embarrassing myself, or you?" I knew it was uncalled for, but sometimes my mouth ran ahead of me.

"Calm down. They're peaceful people."

"Calm down? Peaceful people don't carry hatchets and machetes."

"They're just defending themselves. You did walk into their homes and threaten them."

"Threaten them? They'd know if I was threatening them."

"Abbey, please." Susan tried to calm me down—tried to assure me she was safe and I didn't need to worry about her.

"How well do you actually know them, Susan? Sam and I are here hunting down a possible witness to a murder that happened directly across the river from here. So, please don't patronize me. I'm just doing my job."

"Sorry. That wasn't my intention." She rubbed my back. I tensed to the touch. "I just need you to relax. I'm okay. You're causing a scene and making matters worse. Trust me, please. We're safe."

"Safe?"

Susan's voice lowered to a whisper. "You know they can hear us through the side of the tent."

"I don't care who hears us," I said in a louder voice. I wanted them to hear me. I wanted them to know they annoyed me. I wanted them to realize I had the power to clear them out of this site.

"I do." Susan forced a smile and pointed to a skinny, dirty woman lying on a new sleeping bag. She wore a red and black checkered lumberjack coat and smelled like a soured dumpster. "This is my friend Christy."

I nodded. How did Susan know this woman? How were they friends?

"She's a missionary of sorts," Susan added.

Missionary? She knew that wasn't a comforting thought for

18

me. It was probably the worst thing she could say to make me relax. A witness was hiding somewhere in this camp. He may even be a suspect. "Susan, you may think it's safe, but you don't know that for certain. I want you to leave this place now."

The little woman sat up. I could tell it took great effort to do so. "She's safe as long as she's with me. So are you," she said. I couldn't help but laugh. This woman couldn't even protect herself. She could barely sit up in her own tent. What could she do if they threatened her?

"Abbey, that's rude."

"At least it's honest. I'm sorry, Susan, I have a gun and military training. I can take care of myself," I said confidently and spitefully. "You have neither." Looking at the pile of bones before me, I said, "Lady, you're the one who needs help. I can tell you're weak and malnourished."

"Abbey Rhodes, how dare you! That's why I'm here. She's starving to death."

I took a deep breath and counted to ten. Anyone else would have been lying on the ground. I took a few breaths, but my anger still boiled. "Then take her somewhere she can get a hot meal, a bath, and warm lodging, Susan."

Susan started to say something else, but Christy waved her hand. "This is my mission field. I will stay here to care for these people and share the Gospel of Jesus Christ with all who will listen." Her voice betrayed her condition. She was weak and fragile.

Susan wiped a tear that trickled down her cheek. "She's our version of Mother Teresa."

I could tell the woman had moved her. She didn't, however, move me. Mother Teresa was strong. She could work. She was a physical help to her mission field.

"If she's the missionary, why are you here?" I could tell Susan didn't like this side of me, but I was all business when I was on duty. I was Ever Vigilant, especially now. And I wasn't in any mood for her church talk—not today.

"I bring her food and supplies." The old woman lay on a new sleeping bag and pillow. I also noticed brand-new pots and pans for cooking and boiling water. Susan pleaded with desperate eyes. "I know you don't understand, Abbey, but I need to do this. She needs me."

I knew what she meant, but before I could stop myself, I said, "Yeah, well, Hannah and Danny already lost one parent." I turned away. I knew that hurt her, and it was meant to. The comment wasn't as much about the kids' future as my fears. Susan was my only real friend outside the Daniels family—and they were more parental surrogates than friends. Nothing against Sam, but he was my work partner. Only another woman could possibly understand my problems and my past. Susan accepted me, scars and all. I needed her. She'd accepted my shortcomings and past, yet I still couldn't share everything. I'd known Lieutenant Daniels for four and a half years, and he only knew a sliver of the whole truth. No one knew all of it, and I planned to keep it that way. I was the only living person who knew what I'd done to survive in Guatemala and how I'd finally escaped. I'd buried the details deep inside my mind, never to resurface.

The silence was deafening. Susan stared at the side of the tent. She didn't have an answer for it. She knew the kids were still getting over the loss of Mark Ripley, their adopted father. She knew the pain they carried. She had a load of her own. I knew, deep down, that ministering to these people was Susan's way of moving forward.

"Why are *you* here?" Christy asked. Her voice was disarming, almost comforting—the voice of a seasoned counselor.

I knew that trick, and my walls snapped back in place. "I'm here because a man was murdered across the river last night. A flash of light caught my attention when I left the crime scene this morning. I noticed a man in fatigues watching me with binoculars from this side of the river."

"Did you say a man in fatigues?" She pursed her lips. "Oh, my. I'm afraid he will not be able to help you."

"He who?"

"Have a seat, Miss Rhodes." I glanced at Susan, and she shrugged her shoulders. "Yes. She's spoken of you. We pray for you every week."

They pray for *me*? That didn't sit well. It wasn't that I didn't need the help. I didn't want the prayers—prayers wasted to a God who'd ignored my childhood pleas for help. "I've heard that phrase before from other self-righteous people." Was I including Susan in that comment? I couldn't stand people who thought they were better than others—especially me. I certainly didn't need help from a scrawny, little homeless woman.

She cut off my thoughts, saying, "He's a soldier, and his last name is Rushing—assuming that is his uniform. If I've read it right, he has the rank of Lance Corporal. In my humble opinion, he suffers from PTSD with possible dissociative symptoms."

I suffered from PTSD, but I was high-functioning. She was implying he wasn't. "Dissociative symptoms? Does he have multiple personalities?"

"No, Dear. I think he is confused about time and place. He seems to be acting out his former duty."

I had to mentally discard the *Dear* comment so I could stay on task. "You sound like my counselor. How do you know so much about him?"

"I'll take that as a compliment. I served over twenty years as a licensed social worker and counselor until I got frustrated with the hoops they expected me to jump through." She paused and took a slow, deep breath. Several moments later, she added, "So I became a missionary."

"Just like that?"

She nodded and smiled. So did Susan.

Missionary? That word struck a dissonant chord deep in my bones. I knew it was wrong to judge every missionary by my father's hyper-conservative theology and critical character, but I couldn't help it. The final straw that broke our relationship was his accusation that I tempted and falsely accused the youth leader of rape. I was a fourteen-year-old girl who was led astray by a youth leader's lies and manipulation, who was given alcohol to lower my guard and was then raped. Somehow, that was my fault? That event ruined my life. My father cast me out like garbage, accusing me of intentionally acting and dressing provocatively. Yeah, right. Like I wanted men to ogle and desire me—look at me like an object designed merely for their pleasure. He cast me out of his sight and forbade my mother and sister from having further contact with me. That's what a missionary was to me. I could feel the emotional walls thickening.

I stared at this little woman. I could see her lips moving, but the past clutched at me. All I could hear was its voice—its taunting words of worthlessness and inadequacy. I could feel myself withdrawing, descending into the deep darkness of the pit.

Susan must have seen it in my glassy eyes and muscular stiffness. She put her arm around my shoulder. "Relax," she whispered in my ear. "She's not your father."

I rolled my shoulders, trying to head off the inevitable muscle cramps. I forced myself to lock onto the present, to tune into the woman's words.

"…but my denomination had more important matters, putting its money and efforts into social equity rather than ministering to the truly needy." Christy took another breath. "Would you mind if I lie down before I continue?" I shook my head. I needed a distraction—an escape from the onslaught of my own PTSD. She put her head on the pillow and turned to the side so she could still face me.

"Like Susan, I am a widow. No longer having any significant ties to my community, I sought more immediate and meaningful work here in Nashville. God led me to these people, here on the banks of the river."

God led you? I wanted to say, *Unlike you, she has kids,* but my lips were frozen. If I could bring myself to listen to her tale, Christy would fill in the holes I needed someone to fill. She might explain more about the soldier or this camp's leader, Damien. Sound finally escaped from my lips. "Go on."

"I came here two years ago and camped on my own. If it weren't for Mr. Rushing, I, too, might be dead. I saw him watching over me. While gathering water, I slipped from the bank and into the river one day. He dove in, put his arm around me, and brought me here." She accepted Susan's bottle of water and took a sip. "I said he suffers from a dissociative break because he talks and acts like he's still in war trying to rescue Americans and friendlies."

That made total sense. Many of our faithful warriors returned home only to find they have no home. They'd served their purpose and were discarded—like I was. They wander and search aimlessly for connection and purpose, only to end up in sites like these. I felt sorry for the soldier. Unfortunately, his condition didn't help our cause.

"So," I began, looking for the right words. "You're saying our soldier isn't just suffering from momentary flashbacks but has a whole different reality than ours?"

"I believe so. He has lucid moments, but most of the time, his mind is elsewhere. That's his mind's way of coping with his tragedy." Her eyes flitted shut, and she went silent.

Susan checked Christy's breathing and then motioned to the tent's flap. She and I crawled out and were surprised to discover Sam and Damien missing. "Where's my partner?"

"He's with Damien," said the tall, wiry man with the hatchet still gripped in his left hand.

"And that would be?"

He shrugged his shoulders.

I knew he couldn't have gone far, but I was losing my patience with these people. Even though I had my Sig M17X with twenty-one rounds per magazine, I felt outnumbered and uneasy. He didn't answer.

"Where are they?" He shrugged his shoulders again. He looked at me and smiled. Did that mean he knew where Sam was? Did that mean they'd done something to him?

"They're okay, Abbey. Damien won't harm him." She must have read my mind.

I ignored Susan's attempt to soothe my rising anxiety and stepped forward. He started to pull the hatchet back, but I had the pistol out in a flash and said, "I wouldn't do that." I took another step forward and sensed movement from my rear. I still had the gun pointed at the man with the hatchet. "Whoever you are, you better identify yourself before I turn and shoot you."

"Detective Sam Tidwell, Metro Nashville Homicide."

I spun around and snapped at him. "Are you insane?" He wasn't smiling. I could see in Sam's eyes that something was terribly wrong. "What happened?"

"Come on. I'll tell you back at Homicide," he said. "Let me drop you off at your car first."

"Susan…"

"Don't worry. I'm heading home." She asked Damien to look in on Christy. On the way back to the cars, she asked, "Sam, are you okay?" He nodded. Susan took that as a positive answer. I knew better. I could see he was visibly shaken. "See you Sunday?" she asked me.

I had no excuses. I just didn't want to go—not to church. "Not this week, Susan. I'll be there next week." I knew I'd said that before, so I wouldn't blame Susan if she didn't believe me.

"I'm going to hold you to that, Abbey."

"I'll be there next week. I promise." We parted ways. We waited until Susan was safely back on the main road before pulling out ourselves.

Sam took me back to my car without another word. This case was getting more and more complicated by the hour. Even though the primary crime scene was in the recycling lot, I felt this camp would give us answers—answers to questions we didn't know to ask yet. I stayed in my car, quietly staring at the recycling lot, trying to picture the events of last night. I wondered if our soldier was out by the river. They had to hear the gunfire, and yet no one mentioned it. There was no way under heaven the shots didn't stir curiosity among the residents of the four camps. So, why weren't they asking us about it? Why didn't they want to know why we were there? All they focused on was getting us to leave. What were they hiding? What did they know?

Then I thought of Dean Swain driving into the recycling lot. Was he meeting someone? Was he a part of the East Bank Project? Although there was a sadness and permanence to death, the beginning of a case excited me. My mind began to explore the many possible scenarios. It's what I loved most about being a detective.

Chapter Three

Sam and I returned to Homicide headquarters. After instructing Deborah, our Administrative Assistant, to search for Dean Swain's next of kin, we sifted through the evidence gathered this morning.

"What's Damien's story?" I asked as I spread the bags across the conference room table.

"He claims to be a former small business owner and city councilman from Carbondale, Illinois," Sam explained. "He says he was removed from his position after being falsely accused of selling political favors. Long story short, his reputation was ruined; he hit bottom, wandered around, and ended up in Nashville. He's the self-appointed mayor of the river site."

"Seems like a man with his credentials and experience could do better than this," I said.

"I thought the same thing, but he seems proud of his accomplishments." Sam paused momentarily before adding, "There are three sizable camps and a fourth with just a few scattered tents of loners like our soldier."

"Remind me to look him up." I pulled out my notebook. "Susan's friend says he's a Lance Corporal named Rushing. She diagnosed him as having PTSD with a dissociative something."

"With dissociative symptoms. That makes sense. Damien said he's dangerous and more than a little crazy. He's been seen with a large survival knife."

26

"Where were you, Sam? You looked terrified when you returned."

"He took me to see the other three camps." Sam paused. I noticed the hairs on his arm standing straight up. "Our soldier lives in one of the tents beside the interstate pillar.

"Sam, what happened back there?" I wondered why he was being so evasive.

"Nothing." He rubbed his arm. He tried to focus on the evidence, but there was a distance in his eyes.

"Something happened. Don't tell me it didn't."

"I felt like I was being watched the whole time—expected to walk into a trap at any moment, but nothing happened. Damien kept this creepy look on his face like he knew something I didn't." Sam turned. His face was ghostly white. "It's a complex system—although they are independent groups of homeless people, there's some kind of hierarchy of the sites." Sam shrugged. "I thought homelessness was homelessness."

"That doesn't make sense."

"Typically, a person without a home just lives on the street, next to a bus station, or someplace they can beg for food. These camps are separated from the rest of Nashville by a river and a fence. It's some kind of private community."

I started to understand his point. "You mean like a home-school school where other homeschoolers gather together at a place like a church or a community center to make a larger group?"

"Exactly. You can't call it homeschool if you're not learning at home."

"Okay, Sam. So, you're saying you can't call it homeless if you're part of a camp of other people who are making that place a permanent home or village of sorts?"

"Yes. See, it doesn't make sense." Sam scratched his beard. "They have identical structures with the same kind and color of blue tarps. Where do they get their food and money? Damien established a *law* where a new homeless person can't just walk up and throw down a tent; he has to ask permission to join *the village.*" Sam rubbed his arm again. I could see the goosebumps from the other side of the table. "He's also established some kind of neighborhood watch with their own designated security team." Sam looked up at me. "You already met them. Anyway, Damien made it clear outsiders like us were not welcome."

"Message sent and received. What do they do to a person who won't go away?"

"I asked that before we left for the *tour.* Their answers were inconsistent. They did share an interesting fact. Two men drove up last night in a fancy car. They walked around the parking lot and came down to the river before driving away.

"Think that was Dean Swain and his passenger?"

"Almost had to be. They gave a perfect description of the Bentley. They didn't stay long. Damien said there would have been consequences if they'd tried to stick around longer than they did."

"Consequences? What kind of consequences?"

"He didn't say."

"That land has lain vacant for nearly ten years. Why would anyone care about the homeless living here?" Then, an idea popped into my head. The idea of an organization among the homeless made me wonder if anything nefarious was happening there. That was a farfetched idea, even for my mind. I put gloves on while Sam explained Damien's answers. While he relayed the site's history and future social hierarchy, I opened a bag containing two partially smoked cigars. "Why did you bag these?"

"Smell the small one," Sam said. One cigar had been smoked down to about two inches. The other had barely been used.

I smelled the short one but didn't know what I was looking for. "It stinks." It made me think of Mr. Morales's dance hall back in Guatemala—old, toothless men who wreaked of cigars and alcohol.

Sam laughed. He grabbed the cigar and smelled it. He let out a heavy sigh. "Not to a connoisseur of cigars."

"How would you know?"

"I used to smoke cigars back in the day. I loved the smell." He showed me what remained of the label. "This is a Fuente brand cigar. They cost about a hundred-fifty dollars each."

"So? He drives a Bentley. That's a drop in a bucket to him."

"Look closer, Abbey." I did, but I still wasn't catching Sam's point. "There are two cigars. They were positioned in the ashtray facing two different directions."

"I'm still not following, Sam. Spit it out." I was tired and still chilled to the bone—not in the mood for his games.

"There was another person in the car."

"So? That fits Damien's description. He said, 'they drove off.'"

"You're missing my point, Abbey. The passenger's cigar is common—about ten bucks." He smiled. "We can see if there's a DNA match. I'll bet the Fuente belongs to Dean Swain. The other one would belong to a passenger, possibly someone in the car at the time of the shooting."

"So there was a second man in the car?"

"Yes."

I nodded. I was starting to follow Sam's breadcrumbs. "Who-ever it was started smoking much later than Dean and didn't smoke the same brand. I'll wager it wasn't a friend. If he were, Dean would have also bought the high-quality cigar for him."

"Go on. You're starting to get it."

"Didn't know each other and started at different times." I repeated it. Then the bulb lit up. "It was a random encounter."

"Exactly." Sam smiled. He loved the role of mentor.

"Do you think Dean and his passenger got in a fight and shot each other?"

"It's a possibility. They drove to the homeless camp but ended up at the materials recycling site."

"Two strange places to see a Bentley. And if they traveled together, what set them off? What made them start shooting each other?"

"Remember, Abbey, Dean's gun was never fired."

"That's right!" I grabbed the Ruger .380 we found in Dean

Swain's hand. Turning it over, I read the serial number. I opened my laptop and searched the database for the owner. "Sam." He leaned over and looked at the result.

"It's registered to Dean Swain. That makes no sense."

It made perfect sense to me. "Dean had to get his gun from an ankle holster. He raised his gun, but he never got off a shot. The carjacker killed him with the first shot but fired two others before Dean fell. There was a third person in the lot. Someone defended Dean, firing at least five shots at the would-be thief. We have two people to find: Dean Swain's murderer and the person who came to his defense."

"Possibly three if the passenger who smoked that cigar was still in the car when the shooting started."

"Unless he was the carjacker. If not, where did he go? You only found one blood trail from the Bentley."

"Abbey, you call the hospitals and see if they treated any gunshot victims last night or this morning. There was a significant amount of blood in that car and on the ground heading to the street. I don't know if anyone could have survived the loss." I nodded and made a note to do that. "I'll check around and see who sells Fuente cigars."

We had a starting point—two sets of clues: the blood and the cigars. Follow the first set of clues, and you will usually find more. Eventually, you discover enough to lead you to the killer. "What about the prints and ballistics?"

"We're at the mercy of CSI, and they have a backlog of cases right now. It could be weeks."

"That's not right." I hated having to wait for the results of tests. There should be a quicker system. I knew the equipment existed. Why didn't we have access to it? I was certain the powers that be would claim budget cuts due to the defunding craze. "The forty-four's serial numbers have been filed off. No leads there."

"Send your pictures to the printer so I can study them. We should have the officers' sketches and photos later today."

Sam helped me gather everything back into the evidence box, and we went to our desks to start the tedious process of identifying our suspects. Nashville has over eighteen hospitals. I started with the busiest ones and worked my way down the list. Just as I feared, none of them treated a victim of a gunshot. I called several veterinary clinics and dental surgeons just in case. Still nothing. No surprise. As I was giving up on my line of inquiry, I heard Sam telling someone we'd be over to talk with him.

"Who was that?"

"The manager of Music City Cigar Bar. They sell several different types of Fuente cigars. They sold one last night. The bartender who sold it comes on duty tomorrow at four. With some luck, he'll identify anyone who was with Dean Swain. Can you get a good picture of him—alive?" I nodded. "If we can get a match on Dean, maybe we can find out who left the bar with him." Sam looked at his notes. "Two other cigar stores carry the brand but haven't sold any in the past week. What about the hospitals?"

"Nothing." I thought for a moment. "If he survived, someone probably patched him up without seeking professional help." That meant he was a seasoned criminal who couldn't expose himself to a hospital that was required to contact police in the case of a shooting wound. What else could we do while we waited for the report from CSI? "Hey, Sam?"

"Yes."

"This is an attempted carjacking, right?" He nodded. "Do you think the Auto Theft Unit could give us any leads on organizations running the East Bank?"

He shrugged his shoulders, loosened his tie, and cleared his throat. I knew I wasn't going to like his answer. "That's probably not a good idea."

"Why not?"

"Um…they might throw us a bone, but I'm sure they're busy. Besides, I hear they're territorial about their cases."

"Where'd you hear that, Sam?"

31

"You know. Word gets around." He stuck his hands deep in his pockets and lowered his head. Sam looked like a little boy who'd gotten caught doing something he wasn't supposed to do. "They can't be bothered."

"Surely, if there's a murder tied to an attempted car theft, they'd want to know," I said. I meant it as a statement, but it sounded more like a question. My transition from East Precinct patrol to Homicide was bumpy, but I never felt like anyone had it out for me. We had clear boundaries and established roles during last year's Ripley case. I never felt like we were bothering them. "I think we should bother them. After all, we all work under the umbrella of Metro Nashville." We worked with the officers of East Precinct and Sex Crimes every step of the way while trying to solve Mark's death. Why would Auto Theft be any different?

I was about to find out.

Chapter Four

Thursday, March 20, 2:10 PM—Auto Theft Unit of MNPD

We grabbed some drive-through food on the way to the Auto Theft Unit of the Metro Nashville Police Department and stuffed it down. "Eat when and where you can," Sam always said. This mantra was becoming too commonplace for the detectives of homicide and was playing havoc with my digestive system. Sam pulled into an empty parking spot and said, "I have to admit I don't have a very good history with these guys. I may have lost my temper back in the day and said something ugly. Why don't you take the lead?"

I wanted him to explain, but we didn't have the time, and I could tell Sam didn't want to elaborate. "Sure." I needed to pull out every card I had in the deck—to look my best—so I pulled the band from my ponytail and shook my hair. I hated to rely on my youthful looks, but I did get better responses when they thought I was helpless and clueless. Should I play it cool, cute, ignorant, desperate, or confident and determined? Maybe these were the type of men that resented women on the force and playing it stupid would only serve to solidify their prejudice. The moment we walked into the room of offices, my decision was made.

A tall, older officer with dyed jet-black hair and a goatee to match stood as we walked in.

"Detective Tidwell, long time no see. Slumming it today?" Was he the source of Sam's hesitance?

"Larry."

The officer looked at me and said, "I didn't know this was bring your kid to work day."

I could tell his verbal jab hit Sam in the gut. We were still working through the fact that I looked so much like his deceased daughter, Molly. If this guy knew Sam, he also knew about Molly.

"Oh, that's right. You don't have a kid anymore."

What a jerk! I stepped in front of Sam, flashed my badge, and walked directly to Larry's desk. He seemed to be the kind of bully that was all bark and no bite. I hoped my assessment was spot on. "How original. I heard those kinds of jokes in third grade." His face tightened and turned blood-red. He took a step toward me, intentionally invading my personal space. I looked up and shook my head. "If that's supposed to intimidate me, it failed."

He smiled and raised an eyebrow. He turned to his buddies and said, "The kid's got spunk."

I wanted to put him in place—say something about his dyed hair and beard, but I needed to stay professional—rise above his petty jabs. "Listen. We've got a murder on our hands that involves an attempted carjacking. We thought we might throw you a bone if you're through trying to impress me." He hesitated. I assessed his posture and the looks of his fellow officers and said, "Come on, Sam. You were right. This was a waste of our time." I grabbed Sam's arm and started back for the door. I could tell Sam was on to my plan. He followed, feigning bewilderment.

"What's your name?" It was a different voice—a deeper voice. He didn't call me *sweety, kid, or little girl.*

I stopped and turned. "Detective Rhodes." He was a medium-built black man with dreads, dressed in plain clothes—an undercover detective. This was who we needed to see. Now *he* might know something.

"What can we do for you, Detective Rhodes?" He sat on the edge of his desk, his feet resting on his chair.

"It's what we can do for each other," I said. "We have a homicide and a brand-new Bentley someone tried to steal." He waved us forward. As we passed the first officer, I winked. I could tell Sam was eating it up. I desperately wanted to say, *You stay here while the grownups discuss business,* but I shut my mouth. I had to stay professional. There was more on the line than my pride.

"Let's talk in the conference room." He led the way. As soon as he shut the door, he apologized for Larry's behavior. "I'm Detective Underwood. Tell me how we can help."

Sam and I explained the details we had and where the incident occurred. "Who lifts cars in that area?" I asked.

He thought for a moment. "No one. That's not fertile ground." He looked puzzled. "Did you say the Bentley was inside the lot?"

"Yes," Sam said. "You got a piece of paper? I'll show you what it looked like."

"I'll do you one better," Detective Underwood said. He leaned back in his chair and opened a small cabinet. "Give me the address. I'll pull up a satellite image of the lot." He typed the address on the tablet, and the lot appeared. He stretched out the image of the lot so it filled the screen and said, "Show me where everything was." We pointed to where Dean Swain's body lay and where we found the Bentley. I explained my theory about the third person. Detective Underwood folded his arms; his eyebrows furrowed. "That doesn't make sense."

"Well, that's where we found them," I defended.

"That means one of three things," he said, staring at the satellite image. "First, it was a chance encounter. He saw the Bentley and followed it there. Second, he was tipped off. Someone let him know where the Bentley would be and when. Third…" He looked at Sam. "You have yourselves a conspiracy to murder—not just the owner, but the thief as well."

Conspiracy. That word dropped like a load of bricks on my brain. If that were true, we were not only looking for the injured thief but the third man and possibly his boss. Who could have wanted both Dean and the carjacker dead? And why kill them there? I was glad we came here. It gave me a new perspective on the case. "Which do you think we have?"

Detective Underwood put his elbows on the conference table. "If I were you, I'd wish for option one. Then all you have to do is find the injured thief."

"And if it's not option one?" Sam asked.

"Option two involves an organization, which puts the case in our hands. I have to say, stealing a Bentley is rare. Most Nashville chop shops stay away from high-end cars. Too easy to trace. Option three is messy. You must find that third person and work your way up the chain until you find out who ordered the hits. The quickest solution is to find out which chop shop has an injured or dead member."

Sam nodded. I could tell he decided our next course of action. "Let's work with option two and make it a joint venture. What groups work East Nashville, especially that side of the river?"

He leaned forward. "Two that we know of. El Comandantes is based in Antioch, but their members consider all of Davidson County their territory. It's a Mexican gang that specializes in moving cars. The other group calls itself Shadow Crew, a Black gang that works north and central Nashville. They're much smaller and run two chop shops that change locations regularly." He flipped his head to the right, sending a wave of dreads over the side of his head. "I've worked undercover with them before. I can check them out over the next few days and let you know if they were involved."

"Okay," I said. "Then we'll look into El Comandantes. I speak fluent Spanish." I could tell Sam was already disapproving of my new plan. At least he kept silent, choosing not to embarrass me in front of Detective Underwood. I explained my idea of working undercover, posing as a young Mexican woman looking for a place to belong.

Sam put his information card on the table and said, "Keep in touch."

"This is going to take some time and coordinated planning," Officer Underwood advised as he walked us to the door.

The moment Sam shut his car door, he snapped. "Are you crazy, Abbey? Do you know how dangerous this is?"

I knew he was worried, but this was one of those moments I didn't like him treating me like a daughter, instead of a partner.

"I'll play it cool, Sam. It's not like I'm going deep undercover." He shook his head and said nothing more about it. As we pulled into Homicide, I said, "I'll devise a plan tonight and let you know in the morning. If you don't like it, we'll come up with a plan B."

We got out, and Sam looked over the top of the car. "Better start working on that plan B, Abbey. I don't want you to get hurt."

"Aw, Sam. You're just the sweetest today." I was trying to lighten his mood, but nothing seemed to work. This case rattled him, starting with his tour of the homeless camps. Rehashing feelings of his daughter's death didn't help. I spent the rest of the afternoon researching Damien Jones and Dean Swain. I had to dig deep for Damien's story. Carbondale was a small town; his story wasn't front-page news even in that setting. He was telling the truth, but he was also embellishing his version of the story. Dean Swain was easy to find. He was a social media influencer. He was a playboy prankster, not the kind of man who would intentionally be found in a homeless camp or a materials recycling lot. I'd have to look at him later. I was exhausted and needed a break.

Chapter Five

It's not a good sign when the Mayor's office leaves a message saying, "The Mayor needs to see you first thing this morning." I checked with Sam, and he received the same cryptic message. Why would the mayor want to see us? I hadn't seen him since the Ripley case, and that was a brief official encounter. I didn't know what to expect this time, but a tongue-lashing directly from the mayor, especially on the second day of a new case, was the furthest thing from my mind. Unfortunately, that's exactly what we got. The moment we got off the elevator, the secretary pointed to a glass door with a bronze plaque mounted to its right that read, "Mayor Michael S. O'Reilly."

"This isn't good," Sam said.

I turned my attention from the plaque to the five men standing inside the office. I recognized the Mayor, The Chief of Police, our Commander, and Captain Harris. The only person I didn't know was the man standing to the mayor's right. I took a deep breath as Sam knocked.

"Come in."

"Mayor O'Reilly. Chief Clendenon," Sam said with a slight bow of his head.

"Everyone, sit down," Mayor O'Reilly said. "Let me get right down to it. This is a good friend of mine, Jonathan Thomas, President of JLT Enterprises."

"One of the developers on the East Bank Project?" I asked.

I could tell by the looks on their faces that I wasn't invited to speak.

"Detective Rhodes, is it?" Mayor O'Reilly asked. I tried to swallow the dry lump forming in my throat. "I don't recall opening the floor to questions or comments." I shook my head, not eager for another rebuke. "Just sit there and listen, young lady. I've heard about your inability to keep your mouth shut. I believe you'll learn a lot more by doing so." *Ouch*. Who said that about my mouth? Anyway, who thought the mayor would even need to know such a thing? The last time we communicated, he praised us for our work on the Ripley and Watson cases last year. I had no idea the mayor thought ill of me. In fact, I didn't know the mayor thought of me at all. I blushed with embarrassment. I expected someone in the room to defend me, but even Sam kept silent. Chain of command. Just like the army.

"I received word early this morning that Mr. Thomas's stepson was murdered near the banks of the Cumberland." The mayor paused for effect. Did he expect us to answer? I wasn't going to speak first. What would I say? Was he referring to Dean Swain? We hadn't even heard back on the next of kin search. How did he know? "And none of you had the decency to inform me."

"Who's his stepson, sir?" Sam asked.

"Dean Swain."

"Even if we knew the connection between Dean Swain and Mr. Thomas, how would we know you'd be interested in the case, Mayor?"

"Tidwell!" The retort came from Chief Clendenon. "Did you even attempt to notify the next of kin? I expect Rhodes to make that kind of rookie mistake, but you're a veteran. You know better."

I was feeling even worse after that comment. Was everyone in this room against me? Was I a loud-mouth rookie with no common sense?

"Yes, sir, but we're still looking. As of last night, we hadn't found any kin. This case is a little complicated."

"Well, uncomplicate it," the mayor growled.

"Yes, sir." I saw Sam's eyes dart in my direction. This wasn't about making excuses. Sam was taking the heat off me.

"Do I need to do your job for you?" the mayor asked.

"If we could get to it…"

Before the chief or the mayor could respond, Mr. Thomas said, "Dean is my stepson. He kept his father's name. I can understand the confusion."

"Jonathan," the mayor began.

"Let it go, Mike. They didn't know, and it doesn't matter. What matters is that we find the person responsible and make him pay."

That last part unsettled the room. I think everyone had the same thought as I. He meant to kill the murderer. "We will, sir," Sam assured him, ignoring the implication. "We'll have him in custody within a few weeks."

Then it happened. The mayor blew a gasket. He went on and on about how important Jonathan Thomas was to him personally and to Nashville. The mayor spoke of the upcoming East Bank Project fundraiser and the many developments that came with it, including affordable housing, a new park, shops, and even a major league baseball stadium to lure a team to Nashville. "We can't have an open crime scene on the East Bank. You need to put all other cases aside and focus on this one. And if you two aren't up for the challenge, we'll find someone who is. Is that understood?" He continued to bark out veiled threats. The way he put it, if Sam and I didn't solve this murder by the end of next week, we'd both be out of jobs.

By the time Mayor O'Reilly finished, he'd reduced me to the incompetent little girl emotionally battered by my father. I could feel the images flooding my mind, images of my father yelling at me and telling me I was a lost sinner who tainted his ministry. Images rose to the forefront of my mind. Bad memories. I tried all my counselor's suggestions until I succeeded in stuffing the feelings down, at least long enough to get out of the room. I was dismissed, and Sam was told to stay behind. I left the room, but

I could hear the mayor shouting all the way down the hall. Sam left the meeting like a dog with his tail between his legs.

"What happened?"

"I don't want to talk about it."

"I'm sorry."

This was the second time I'd seen Sam's confidence stripped away in two days.

"It's not your fault."

We rode to Homicide in silence. This was becoming his new pattern, which put distance between us. I wanted desperately to tell Sam about my undercover plans, but they sounded stupid now, even to me. I wanted to reach out and give him comfort and support, but I kept to myself. We both left licking our wounds from the verbal beating.

Chapter Six

Sam kept isolated and busy after we returned from the mayor's office; he avoided me like the plague. I desperately wanted to ask what they said when I left the room, but Sam clarified that he didn't want to discuss it. I'd heard the yelling, but I couldn't make out the words Mayor O'Reilly used. I couldn't interpret Sam's mood. Was he mad at me, embarrassed by me, or just sulking from the meeting? I could stand it no longer and turned to ask, but his phone rang. I listened to his side of the conversation as I pretended to work on the clues we had so far. He said, "Thanks," and hung up the phone.

Sam opened the attached file on his computer and said, "Abbey, come take a look." He scooted his chair to the right and allowed me to roll over to his left. "She said to look at the ballistics first."

"Have we already received the results? I thought you said they were backed up and it could take weeks."

"When Mayor O'Reilly and the Chief get involved, mountains move." He scrolled up.

"Stop." I pointed to an image showing the scoring of the nine-millimeter bullets. "Two different guns? Both are nine-millimeter handguns, but they have different barrel scoring. This is getting complicated."

"That's what it looks like, Abbey." We turned and stared at each other. I knew he was thinking the same thing as I. The mayor was not going to be happy because this was not a black-and-white murder case. It would not be solved by the end of this week—or next.

"Sam, we had at least four people at that crime scene. What's going on?"

His head sank. "What's going on is that we can rule out options one and two. I hate to say it, especially with the mayor on our case, but we have the worst scenario. For some reason, someone conspired to kill both Dean Swain and our missing carjacker. That's not good."

"What would a millionaire playboy and an East Nashville carjacker have in common?"

"I don't know, but Mayor O'Reilly wants this solved by next week, or as he put it, 'There will be two openings in Homicide.'" He scrolled up. "The slugs in Dean came from the forty-four lying in the car. At least we only have one murderer to find."

"Do you think Dean arranged to meet the man at the lot and was double-crossed?" Sam didn't answer. He just scrolled through the report to the fingerprint section. "We have a hit on the prints." Two photos appeared on the screen: a Mexican national with dark features and a white male.

"You've got to be kidding." I couldn't believe my eyes. "It can't be him."

"Who is it?"

"Sam, that's the rookie I told you about last year—the one from East Precinct who grabbed my breasts and was forced out of Metro PD." I looked at the image and read the name to be certain, even though I knew it was him. "Chase Martin. He was in Dean's car. That would explain the cheap cigar."

"He fits the description Damien gave me of the second man. You're right. This says he's an ex-cop. This case is getting worse by the minute." Sam printed two copies of the report and gave me one. We read in silence, marking critical evidence we needed for the case.

"You were right again, Abbey; his DNA is also on one of the

cigars." The last thing I wanted was another encounter with Chase Martin, but fate was forcing my hand.

"This man," he said pointing to the illegal alien from Mexico, "left his prints in several places. It says they were on the driver's door, the steering wheel, the start button, and the inside of the passenger side door." I read his name and rap sheet. Tito Ruiz. Class B felony theft, aggravated assault, criminal trespass, DUI, and the list went on. "How is he not deported or in jail?"

"You can thank a justice system that gives more rights to the aliens and offenders than the citizens and victims. He may have been lucky in the past, but his luck just ended. The Mayor will see to it personally that he rots in prison."

"What would be the link between Dean Swain, Chase Martin, and Tito Ruiz?"

"A social influencer, whatever that is, a washed-out rookie cop, and a petty criminal? I don't know, but we'll find out, and we have a little over a week to do it." Sam looked through his notebook, dialed a number, and put his phone on speaker. "Detective Underwood, this is Detective Sam Tidwell from Homicide. I have you on speaker, and Detective Abbey Rhodes is listening. I'm afraid we have option three." Sam shared the report with him and highlighted specific details that pertained to the Auto Theft Unit. "We need your help finding Tito Ruiz. It looks like he's a member of El Comandantes. If you can find their current base of operations, I'll get the warrant. Want to tag along?"

"Absolutely. I'll let you know as soon as we locate him."

Sam hung up and looked at me. "Okay, Abbey, while he looks for their new base of operation, we have a four o'clock appointment at the Music City Cigar Bar. Print pictures of Dean Swain, Tito Ruiz, and Chase Martin. Oh, and bring the cigars."

Chapter Seven

Friday, March 21, 4:00 PM—Music City Cigar Bar

Outside, the Music City Cigar Bar looked run down and abandoned. Its two-story brick exterior was stained and missing a chunk of its ornamental façade on the second story's west side. You could tell pieces had fallen off before because the bricks didn't match. Sam pulled into the parking lot at the building's rear, and we made notes on the lot and the building. I wasn't impressed. Why would a millionaire frequent this place?

But the moment Sam opened the door and we walked inside, I felt like Dorothy stepping into Oz. The deep blue walls and bright white contrasting trim mesmerized me. My eyes followed the stairs to a loft directly above the cigar store. It was colorful and bright. The room to our left was quite different, painted in earth tones. A smoky haze gathered at the ceiling, giving the chandeliers the look of headlights on a foggy morning.

The bar lined the far wall. Dark brown leather couches and winged-back chairs filled the space between the bar and the entrance where we stood. A few tables were scattered here and there. Sam headed to the bar and flashed his credentials. "Detectives Tidwell and Rhodes. You the fellow who worked Wednesday night?" The bartender nodded.

He turned to a fellow bartender. "Hey, Veronica, watch the bar for me?"

"Sure. You in trouble?"

I answered, "No. We have a few questions for him about a

current case." He motioned us to follow him up the stairs to a large sitting area. We had the place to ourselves.

"My name is Jimmy Denton. Have a seat."

As soon as we sat down, Sam dropped the picture of Dean Swain on a small table between our chairs. "Recognize him?"

"Of course," he said. "He made sure everyone in the place knew who he was."

"Did he give his name?" I asked.

"Yeah. Dean Swain, social media influencer. He attracted a lot of attention. He was throwing money everywhere...not literally. He was buying people drinks and cigars. Made a big deal that he was rich and could afford it."

This was beginning to make me think our theory was all wrong. The guy practically invited everyone to follow him outside and rob him. "What time was that?"

"He was here from ten to about midnight."

"Was he drunk?"

"He should have been, but he didn't show any signs of it."

Sam pulled the bag out of his jacket pocket. "Recognize these?"

The bartender took the bag from Sam and looked at the two cigars. "Sure."

Sam tossed the other two pictures on the table, "What about them?"

He fingered the two photos. "Never seen him before," he said as he tossed Tito's picture back on the table. He shook Chase's photo. "Yeah, he was here that night."

Okay. Now we were getting somewhere. Chase Martin was in the cigar bar at the same time as Dean Swain and somehow made it inside Dean's car. "Tell me about him."

"They were a dichotomy of sorts," he began. Big word for a bartender.

"Meaning?" Sam asked. He hated fancy words.

"Well, Dean was boisterous and a tad obnoxious." He smiled. He was doing this to Sam on purpose.

"What's with the big words?" Sam asked.

"I'm sorry." He wasn't. "I used to be a psychology professor. I discovered I could make more money tending bar. I use some of the same skills here to offer advice." He made an odd face as he said it, as if he couldn't believe the statement either. "He made everyone feel inferior. On the other hand, that guy sat by himself, smoking our cheapest cigar."

"Was he drinking too?"

"No. That's the thing. He couldn't. He had a concealed firearm."

Sam perked up. "Did he show it to you?"

"No. He identified himself and let our manager know he had a firearm under his jacket."

Interesting. "Why would he do that?" I asked. Surely, Chase didn't still consider himself a cop.

"Said he was here for a business meeting, but the guy stood him up. He wasn't with Dean, but when the two men on either side started to squeeze Dean at the bar, asking for money, that guy stepped in, pulled his jacket aside, and told them to back off."

"Did they?" I asked. He nodded. "And you say there were two of them?" He nodded again. Maybe I had this all wrong. Maybe he went with Swain to protect him, and those two guys followed him to the lot. Maybe some of the blood belonged to Chase Martin.

"What happened next?" Sam asked. "Did he push Swain for money?"

"No. Oddly enough, he offered some friendly advice to Dean about keeping a lower profile and started to walk off."

"Then what?" I asked.

"Dean followed after him and tried to hire him on the spot— said he was looking for his own security team and could use a man like him." The bartender stopped as if he'd answered all our questions. He looked over the railing to see if Veronica was doing okay. "Anything else?"

"Yes. Did Swain hire him? Did they leave together?" I could

have rattled off a hundred more questions. I could tell he was missing tips and anxious to return to the bar.

"I'm uncertain about the job, but they left together."

"What about the two men asking for money?" I asked. "Did they follow them out?"

"No. They were here until we closed."

"Ever see them before?"

He looked down at the bar again. "Yeah. They've been here a few times. Always looking for a handout."

"How can they afford to drink in a place like this?" Sam asked.

"Oh, they have money. They just don't want to spend theirs."

We thanked him for his time and walked to the parking lot. I noticed the surveillance camera mounted on the corner of the building, which I hadn't seen when we arrived.

"Sam, I'll be right back."

Having secured a digital copy of the bar footage between nine and one of the night in question, we headed back to Homicide to look it over. It was just as the bartender said. We filed for a search warrant for Chase Martin's apartment, which just so happened to be only two blocks from the cigar bar.

Chapter Eight

Friday, March 21, 7:05 PM—Chase Martin's Apartment

W e obtained a search warrant within two hours—with help from the mayor's office. Seeing how quickly things could be processed if someone with clout was involved made me sad. Was one life worth more than another? Why couldn't it go this quickly every time we had a case? We needed the information just as much then as now. Apparently, Dean Swain's life carried a higher price tag, and, as they say, the wheels of government were greased.

Sam contacted the management office for Chase Martin's apartment building, informed them of the warrant, and they met us at his door. Sam produced the search warrant, but she didn't even look it over. I knocked several times and announced that we were from Homicide, but no one answered the door.

The representative unlocked the door and let us in. She tried to peek in over his shoulder, but Sam instructed her to stand by the door while we searched the premises. I honestly expected to find Chase dead on the carpet, full of bullet holes—no such luck. I didn't really want the man dead, but his kind annoyed me to no end.

It was a long but narrow apartment in Nashville's plethora of new buildings. Sam started on the left, searching the open shelving and cabinets for any connection to our case. I took the right side. We planned to meet at the other end. I opened the small coat closet directly outside his bathroom. The closet was empty except for a few jackets, coats, blankets, and a pillow. I entered the bathroom next. Chase Martin was a neat freak. Everything was pristine and in its proper place. The shower must have been cleaned this morning. His medicine cabinet behind the mirror over his sink looked staged for a showing. The first shelf held a toothbrush and toothpaste, which looked brand new. The second shelf had a deodorant stick, dental floss, a hairbrush, and a bottle of Tylenol. On the top shelf, Chase had three bottles of medicine. He was taking Sertraline, Escitalopram, and Trazadone.

He was dealing with anxiety or depression, and he was having trouble sleeping. But why take both Sertraline and Escitalopram? I took pictures of the prescriptions as evidence. I opened the door on the other side of the commode and entered a small laundry room. It was more of a laundry closet. I was getting claustrophobic just standing there. The washer/dryer combo to my right looked brand new. I opened the cabinet above and felt like I was part of a television commercial. It only held a bottle of detergent, a small bottle of fabric softener, and a box of dryer cloths. My apartment was always clean, but this was obsessive. To my left, the closet made a backward L. His clothes were organized by type and color. His slacks all hung at the same height with beltline and ankle lines all with the same pattern, evenly dispersed on the rack. His shirts were hung by sleeve length and color and were arranged from dressy to casual. They, too, were evenly spaced across the rack. You would have had to use a ruler to make them this symmetric. His shoes had the same pattern on the floor below. Now I knew why he was taking both meds. He suffered from OCD with anxiety. That's why everything had to be in its proper place.

I grabbed a small step stool from the left of his closet and stood on it to examine the top shelf. There were five ammunition boxes for a .357 magnum, two small storage boxes, a backpack, and a pillow. I photographed the evidence and removed the storage boxes and backpack for further examination. Just as I unzipped the backpack, Sam joined me in the closet.

"This guy is some neat freak. Are we sure he actually lives here?"

"I think he has OCD, Sam. Look at this closet." The backpack had climbing accessories: a neatly bundled nylon rope, several carabiners, gloves, a small rock pick, and grip shoes. Nothing else. The boxes held files, notes, awards, records, and a few books on how to run private security. "Take a look at these."

Sam started to flip through one of the books.

"What are you doing? Don't touch that!" Chase Martin burst through his bedroom door, making a beeline for his closet and us. "Get out!" He looked at his boxes and backpack. "Hands off."

Sam stood and presented the warrant to search the premises. "Calm down, Mister Martin."

"You!" He pointed at me. "Why are you here?" Guilt, shame, and fear suddenly gripped me, and I felt like I was falling from that platform at Soar Adventure Center all over again. I felt the rope snap, and I scrambled to untether my cable. "Get out!" he screamed.

It snapped me out of my vision, and I realized I had pushed myself back into the corner of his closet, knocking his shoes aside. Chase dropped beside me and scrambled to rearrange the shoes, putting them back in the exact order we'd found them. "Look what you've done." Beads of sweat began to fill his forehead. His hands were shaking.

A few minutes later, after Sam succeeded in calming us both down, we sat around Chase Martin's small kitchen table. "I don't understand," Chase said. He stared at me. "Are you still pissed at me for that stupid prank?"

"I wouldn't call that a prank, but our search has nothing to do with your inappropriate groping," I said, gritting my teeth. I wanted to lash out. Instead, I took a deep breath and let it out over three seconds. "Your prints and DNA were found in Dean Swain's car."

"So? Is that why you're searching my apartment? Did he accuse me of stealing something?"

"Not exactly," I said, enjoying this too much.

"Then what are you looking for?" He searched the room with his eyes. He was taking a quick inventory.

"A murder weapon," Sam said.

"A murder weapon? Who's dead?"

I stole a glance Sam's way. Was Chase Martin truly ignorant, or was he trying to play us? "Dean Swain."

"Dean's dead? He was alive Wednesday night."

"So," I said, "you admit you were with him the night of the murder."

The expression on his face changed immediately as the reality of our presence there hit him. "Wait—what—you think I killed him? Why would I do that?"

I had to admit. I was surprised Chase was alive and uninjured. I expected him to be the second victim. "To steal his Bentley."

He laughed. "Why would I want that gaudy car?" Then, he must have realized the poor timing of such a comment.

"So, why were you in his gaudy car?" Sam asked.

"He wanted to show me this tract of land by the river—said he wanted to buy it and make a parking garage."

"Why show you?" I asked. "What made you so special that a random millionaire would take you for a ride?" I couldn't help the bitter sarcasm that flowed from my lips, even if I wanted to.

"I don't know." His eyes darted from mine to Sam's. "He asked me."

"How did you know him?" Sam asked, keeping the conversation moving.

"I didn't. Some guys were moving in on him at this bar. He was so naïve, flashing his money around." He paused as if he was replaying the scene in his mind. I noticed he turned his water bottle three times, making sure it was centered in the ring of water on the table. "One guy was keeping him busy while the other was reaching for his wallet. I couldn't just sit there and let it happen, so I told them to bug off."

"And two men stopped their scheme just because you told them to?" His story was too easy. The bartender said the same things, but it sounded like a rehearsed summary of the events. I waited to see if Sam was going to follow up. He didn't.

"And he invited you for a ride in his very expensive car just because you came to his rescue?" I asked.

"No." There it was—a glitch in his story. I let the silence set in heavy like an impending storm. "He said he was looking to hire some personal security. Imagine that."

"Yeah. Imagine that." I made it obvious that I wasn't buying his tale.

He continued anyway. "It was like a sign from God."

"Leave God out of it," I snapped. That kind of comment still bit hard. I'd heard too many people use the name of God to cover for their selfish desires like God cared one way or the other.

Chase stared at Sam's chest, his eyes now downcast and glassy. "He needed security, and I needed a job. So, yeah, I got in his car. He drove down by the river and talked about the opportunity to make a killing. He was so proud of this stupid idea."

"A killing, huh?"

"Go on." Sam prodded him to continue while holding his hand up so I would be quiet.

"He thought with all the development on the East Bank that Nashville would seriously need more parking. He's right about that. But he wanted to build a ten-story parking garage on this side of the river. He thought he could talk Nashville into building another pedestrian bridge from his parking garage to a landing."

"A landing? Where?" I asked, now interested in what Chase had to say.

"Let me see…" He thought for a moment. "I think he said it's a little recycling lot on the other side of the river."

It started to come together. "And where is this land he wanted to buy?"

"The parking lot side is in the shape of a triangle whose sides are formed by the railroad, the river, and the Interstate. It's just four blocks from here."

"The homeless camps." So, he was one of the two men in the fancy car.

"Yeah. That's right. You know the place?" Chase asked.

"We do." I looked at Sam and wondered if he was thinking the same thing. He didn't follow up with a question, so I asked, "And then you went to the recycling lot?"

"No. I didn't want to take advantage of him. He'd had a lot to drink."

"But you let him drive anyway?" Sam asked.

"Like I could stop him. Anyway, I gave him my card and said if he was still looking for security tomorrow, call me. He never called, so I assumed he didn't remember the offer or changed his mind."

"Did he drive you back here?" Sam asked.

"No. He was all fired up about the idea and wanted to go see the other side. Said he had to envision it one more time before he put an offer together. I just walked home."

"You didn't leave in his car?" I didn't know whether to believe him or not. Damien's people said two men left in the Bentley. But Chase's story made sense, and he appeared sincere. It was hard not to want him to be guilty, knowing he was the kind of guy who would give up a career as a cop to fondle a perfect stranger. Maybe he learned a lesson from that. Maybe not. "You gave him your card?" I asked. He nodded. "I didn't see it among the evidence. Could we have one?" He nodded again and pulled one from his wallet.

"When did he die?"

"Shortly after he left you," Sam said softly. "He was shot in the recycling lot just across the river."

"That's where his bridge was going to go. So, if I had gone with him, he'd still be alive?"

"Possibly," Sam said. "Or you might have died also."

"He needed security, and I let him go. That's going to be hard to live with."

Sam put his hand on Chase's shoulder. "You barely knew the man. Cut yourself some slack."

Slack? Right. "Do you own a nine-millimeter?" I asked as I took the card from Chase's hand.

"Haven't had one since I was a rookie, and you know how that turned out." It had a little dig to it. Like it was my fault he quit. Why do men think women are asking to be used? "Just the thought of one reminds me of what I lost."

Sam must have seen this turn toward me. He handed Chase his card and said, "Stick around Nashville. We'll need you to come to the station around eight and make an official statement. You can either come on your own initiative, or I can send a ride."

"Tomorrow's Saturday," Chase said.

"I'll be working tomorrow," Sam said. "I'll be there from eight to one."

"I'll be there first thing."

"In the meantime, if you think of any other details, call me." Sam grabbed me by the arm and gently guided me out of Chase Martin's apartment.

I pulled away. "Oh, one last question. The bartender said you were there for a business meeting, but the guy stood you up."

"Yeah. So?"

"Who were you meeting?" I wanted to see if there was a meeting or if Chase came to see Dean Swain. I didn't trust him.

"A potential client."

"This client have a name?" I pressed.

"Of course he did." Chase shut the door in my face. Sam led me to the elevator. When the elevator doors closed, I asked, "So that's it? We're letting him slide?"

"For now." Sam directed my chin his way. "Are you okay? I know that had to be hard."

I nodded and said, "Thanks."

But I wasn't okay. I never expected that stupid incident and this chance encounter to get to me. Unfortunately, they would be the first in a series of deep cracks in the dam that held back more dangerous and damaging memories.

"Listen, I'll get Spence to sit in on his statement tomorrow with me. I'll follow up on the potential client's name. You take the day to relax." Before I could object, Sam said, "We'll probably have to hit this hard next week, and I want you at the top of your game."

I just nodded. Honestly, I was relieved not to face Chase again. I know it was just a stupid act by an idiot, but it made me feel cheap. As much as I tried to escape my past, it kept rearing its ugly head. There was one way I could escape for the moment. I'd spend the day with the Ripley family.

Chapter Nine

Saturday, March 22, 11:30 AM—Ripley Home

After a rough week, relaxing and kicking the ball with Hannah Ripley was refreshing. I couldn't believe she was turning fifteen this summer and would be getting her driver's permit. Hannah progressed well with our soccer lessons. Her confidence rose exponentially. She'd even asked Susan to sign her up for the summer girls' league in hopes of making the school soccer team. I was so proud of her.

"How do you do that cool entry pass?" she asked.

"You mean the flip throw?" Of course, I knew that was what she wanted, but I was giving her a subtle hint about the terminology. She nodded. I scooped the ball with my right foot, bounced it off my knee, and tapped it a few times with my head before catching it. "First, prove to me you can do a forward handspring. If you can do that without the ball, I'll teach you to do it with it."

Hannah ran a few feet, put her hands on the ground, and flipped to her feet. "Good job, Hannah. It's harder with the ball. You'll need a good grip and firm arms." She nodded. "Okay, first, you need to measure the distance. The closer you can land to the line without touching or passing it, the farther the ball will go." I demonstrated. "Toss it back." Hannah kicked it back to me, and I repeated the throw.

"You do it once without worrying about the spacing. I'll help you mark it for the next time." Hannah took a couple of steps and put the ball to the ground. Her arms crumbled under her weight, and her head crashed right into the ground. Been there; done that. I made a mental note to get Hannah some weights for her arms. "Brush yourself off and try it again." I could see the glisten in her eyes, but she was tough. Hannah wouldn't cry about it, at least not in front of me. It took three more tries before she locked her arms and flipped over. I smiled. The ball went straight up in the air. She grunted. "Getting close, girl. Don't quit now."

I noticed Susan flinching every time Hannah tried the flip. After about the tenth try, the ball went straight. "Okay." I approached her launch point and said, "This is where the ball hit the ground." I took two strides and said, "And this is where you landed." She nodded and smiled. "All you need to do is start with the desired landing spot and take two giant steps to the launch point. Make sense?"

"Yes. Think they'll be impressed?" she asked.

"I know I am." I winked and gave her an encouraging smile.

We kicked the ball around, taking turns passing and kicking the ball into the goal. Susan opened the back door and said, "Come wash up. It's time for lunch."

Hannah tagged my shoulder and ran, "Beat you to the house."

"Not fair," I said and ran after her. It was so nice to see her talking and having fun. We shared a special bond—a bond forged by darkened pasts. Hannah and I both experienced abuse, and we were still learning how to rise above it.

"Oh, hey, Doctor Pederman. I didn't realize you were here." It was Susan's father. Her parents moved from St. Louis to Nashville shortly after Mark's death. They were supportive parents. I was a little envious. I often wondered how my life would have differed if my parents had encouraged and supported me.

"Abbey, how many times do I have to tell you? It's just Charles. I retired three years ago."

"But you earned a degree. You were and are still a doctor."

"Please, Abbey."

"I'll try. It just seems disrespectful not to call you doctor." It was the same struggle I originally had with Sam. I called him Detective Tidwell until he urged me to be more informal. That wasn't natural for me. I knew the Daniels family a lot longer, and I still called him Lieutenant Daniels. It was part of my defensive walls; keeping things formal with my peers provided a sense of distance and safety. At least, that's what my counselor told me.

Hannah and I washed up and returned to the kitchen. "Smells good. What is it?"

"Nothing fancy, just sloppy Joes." Susan put a plate of buns on the table, each full of ground beef in a red sauce.

"Sloppy what?" I asked.

Susan was taken aback. "You mean to tell me you've never had sloppy Joe's?"

"I don't even know what they are, but they smell terrific."

She said it was the kids' favorite. She rattled off the ingredients, but I didn't really listen. I had no intention of making them for myself.

Susan's mother bowed her head. Everyone else followed. She began to pray. I closed my eyes in compliance and respect—for them. "Our dear Heavenly Father, we thank You so much for Your bountiful blessings—blessings of food, shelter, family, and friends. Bless us, Lord, that we might be a blessing to others. Amen."

I watched everyone take a sandwich, a spoonful of tater tots, and fruit before putting some of each on my plate. It didn't take long to understand why they called it *sloppy* Joes. You couldn't bite the sandwich without the meat falling out the other side. It wasn't the kind of food I normally ate, but it was good.

"I'm so glad you had some free time today. The kids have been dying to see you," Susan said with a smile.

I winked at Danny. "Missed you too, little man." He grinned and elbowed Hannah. "It's nice to have a place to unwind and get away from work."

"Mom, can I go to the movies with Annabel tonight?"

"Now's not a good time, Hannah."

"You're always saying that. When *is* a good time?"

"Hannah Ripley!" Susan's face was red.

"Come on, Mom. You never let me go anywhere."

Susan looked around the table. We were all waiting for her to answer. "Fine! But you have to turn your location on."

"Why? So, you can stalk me?"

Before Susan could say anything, I had Hannah halfway down the hall. "That's not the way to get anything, and it's extremely disrespectful."

"Who do you…"

I had my finger to her lips and was giving her my best, *Oh no you didn't, girl,* expressions on my face. "Be quiet and listen. Your mom is stressed right now. If you really want to go with your friend, you'll take a different approach." She nodded. "You'll go back in there and apologize." Hannah started to say something, so I put my whole hand over her mouth. "You'll apologize and give a counter-offer."

She huffed and pulled back from my hand. "What's a counter-offer?"

"Something like, 'I'll turn my location on if you will.' See you both give a little and you both win."

We returned to the kitchen and Hannah did as I suggested. "I'm sorry, Mom. That was disrespectful of me. I will turn my location app on if you will. Then we'll each know where the other is."

Susan had a look of complete shock. She put out her hand and shook Hannah's. Without looking at me, she said, "You know you're welcome any time, Abbey." Susan topped off my glass of sweet tea even though I'd only taken a sip.

I studied her for a moment and realized her hands were shaking. "You okay?"

"Me?" she asked, somewhat taken aback by my question. "Why, of course."

"I'm sorry, Mom," Hannah said, thinking it was about her.

"You're okay, Hannah. It's been a tough week."

"Something I should know about, Sweety?" Mrs. Pederman asked, now following my glance to Susan's trembling hands.

"No, Mom!"

I'd never seen her snap at her mother before.

"I'm sorry. I shouldn't have said that."

"Oh, Susan, is your blood sugar low?" She looked at Susan's plate. "You're so worried about everyone else that you haven't eaten anything."

Susan grabbed her sandwich and took a bite. She shot me a glance that, if I had to guess, was saying, *Thanks a lot, Abbey*. She forced a pretend smile. She was an emotional wreck. Usually, she was the rock.

I took the gesture as a hint and turned my attention to Danny. "So, little man, what are you doing this summer?"

"Summer? That's like forever from now," he said. "But Sunday night, Grampa Charles is taking me to see the Predators."

"Oh, I love hockey," I said. It was the closest thing to soccer. "I saw my first match in Germany while on leave. It's like soccer on steroids—much faster."

"What's steroids?" Danny asked.

"Nothing important. I meant to say it's much faster and rougher than soccer." I'm sure that didn't help either.

"I've never been," he said. "I don't know the rules, but I think it will be fun."

"It will, Danny. Trust me."

After several minutes of listening to us talk about hockey, Susan said, "When you get a chance, Abbey, could you come to talk with Christy? She's worried. Her friend is missing, and she can't find her."

"Her friend?"

"Yes. Her name is Alice. She lived in a tent on the hill."

"Maybe Alice just moved on," I suggested. "After all, she is homeless."

"But all her stuff is still at the camp. The only thing missing was her water bucket." Her hand began to shake again. Susan slipped it below the table, out of sight.

"Maybe she left in a hurry."

Susan stared at her plate.

"Okay, if I get a chance. Right now, the mayor has us working nonstop on this case, and he expects us to solve it by next weekend."

"So, you didn't catch your murderer yet?" Susan asked. "I thought you found blood all over the scene. He couldn't have run too far."

"No. It's a lot more complex than we first thought." Before she could ask a follow-up question, I added, "I don't think that's something we should discuss in front of the kids. Do you?" Normally, Susan would steer me away from adult conversations in front of the kids. Today, her mind was elsewhere.

"Let's discuss something more appropriate, Susan."

"I'm almost fifteen years old," Hannah said. "I can handle it."

"Yes, but Danny's eight." I persisted in my argument. Susan's parents agreed with me.

Returning the subject to the homeless situation, Mrs. Pederman asked, "Abbey, don't you think it's too dangerous for Susan to be helping them by herself?"

I didn't answer. The homeless camp was irrevocably connected to the murder, so talking about one would lead to the other. She noted my silence and said, "Maybe Charles could take the kids out back, and we can chat." He took the hint and asked the kids if they wanted to play outside. I could tell Hannah would rather stay with us, but she went without further argument.

When the door closed behind them, Mrs. Pederman turned to her daughter and said, "Susan, I'm scared. You're going to get hurt."

"I'm fine, Mom."

"For now, but the kids need you here. You're talking about missing people, for goodness sake. That could be you one day. I don't think you should be involved in such things."

"Mom, you can't pray that God would use us as a blessing to others and then refuse to be one," Susan snapped. "It's hypocritical."

She stood and whisked plates from the table, not wanting to face her mother. "They need me."

"So do the kids."

I thought it; her mother said it.

"I need to do this." She returned to clear the rest of the table. I noticed her lip quivering.

Mrs. Pederman looked my way. I wanted to support Susan, who was my friend, but I agreed with her mother. I was torn. I kept silent and observed. That didn't work. "Is there something about that site that's important to you?" Susan didn't answer. "Is it Christy?" Still, no answer. "Susan, help me understand. Those people…"

"I miss Mark!" She rushed back to the sink and began washing the dishes. "Helping *those people* brings me…"

"Oh, Honey." Mrs. Pederman ran to her daughter's side and hugged her. Susan crumbled in her mother's arms. They both slid to the kitchen floor and sobbed.

I didn't know what to do. Should I join the embrace? Should I let them have their moment? Should I go out back with the kids? Should I slip away quietly? Emotions weren't my strong suit, so I took the path of least resistance.

Mark was murdered over a year ago. Susan had a momentary breakdown after the funeral, but she seemed to manage okay. What a detective I was. She'd been mourning him quietly all this time, and I made our friendship a one-way relationship. I'd used Susan as my counselor and advisor, never stopping to wonder what she needed. Sure, I'd helped Hannah, but that, too, was a mutual benefit. I watched a mother and daughter share a meaningful embrace; their bodies shook as one. I did what came naturally. I got in my car and drove away.

Shame filled my heart. I hadn't been a good friend to her. I'd taken from the friendship but not given back. Was I that way with everyone else? I made a mental note to discuss it in my next counseling session.

Chapter Ten

Monday, March 24, 6:15 PM—El Comandantes base of operation, Antioch, Tennessee

Homicide and Auto Theft obtained our respective warrants, ours to search for Tito Ruiz and theirs to search for stolen vehicles. We met Detective Underwood and his team from Auto Theft Unit two blocks from the alleged new base of the gang, El Comandantes. Two SWAT teams from Nashville joined us and readied themselves for a violent response to our search. Twenty-seven officers in all: two from Homicide—Sam and me, five from Auto Theft Unit—including Detective Underwood, and two ten-person SWAT teams. Chief Clendenon insisted on *a surplus of officers* to handle the gang. Blow this raid, and heads would roll, beginning with his.

I watched as everyone donned protective gear, amazed that this operation was put together in three days. I strapped my protective vest in place and nodded. We'd scoped out the place earlier in the day and made our final plans. According to the intel, the El Comandantes gang had taken over an abandoned Bargain Depot warehouse on the south side of Nashville, making it easy to move stolen cars in and out without detection. We expected anywhere from fifteen to thirty members to be present when we breached. I imagined a major shootout.

I thought Detective Underwood and I would first enter and present our respective warrants at the main door, and if they resisted, we'd lead the SWAT team into the building like I'd seen in so many police drama series. That was not the reality. Since the building was still the property of Bargain Depot Incorporated and reportedly vacant, we were not required to announce ourselves. It was obvious by the number of cars present that several people were on site illegally. The Auto Theft officers positioned themselves by each of the four dock bay doors, assuming that was where the vehicles would be stationed. Sam and I were positioned near a small side door. Each of the SWAT teams handled the two main entrances and exits.

When the time came, they used a doorbuster to smash open the doors. They announced themselves as "SWAT" and tossed concussion grenades inside. Not only did they initiate the breach of the building, but they subdued everyone on site without a single shot fired. It was impressive! I could have watched the body cam footage over and over again. I anticipated a bloodbath, a shootout until the last man fell. Thankfully, I was wrong. The gang gave up immediately. I suppose, in the grand scheme of things, they thought their chances with the legal system were better than they were against two units of SWAT officers.

Once we were given the *all clear*, Homicide detectives and Auto Theft Unit officers entered and searched the facility. For the Auto Theft Unit, it was like discovering the famed city of Eldorado. High-end and specialty cars were in every stage of the alteration process, preparing the new versions of these autos for distribution and sale. It was the Mother Lode—twenty-six cars in all, mostly American muscle cars. It looked like a scene from the *Fast and Furious* movies. Detective Underwood and his team began the tedious task of processing the cars. He didn't seem to mind.

For Homicide, it was an arduous undertaking, trying to extract information from an organization that quite literally made weak links disappear. I spoke fluent Spanish, but it was of no use. They were tight-lipped to the death. Sam and I were relegated to a face-to-face search of the members of the El Comandantes for Tito Ruiz.

SWAT had the men and women lying face down on the hard, cold cement floor of the warehouse with their wrists zip-tied behind them. We would roll them over and hold the picture of Tito Ruiz next to each man's face. We'd exhausted our supply of gang members and were mentally kicking ourselves when I heard one of the SWAT members shout, "Detectives." He was standing on the deck of an office platform in the southwest corner of the building. He waved us forward.

I ran on ahead, and Sam hurried after. As I took the steps three at a time, I landed on the decking quickly. He pointed into the small office with two desks covered in money and keys. I noticed a body on a couch in the back. "Is he alive?" I asked.

"Barely. Ambulance is on its way." He turned the man's head my way. "This your guy?"

"Yes."

It was Tito Ruiz. They'd patched him up, but he was clinging to life. "You join your team downstairs. We'll handle this." He met Sam at the door to the tiny office and went to the main floor to process their catch.

Piles of rags and bandages lay on the floor beside the small couch. They were all soaked with blood. I bagged one for a blood-type match with the Bentley. By the looks of things, the shooter hit Tito four or five times. I was surprised he had enough stamina to make to the street and into his accomplice's car. I shook him gently and called his name. His eyes stayed shut. We stayed with Tito until the ambulance pulled away.

When we turned around to go to our car, we noticed Detective Underwood walking our way. He shook our hands and said, "All said and done, twenty-one men, two women, and over eighty-five thousand in cash. It was a great bust for all parties. Thanks for the teamwork." He walked away. Sam had the biggest smile. Whatever the rift was between Sam and the Auto Theft Unit, this bust went a long way in healing it.

Chapter Eleven

Tuesday, March 25, 9:45 AM—Davidson County Mayor's Office

The Mayor's office didn't take long to jump on the good news. They ran with it before all the facts could be confirmed. Even though the Auto Theft Unit's bust was bigger news than ours, Mayor O'Reilly put all the focus on Homicide. We still had questions—questions about the owners of the nine-millimeter handguns. Who told Tito about the Bentley? Who picked him up from the scene? All we knew was Tito's prints and blood were in the car and on the gun.

For now, the mayor only seemed to care that the alleged murderer of Dean Swain was in custody, lying in a local hospital bed under constant guard. The DNA and fingerprints were enough to pin Tito Ruiz as the alleged murderer of Dean Swain. His gun matched the bullets in Dean's body. For the mayor, that finished the case. He didn't seem to care about the car theft bust like I thought he would. Bringing down one of Nashville's two major gangs was quite an accomplishment. Why wasn't Detective Underwood invited to the mayor's office?

He was obsessed with the Swain case. In less than a week, Sam and I went from victims of *Alice in Wonderland's* Queen of Hearts to Mayor O'Reilly's two favorite people. We stepped off the elevator into the welcoming arms of reporters from channels two, four, five, and seventeen. We were the golden children once again. And leading the song of praise was no one other than Jonathan Lee Thomas, Dean Swain's stepfather.

"Ladies and gentlemen of the press, let me present our heroes."
He ran up and put his arms around us—Sam on his right, me on
his left—just like we were the best of friends. "Nashville's own
Holmes and Watson: Detectives Tidwell and Rhodes."

I assumed I was Dr. Watson. Mr. Thomas had a reputation
of being a little misogynistic—if one could be a *little* misogynistic.
I was surprised he included me at all in his praise and gave my
correct title as a detective. He built us up as heroes, enhancing
little details occasionally, forgetting to include the real heroes of
SWAT. No matter how hard we tried to get words in edgewise,
the press took his version and ran with it. He made a better story
for their audiences. Where ours was black and white, Jonathan's
was a kaleidoscope of color with villains and heroes. This wasn't
his first rodeo, and by praising us he inadvertently put himself in
the limelight. But he had the added pleasure of coming across as
humble and appreciative—the perfect man to head up the East
Bank Project.

I told Mr. Thomas we still had at least two more shooters
out there. When he learned they shot Tito and not Dean, he said,
"Why search for them? They deserve medals as far as I'm concerned."
He and Mayor O'Reilly made it perfectly clear the only life that
mattered was Dean's.

Mayor O'Reilly said, "This is a time to celebrate, detectives.
Relax and enjoy the moment."

He said these moments don't come often, but once a year
was too often for me. I loved my job, but I despised the notoriety.
A simple thank you would do for me. I could tell Sam felt the
same—if not worse.

Sam finally managed to pull the captain aside and appraise
him of the remaining aspects of the case. Captain Harris told us,
"The mayor is right. Savor moments like this. They are too far and
too few." He added we could continue wrapping up the case when
all the hoopla died down.

We tried to escape the scene. Sam and I easily evaded the

reporters who were more interested in Mr. Thomas than us. We slipped along the far wall and cut back to the office door. He and I stole a glance back at the mayor and his party before Sam pressed the down arrow. As I stepped onto the elevator, I heard a voice calling out, "Detectives Tidwell and Rhodes."

Sam held the elevator door open. "Yes, Mr. Mayor?"

"You're not leaving already, are you?"

I let Sam answer. "We were heading back to Homicide, Mayor."

"Don't leave yet. This is all for you," he said with a sweep of his hand about the room. "We are so proud of you. I feel that I need to do something more to honor you for solving this case so quickly and efficiently. Jonathan gave me a wonderful idea." *Oh great. It never goes well when mayors or their friends have wonderful ideas that included rank and file members.* "He thinks we should present you at the fundraiser this weekend."

"That's not necessary," Sam said. "This was quite enough, sir."

Jonathan stepped forward. "Nonsense, my boy. You and your pretty lady here will be my personal guests."

"Pretty Lady?" I asked. "I don't do well at those kinds of things." It was like they didn't even hear me speak. No one acknowledged my comment. I was to be seen and not heard.

"I don't have anything appropriate to wear to that kind of event," Sam said. I hoped desperately that he could wiggle himself and his *pretty little lady* out of this.

Just for good measure, I said, "Me either. I don't have anything that formal, but thanks for the invitation."

"I wouldn't dream of letting you go without showing my deepest gratitude." Then, in front of everyone, he looked me over and gave me precision estimates of my height, weight, and measurements, including bust size. The sad thing was that Mr. Thomas was right. It better not make the news, though. He gave Sam an accurate sizing of his coat and pant sizes. I had to admit, he was good. He turned to the mayor. "I assume you have their home addresses, Mike?"

THE LEAST OF THESE

"We sure can get it." Wasn't that illegal? Could he give out our personal information?

"Great!" Mr. Thomas said. "I'll have a seamstress meet you, Miss Rhodes, to fit you for a ballgown." Looking at Sam, he said, "And my personal tailor will take care of your needs, Detective Tidwell." Yeah, I noticed it too. I was *Miss Rhodes*, and Sam was *Detective Tidwell*. No respect. So much for my earlier comment. "I'll send my driver to retrieve you both Saturday night."

"Uh, well…" Sam said it all.

"Wonderful! Then it's settled." With that, we were dismissed. What had we done to deserve all the attention? Better question: What had we gotten ourselves into? A formal event that the mid-south would watch with interest.

As soon as the elevator doors closed, Sam asked, "This is a dance, isn't it?"

"Of course, it's a dance, Sam. It's a fundraiser ball. You didn't think that referred to sports, did you?" I was taking my frustrations out on Sam because he was safe. *A dance?* It was the last thing I needed—to be paraded around a fundraising dance like fresh meat for the photographers' pleasure. Once again, I had to push the past down. I couldn't afford to let it surface now, especially not with a public event looming.

70

Chapter Twelve

Sam and I were digging into the physical evidence and CSI's report, searching for leads for the other shooters, when the Captain opened the conference room door, leaned in, and praised us on a job well done. He also made one more comment specific to me. "This happens when you stay in your lane, Rhodes, and let everyone else do their respective jobs. Your job is homicide. Nashville has competent departments that can handle everything else." As he walked off, he added, "Drive in your own lane, Rhodes."

Sam closed the door and rolled his eyes. Just then, I received a frantic call from Susan Ripley. She was rambling on and on about missing people. I'd never heard her so hysterical. Even when Sam and I broke the news about her husband's death, she'd been stoic. I remember referring to her as a Stepford wife. Of course, that perception had changed over the months of our budding friendship—a friendship where I was more of the needy little sister. Now, she needed me, but I needed to dig in and wrap this case up as soon as possible. Susan's timing couldn't have been worse.

"Susan, take a breath. I can't understand a word you're saying."

"She's gone, Abbey. No one knows where, and Judith just moved right in like it was hers to take."

"Slow down. Who's gone? Who's Judith?"

She rambled about Christy, who wouldn't leave her mission field without telling someone. "She's gone, and she left all her stuff."

71

"She probably went to see someone in need. Susan, she'll walk back there any moment. You'll see."

"She's gone, and no one cares. Judith just moved into Christy's tent and claimed everything. I need you, Abbey."

I tried to explain that I couldn't jump in a car and drive to the homeless encampments on the west bank of Nashville's Cumberland River. We had tons of work on the Swain case. I couldn't drop everything and break free right now. My superiors were breathing down my neck. When she relentlessly pushed the issue, I snapped.

"I can't leave my job and be your personal police force, rushing to your aid every time you get scared."

I know I hurt her feelings because the phone went silent for nearly a minute.

Then, with a broken voice, Susan said, "It's not just Christy. Three other people are missing. Maybe that's important enough for your little police force." She hung up.

My pride puffed up like a peacock's. I looked at the phone but refused to give in.

"That was rude," Sam said.

"I know. Doesn't she know how busy we are? Besides, I told her that place was dangerous."

"I meant you, Abbey. You were rude to her. If she needs your help, it's probably important."

"You heard the captain, Sam. He was clear about my short leash. My neck hurts from the yo-yo of praise and criticism. What about my lane? I'm supposed to stay in it. Remember?"

"Don't take it personally, Abbey."

"Oh, I don't. I know that's just the way things are. Our superiors bark orders, and we're supposed to obey."

"Maybe, but they don't have to know everything."

"I have a job to do, Sam. We have a job to do." I busied myself with the reports. "You know that as well as I. We can be on the mayor's mountain one moment and in his dungeon the next. Let's do what we can to stay on the mountain."

Sam wore me down. I finally gave in, but I insisted he come too. He drove and had to listen to my bad attitude the entire trip. By the time we got to the camp, Susan was in a physical altercation with a homeless woman named Judith. Damien Jones and his helpers were attempting to break up the fight.

"Get out of my tent!" Judith screamed as she pushed Susan to the ground. She lifted a small log and swung it hard. Susan barely rolled free. A piece of the log broke free and bounced our way.

"Police! Drop the log," Sam shouted.

Judith either didn't hear him or chose to ignore his command. As she brought the log up for another swing, I tackled her, throwing us both into the side of Christy's tent. The woman screamed and flailed wildly. I subdued her and cautioned her about making any other attempt at violence. "Get off me. She's squeezing in on my find. I was here first. This is my tent! She can't have it."

Susan brushed the leaves and dirt from her shirt and said, "This is Christy's tent. I know because I bought it for her."

"She's gone. It's mine now!"

It took several minutes before Judith settled down and took a breath, but she continued to mumble that she had the right to the empty tent and its contents. Damien was trying to explain that she was an outsider and that the first dibs on the tent went to someone in his camp.

"You just want it for yourself," she screamed and struggled once again to find a suitable weapon.

She was a big woman. It appeared she had not struggled to find ample food as a homeless woman. Sam finally decided to zip-tie her arm to a small tree. "I'm telling you one last time, Judith. If you try anything, you'll head to jail in the back of my car."

"You have no right!" She kicked his leg. At that, Sam read Judith her rights and cut the zip tie. He did as promised; he put her in handcuffs and stuffed her in the back of his car.

"I suppose you'll be coming back for the rest of us," the tall, skinny man said as he pulled his little hatchet from his belt.

"You holster that hatchet, or I will have you in cuffs," I said, stepping in his direction. I was begging this piece of crap to challenge me. I was ill-tempered and needed someone to vent my frustrations on. He glanced down at my Sig and complied with my order. The hatchet slid back in its place. Once everything finally settled down where we could have a decent conversation, I asked, "Where's Christy?"

"I don't know, and no one will help me find her."

I turned to the men. "When did you see her last?"

Damien shrugged his shoulders. I doubt he even cared. Like Judith, Christy's absence was an excuse to confiscate her possessions, including the new sleeping bag and set of pots. He looked at Susan and said, "Ask her. She's always with her." I looked her way.

"I don't know. That's the problem. She makes the third person missing from the camps," Susan said, running her fingers through her hair, dislodging a small twig. "Or is it four?"

"Four," an older man said from the campfire. "Four in the last week, and they're all women."

Damien turned and said, "Nobody asked you, Freeman." The man shriveled, fading into his black hoodie.

"Who all is missing?" I asked.

"Alice, Grace, and now Christy. I forgot the other woman's name," Susan said. She approached the fire and asked the man, "Who else is missing?" He glanced out from the darkness of his hood but said nothing. "Please, tell us. Who else is gone?"

"Millie," he whispered.

"She doesn't count," Damien snapped. As soon as he did, the man's face slid back into the black hole of his hood.

"Who's Millie?" I asked. Damien glared at the older man. Susan shook her head. She didn't know the woman. "Will someone tell me? Who is Millie, and why doesn't she count?"

Damien explained that Millie was previously a part of their camp but had been caught stealing from his tent twice. They'd

banished her from the main camp, and she made a home underneath an old set of box springs on the side of the hill. Then, she
moved to the area under the interstate. She had occupied a tent
next to the soldier.

"She doesn't count because nobody wants her around. That's
why she wanders from place to place." Damien turned to Sam.
"Her kind doesn't belong here." I knew he meant that about us as
well. He turned to Susan and said, "Neither does she. We're fine
on our own."

The hair on my neck bristled, and my shoulders tightened.
"How dare you! She's done nothing but give to this community."

"She's not one of us. We don't need her pity or her things."

"You sure are all twisted up over the things she bought Christy,"
I said.

I was about to go all over him when Sam redirected the
conversation to the missing individuals. "Okay, so we have three—
possibly four—women missing, and no one knows where they are?"

Susan said, "Abbey, something terrible has happened. Christy
left her belongings."

"Whatever they left is ours to divide," Damien said. "It's our
way. Our place, our rules."

I gritted my teeth. Sam glanced at me, letting me know he
felt the same way, but I should be quiet. He announced, "I'm going
to take a quick look around. You and Susan search Christy's tent
and see what you can find."

"You don't have the authority to search it. That tent is our
property now," Damien said.

"So sue me," Sam said.

"If she left, the property reverts to us," Damien persisted.
"That's our law."

"If Christy is missing, this may become an official crime scene,"
Sam said, and Susan began to cry. "Maybe I should call South
Precinct and have them come look around. They can scour the
entire site from the river to the road."

That caught Damien off guard. He and his men immediately backed off.

"Look in the tent, if you must. You can take her personal items, but the tent and the pots stay with us."

"Come on, Susan." I took her by the arm and led her inside Christy's tent. The moment I stepped inside, something caught my eye. A flyer lying on top of her sleeping bag. "Cleaning Up Nashville rally," I read, and soon realized *cleaning up* meant ridding Nashville of the homeless. The rally was set for tomorrow at noon at Shelby Park.

Why would this flyer be in Christy's tent? Christy had no form of transportation and, as of one week ago, could barely sit up on her own. It was evident to me someone had moved her. Whoever moved her put this flyer in her tent. It was in pristine condition: no smudges, tears, or creases where it had been folded. Too good to have been found and brought back by Christy to her tent. Was it a message from Christy or to her? Was it a clue to her whereabouts, or was it a diversion meant to draw us away from the homeless camp? Nothing else in the tent looked out of place. There were no signs of a struggle.

"Her money pouch is here," Susan said, producing a small bag from within the lining of Christy's sleeping bag. "But it's empty. Who'd take the time to empty the purse and leave it here?"

"Well, Judith was in the tent when you arrived. She probably found it and emptied the bag."

"If she thought she would keep the tent, she would have left it here." Susan dug further inside the sleeping bag. "And here's her Bible. Abbey, she would never leave this. If she did go somewhere to minister to someone, she would have taken her Bible."

"Okay. Let's piece this together. Who all is missing? What do they have in common?"

"Of the four women, two made their homes along the bank of the Cumberland. Christy here and Millie up there," Susan said, pointing to the pillar to our east. Christy lived on the land Damien claimed as his city. Millie lived beside the soldier. "The other two women made their homes that way." Susan pointed toward the road. "Alice lived at the top in one of the old campers. Grace lived on the side of that trash pile." One from each of the four camps. Was that significant? If so, what did that mean?

Susan finished her search of Christy's tent. "The only thing missing besides the money is her new water pot," Susan said. "That's her lifeline. Do you see it outside?"

Susan and I scoured Christy's tent and the area around it for the pot or any clues to her disappearance—much to the frustration of Damien and his men. Nothing we found indicated signs of forced abduction or murder. The other residents had trampled the ground around the camp. No hope of finding a trail. "Someone probably took it when she left," I said. "If it was a new water pot, it would be in high demand here." Nothing I could think of off-hand gave any insights into the four disappearances. The only thing they had in common was their homelessness, which brought me back to the flyer. Maybe someone was beginning to *clean up* Nashville, starting with this site. I wondered if Sam was having better luck searching the other two areas. "Susan, I'm going to check with Sam."

"I'm coming with you," she said, hurrying to my side. She whispered, "I'm scared, Abbey."

"Just stay with me. I'll keep you safe." I was secretly hoping Damien or one of his henchmen would make a move so I could put him in his place.

"Thanks, but I meant I was scared for Christy. This isn't like her to leave the area."

There were four distinct areas where people gathered on this side of the river. The main camp with Damien was by far the largest. After we walked across the railroad tracks and climbed a hill that had become a dumping ground for old mattresses and furniture, we ran into Sam. He was talking with a young couple in a rusted-out, old camper.

"Well, please call me if you see or hear anything." He handed them his card and turned to address us.

"How'd it go?" he asked.

"Not good," I said. "Christy left precious possessions in her tent, but there are no signs of foul play. Only things missing from Christy's tent were the contents of her money bag and a water pot."

"I'm finding the same here," Sam said. "The missing woman up here left everything but her bucket, but they think someone from the dump stole it. They said a man down there tried to take it once before."

"So they're both missing water buckets?" I asked.

"That's understandable," Susan said. "Anything they could use to get water from the river would be priceless—a major tool for survival."

"Is there anywhere else Christy would go?"

"She goes between the four camps, checking on people and sharing the Gospel every chance she gets."

"Nowhere else?" Sam asked.

"She occasionally makes her way downtown to solicit support for her ministry."

"You mean she begs for money?" I asked. No reason to dress up the truth. Susan pursed her lips and nodded. I'd struck another nerve. I was getting too adept at getting in my discriminating digs. "Where would she do that?" I asked, trying to move the conversation along to the investigation.

"Down on Broadway," Susan said, "but she'd take her money bag and Bible if she went there."

"Maybe that's where she got the flyer," I said.

Sam's phone rang. "Tidwell." He turned to me and pointed to his wrist. "Yes, sir. We're just canvassing the homeless camp for clues. No, sir. Yes, sir. Right away, Lieutenant." Sam put his phone back in his pocket and said, "Abbey, the captain wants an update on the case right away."

"Does he know about the missing women?" Susan asked.

"No," Sam said. "This is our secret for now. There's no point in stirring the hornet's nest unnecessarily. He wants to know how the Swain case is going."

Susan turned to me and said, "I thought you solved that case. It was all over the news."

"We found Dean Swain's murderer, but there's still a lot of loose ends we have to tie up."

"But what about the women?" she asked.

"The Swain case takes precedence. It's definitely a homicide, so we're allowed to work it." We walked Susan to her car before returning to speak with Captain Harris. On the way back, I told Sam about the flyer. He agreed that it was probably planted, and he said we should follow up with it later. Then he looked at me and smiled. "But if you want to stay in your lane, you could always pass it on to South Precinct."

"We need to find that soldier, Sam. He's the only lead we have."

"Good luck with that. I don't think we'll ever catch him until he wants to be caught. Until then, let's work with what we got so far and build a case from there."

Chapter Thirteen

Thursday, March 27, 7:35 AM—Homicide

Once the M.E. narrowed the time of death between twelve and two on the morning of March 20, Sam and I scoured the streets and buildings near the crime scene for cameras. We located one on the east end of the building adjacent to the recycling lot. It was a large warehouse comprised of four businesses including a go-kart track and an airsoft course. The owner of the building sent a digital copy, which confirmed Tito's ride the night of the murder. It caught him staggering down the road until someone picked him up in a black Dodge Challenger with Colorado plates. The car belonged to a member of the El Comandantes gang—a man presently in custody from the raid on their last chop shop in Antioch. Through a series of individual cameras in the other direction, we were able to piece together a timeline.

We secured the footage and scanned everything between ten and two. Piecing the clips together, we discovered eight vehicles leaving the area. Unfortunately, only four of those vehicles had identifiable plates. We ran them through the system and noted the owners' names and addresses. I printed images of the other two to keep on hand during the investigation.

We put Spence on Dean's phone records, including calls and text messages. He was going to attempt to identify patterns, regularly called numbers, and check for any communications the night of Dean's murder. Detective Baxter was doing the same for Tito's phone. We reviewed the report on the plasters—five different sets of shoes, one set belonged to a worker for the recycling business, and another belonged to Dean Swain. We took the photos back to the crime scene.

Sam matched the prints to the sketch of the crime scene. It was amazing how it told the story of the other two shooters. Their tracks began at the edge of the paved drive, indicating they parked their vehicle or vehicles near the back of the lot and never drove off the pavement. Two men: one wearing size ten and a half and the other size twelve. Both imprints were from tactical Fast-Tac Low brand shoes. What we could tell of the pattern of their shoes was that they both left the pavement and walked directly to an unhitched semi-trailer. Each track stopped behind a set of wheels. From there, the smaller set of prints led to the spot where Dean died and then returned to the pavement.

"I don't know about you, Sam, but this tells me they had a plan and worked in unison. This wasn't any chance encounter. They purposefully hid their car or cars, took cover behind the trailer, and waited for the chance to shoot Tito."

"I agree. It may be chance, but they have identical shoes—maybe a gang or a unit of some kind."

"Remember when I had to move from his body to the east to get a clear line of sight on the driver?"

Sam nodded then knelt behind the back tires, pulled out his Glock, and lined up the shot. "If the Bentley were still here, I could hit the dash."

"And if I shot from here," I began, kneeling behind the other set of tires, "I would hit the passenger door and driver's seat. But don't forget the car was originally over there," I said, pointing to the beginning of the ruts and streaks.

"We need to confirm that with ballistics. See if the slugs are consistent with each gun."

I asked Sam, "What would that tell us?"

Sam stood and brushed the gravel from his pants. "They never targeted Dean. They counted on Tito shooting him, or they wanted

Tito to steal the car and were positioned just in case he tried to kill Dean."

"The first scenario is a pretty big gamble," I said. "If it's the second scenario, they screwed up royally." I imagined the scene again, watching Dean's movements, inserting Tito and the other shooters. "If Dean was down by the fence looking across the river to the potential parking garage, Tito could have slipped in and out unnoticed."

Sam scratched his beard. "So what made him turn around?"

"The sound of the engine starting," I offered. "It would have startled Dean, causing him to turn around and reach for his gun."

Sam snapped his fingers. "But the officers said the engine wasn't running when they arrived. If Tito started the Bentley, it would have idled until it ran out of gas."

"That's right. Dean didn't turn it off; he was dead. Tito wouldn't have bothered to turn it off. He was wounded and running for his life. Who does that leave? There were no prints leading from the semi-trailer to the Bentley."

"Did the shooters' shoeprints go to the car?" Sam asked.

"No."

"What about the worker's?"

"No. His prints were over by the parking area, and he said he didn't touch anything. When he came in and saw the dead body, he called nine-one-one and waited for the police." I ran to the spot where Dean parked the Bentley and looked around for more prints. "Sam, look." I slid my shoe over the gravel. "This is pavement. It's only covered with a spattering of gravel."

"Someone else turned off the car," he said. "Someone who didn't want it drawing unnecessary attention. Someone standing on this side of the car. Abbey, we may have a third person—someone making sure the shooters did their job."

"This was an orchestrated kill zone intended to look like Tito and Dean exchanged gunfire and died; only Tito ruined the scene by living." I took a deep breath and tried to make sense of it all.

"If they wanted Dean dead, why not do it themselves? Why rely on a wildcard like Tito Ruiz?"

"Why not pay Tito to kill him and take the Bentley? They could have dumped the body anywhere after that."

"I assume they didn't want to risk Tito talking, Sam."

We discussed the paradox of the scene. In some respects, the orchestration was brilliant and professional. In other respects, it was sloppy and haphazard. Setting the scene up to look like a botched carjacking would have ended the investigation there. But putting an unused gun of the wrong caliber in Dean's hand betrayed the amateur nature of the scene. It was almost as if two different people planned the hit. Who would the observer be? Why not leave the Bentley running? Why let a wounded Tito Ruiz run right by you?

My phone rang. "What? Slow down, Susan. You're not making any sense. You're where? What happened? I'll be right there."

"What happened?" Sam asked.

"They took Susan to East Precinct for disrupting the Clean Up Nashville rally—accusing the leaders of killing Christy."

Chapter Fourteen

Thursday, March 27, 10:00 AM—East Precinct

We pulled into East Precinct and made our way to the interrogation rooms. Lieutenant Daniels greeted us. "She's in room two. They're in the middle of taking her statement."

"What happened?"

"According to the event coordinator, she started yelling at the speaker, calling her a murderer—something about a woman named Christy."

"No way. Susan would never do that," I said. She was such a sweet, reserved person.

"Several witnesses on site corroborated the story. She tore down their banner and turned over their volunteer tables."

"Are you sure this is Susan Ripley?" I asked. "I've never seen her lose her temper."

"Yes, Abbey. She wasn't so reserved today. It took two officers to pull her off of the stage. I called you out of courtesy when she mentioned she was your friend."

"Thanks, Lieutenant Daniels. I still can't believe it. She's the kind of person that prays for her enemies. I mean—she prayed for her husband's murderer and asked God to help her forgive him."

"What can I say," Lieutenant Daniels said. "She hit her breaking point."

All the signs were there, but I failed to see them. She was missing her husband, Mark. She was trying to raise two kids alone and just lost her friend, Christy. To top it off, she asked me for help, and I turned her away. "What's going to happen to her?"

"Stacey Hopkins, the leader of Clean Up Nashville, is pressing charges, so unless you can talk her out of it, I'll have to process her."

"Where is she?" Sam asked. "I'd like to talk with Stacey Hopkins."

"Let me talk her out of it, Sam. Susan is my friend, and this is my responsibility."

"Agreed, but you're too close to it. Let me do this. I have more experience in negotiations than you do." I turned to see what Lieutenant Daniels would say, and he nodded.

"She's in room three."

"Can I watch?" I asked.

"You know where it is," he said.

I waited for him to walk down the hall and around the corner. I acted like I would watch Sam and Stacey but stepped into Susan's observation room instead. I listened as she repeated her story to the officer. "I pulled into Shelby Park just moments before the festivities started. There were tents for food, activities for the children, and a main stage for the speakers." She sounded normal to me. "I grabbed a chair in the back corner. I wanted to hear what they had to say and see who could have given Christy the flyer."

Susan took a deep breath and tried to steady her shaking hands. "They introduced the woman who organized today's meeting. An older woman rose and waved at the crowd. She was met with moderate applause. Two speakers later, I was growing impatient. It was boring; lots of statistics. I felt defeated, like I wouldn't find anything here that would lead me to Christy. A young woman rose and took her place at the podium. She could have been a fashion model. She was so pretty."

Susan looked in the two-way mirror and reached up to push a strand of hair behind her ear. The red marks from pulling against the handcuffs reminded her where she was. They must have needed to restrain her. I still couldn't believe it.

Susan continued her story, "She said, 'My name is Stacey Hopkins, and I'm passionate about cleaning up Nashville.' She had such a sweet voice, but she had a bitter tongue. 'Our typical brand of homelessness has come and gone in the wake of a tidal wave of illegal immigrants. They're making their way to Nashville and bringing drugs, guns, and crime with them.' More applause. 'If we don't get a handle on homelessness today, we're going to lose Nashville to them.'"

Susan huffed. "She said, *Them* like the homeless were a plague. It triggered something in me. I was upset, but the crowd applauded louder. She churned the fire hotter, saying, 'And when we lose our city, we lose our ability to keep our children safe.' She was so passionate in her speaking that more people gathered at the rally."

Susan shifted in her seat and rubbed one of her wrists. They were probably sore from the cuffs. "The woman had them in the palm of her hand. She said, 'I may look like a typical soccer mom, but you endanger my children, and I become a momma bear—wildly protective.' People were whistling and cheering her on. She was just getting started. Her voice inflection and volume rose and fell like a heartbeat. She was a master orator, not some soccer mom or model. 'Our parks, like Shelby Park here today, were designed and maintained for citizens—citizens who support them with their finances and labor. We deserve safe and clean parks—safe and clean streets—safe and clean neighborhoods.' The crowd erupted in cheers. Others in the park began to move in our direction."

Susan leaned in and said, "Can you believe it? She told them, 'We need to band together and clear our neighborhoods of the homeless like we do of weeds or our trash.' That's when I lost it. I screamed, 'They're not trash! They're people just like you and me. What did you do to Christy, you murderer?' Next thing I knew, you were putting me in handcuffs."

"Do you remember what you did?" the officer asked.

"Only what you told me," she admitted. "You said I ripped her banner and overturned their tables."

Oh, Susan. I'm so sorry. I should have been there for you. I left the observation room to watch Sam's conversation with Stacey Hopkins. I turned to the right and bumped into Sam, who was shaking Stacey's hand, thanking her for understanding. I watched in awe as she told Sam she appreciated the insights. Stacey turned and walked away.

"What happened, Sam?"

"She's dropping all charges."

"How did you manage that?"

"I told Susan's story, starting with her husband's death and ending with her friend's disappearance." He put a hand on my shoulder. "I appealed to her soft side."

Sam and I waited in the lobby for Susan's release. A woman entered, demanding to see the officer in charge. She demanded they drop the charges on Susan Ripley. She introduced herself as Lyndsey Franks, co-founder of The Least of These Ministries.

I stood and said, "I'm Detective Abbey Rhodes."

"Are you in charge here?" she asked.

"No, but I'm Susan's friend."

"I want her released. They have no right to keep her."

"Calm down, Lyndsey. They're going to release her in a few moments."

"Thank God," she said. "He answered our prayers." She put her hand on my shoulder.

I immediately bristled. *God had nothing to do with it. Thank Sam.* "How do you know her?" I know my voice held a little attitude. I couldn't help myself.

"She's helped us in our work with the homeless," she said. "Susan wouldn't hurt a fly." She paused for a moment. "Although, I've been tempted to give Stacey a punch in the face on more than one occasion. The woman is heartless."

"Well, that heartless woman," Sam began, "just dropped all charges against Susan Ripley."

"Praise God! He still performs miracles."

Before I could object, Susan entered the lobby and saw us talking. "Oh. You know each other?"

"We just met," Lyndsey said. She gave Susan a big hug. "I'm so sorry. Jerry called me and told me what happened."

"I still don't remember all of it," Susan said. "I'm so embarrassed." Then she turned to me and said, "I'm sorry to be a bother."

"Oh, shut up." I hugged her and held on as long as I could. "I'm sorry I wasn't there for you."

"I hate to break up the love fest," Sam said, "but we need to get back to work."

Before leaving, I told Lyndsey I would need to follow up with her on her homeless ministries. She handed me her card and said, "Let's do lunch tomorrow and talk. I'll tell you everything I know."

"Susan, need a ride to your car?"

"I'll take her," Lyndsey said. "I might need to wander around Shelby Park to undo some of Stacey's brainwashing."

I hugged Susan again and left.

Chapter Fifteen

Thursday, March 27, 4:06 PM—Home of Stacey Hopkins

Sam and I waited in the parlor of Stacey Hopkins's home, a mansion in a neighborhood of mansions. Stacey lobbied for a Nashville free of homeless *vagrants and criminals*. She was openly opposed to Lyndsey Franks, who headed up the organization The Least of These, which fought for the rights of *the disenfranchised*.

Not knowing my background, Sam joked, "One woman's trash is another woman's treasure." I didn't let on that it was a personal subject for me. Even though I'd been homeless myself in my mid-teens, I held a callous attitude toward those who depended on the help of others—who felt they had the right to expect aid from those who were somehow better off. I'd worked hard as a young teenager to provide myself with food, clothing, and lodging. I'd done what I could to ensure I was off the streets and earned my way. I made sacrifices to earn my way. I wasn't always proud of my choices, but I wasn't a beggar on the streets.

Even with that attitude, I resented Sam's comment implying the homeless were *trash*.

I knew exactly how Susan felt about the subject. She said the people not only needed a *hand up*, but they also needed love. She meant God's love. Somehow, she considered her hands and gifts an extension of God's. My dad used those exact words about his ministry. Unlike my father, Susan meant them—she lived them. Now, because of her breakdown, Sam and I were pulled into the middle of a feud between two lobby groups: parents who wanted to protect their children from the homeless and citizens who felt it was their civic duty to provide for the less fortunate.

"Detectives." I stood as Stacey entered the room. She was immaculately dressed, like she would host a dinner party for the rich and famous.

Sam started the conversation. "Thank you again, Mrs. Hopkins, for your gracious gesture toward Mrs. Ripley."

"No problem, Detective Tidwell. What can I do for you?"

"I appreciate your willingness to help us in our investigation. This should only take a few minutes."

"Anything I can do to help. Would you care for something to drink?"

"What we would like is to know what your organization does in its efforts to clean up Nashville," I said. "I looked at your website and understand your views and lobbying efforts. What else do you do to clean up Nashville."

"Do I detect a little sarcasm, Detective…"

"Rhodes. No, Mrs. Franks. I understand your position. I'm just curious as to *how* you work to rid Nashville of the homeless."

"We lobby for changes in the law—changes that will protect us and our children from—" She crossed her legs and folded her hands over her knees. "Protect us from those who infringe upon our land and our rights."

"Yes," I persisted. "I read that on your website. I'm asking *how* you intend to rid Nashville of them."

She gave me a condescending smile. "First, when we gather once a month, our group spends a day cleaning the trash from the neighborhoods."

"By *trash*, do you mean actual garbage—or the homeless?"

She stood sharply. "I'm sorry, but I thought you were here seeking my assistance, not to criticize our valuable work."

"Please, Mrs. Hopkins, sit. My partner meant nothing derogatory by her question." Sam pointed back to her chair and waited for her to sit. "But we do need details as to the cleaning up process. It's critical to our investigation."

"I don't think she likes me," Stacey said. "I can tell in the tone of her voice."

"I'm sitting right here, Mrs. Hopkins. I can answer for myself." That was said as much for Sam as it was for Stacey Hopkins. "Do you physically remove homeless persons from these locations?"

"We have—on occasion—relocated certain individuals if they refuse to move," she said matter-of-factly, looking at Sam instead of me. "But that is rare."

I rolled my eyes, so Sam followed up on her statement. "By any chance have you relocated any individuals who were camped on the southeast bank of the Cumberland, east of Riverfront Park?"

"Move them from that site? Why heavens, no. Why would we do that?"

"To *clean up* Nashville," I said, somewhat confused by her reaction.

"Where else would we put them?"

"I'm not sure I understand." I didn't. "There's a huge settlement there, and it's in Nashville."

"My goodness. They can have that land. No one else seems to want it." She looked at me. "I thought you wanted to chastise me some more."

"For what?" I asked.

"Exactly! They think I'm a selfish pig—oh, sorry. No offense."

"None taken," Sam said. "I know what you're trying to say." After the pig comment, he was suddenly less kind in his tone. "So you don't care if the homeless live on the banks of the river? You're not concerned with cleaning that area up?"

"Well," she said. "If they were making their camp at Riverfront Park, it would be different. As it is, that group keeps to themselves and lives away from the neighborhoods."

That still didn't make sense to me. "So, help me understand. You're not against the homeless?"

"Yes, of course I am."

"But not if they live under the interstate or on the junky side of the river."

She pointed to me and told Sam, "See, she understands. I cannot get those people from that Least of These organization to understand. Thank God, you do."

"No, I don't." *Why is everybody bringing God into this? Can't we just focus on the homeless?* I understood Sam's and Susan's frustrations with this woman. This time, I didn't hide my disgust. "You just don't want them around *you*."

"Around my children," she corrected. "It's unsafe." She did have a point there. I knew first-hand, homeless people were not safe to be around. They may not threaten your life, but they would help themselves to anything you possess.

"We didn't come here to debate policies," Sam said, pointing the conversation back to the investigation. "We are looking into some disappearances from that camp."

"What does that have to do with me?" she asked.

"In your speech, you encouraged people to rid Nashville of the homeless." I studied her expression.

"Encouraging them isn't the same as doing it myself." She gave me a coy smile. "If my speeches inadvertently inspire some to act inappropriately or do something questionable, it's not my fault."

She didn't mind taking the credit or passing the buck. This woman could do them both at the same time. Unbelievable.

"I suppose you don't think you're responsible when they protect the children and clean up the neighborhoods?" Sam asked.

"Well, of course I do. They wouldn't have acted if I hadn't organized a movement. Nashville is going to be a better place to live and work because of me and my organization. They need me."

She was a piece of work. She sounded just like the people in Washington. If things go well, take credit. If they go bad, blame someone else. This was getting us nowhere.

"Have you ever visited the campsite on the river?"

92

"Why, good heavens, no. Why would I do that?" She seemed quite perplexed by the question. "Those people don't bother me. They know where they belong. I wish the rest could follow their example."

I pulled out the flyer. "Is this one of your flyers?"

"Well, of course it is. You can read, can't you?" She had a snide side of her own. I could respect that.

"Could you tell me how this made its way inside one of their tents?" She looked at the flyer and shook her head. Sam's phone rang. It had a knack of doing that in the middle of interviews.

"Excuse me," Sam said. "I need to take this." I could hear him mumbling as he stepped away. A moment later he returned and said, "Abbey, we need to get back to the office. Sergeant McNally wants a word with us."

"Now?"

"Now." He thanked Stacey for her time and rushed me to the car. "We need to hurry because he's not wanting to congratulate us. We have something to answer for, and he wants us to do it in person."

That didn't sound good at all.

Chapter Sixteen

Friday, March 28, 7:03 AM—Homicide

My butt still hurt from the chewing-out Sergeant McNally gave us yesterday afternoon. I felt bad for getting Sam involved in my favor for Susan Ripley. I tried to tell Sarge that we legitimately investigated the possibility of an eyewitness, which led us to the other side of the river and the homeless camps. Once there, we were told that people were missing from their tents and shacks; we naturally followed the clues. The flyer in Christy's tent directed us to the Cleaning Up Nashville group. Susan's actions brought us to East Precinct, where we met Lyndsey, who just happened to lead the opposing cause.

Sarge didn't see it that way. He didn't care. Just like the rape and child abuse aspects of the Ripley case last year, I had to let this go. Homeless situations were not a part of Homicide investigations.

I could still hear Sergeant McNally's voice in my head, shouting, "How many times do I have to tell you, Rhodes? No body—no homicide. And even if there *was* a body, you wait until I assign it to you. Do you understand?"

I thought his head was going to explode. I'd never seen it that red, with that many veins bulging. One single cut, and he would have bled to death in seconds. I wanted to tell him the camp connected to our case, and we were following up on a witness, but I've learned to keep my mouth shut. Sam might disagree, but it's true. I wouldn't be known for talking when I should be listening. Sergeant McNally reiterated the captain's warning to stay in my lane.

94

I'm sure when I die, that's what they'll put that on my tombstone: *She couldn't stay in her lane.*

"Rhodes!"

Oh, no. What now? "Yes. Sergeant?" I asked as I was already in motion. "I'm coming."

I turned the corner into his cubicle and realized Sam was already sitting in his *office.*

"He's conscious."

"Conscious?" I asked.

Sarge was about to blow another gasket. "If you two would stay on the case at hand instead of chasing fights that don't belong to homicide, you might have known this yourselves."

I really didn't want to ask, but I had no clue who *he* was. "I'm sorry, Sarge, who are you talking about?"

"Tito Ruiz! Get your head in gear and work on your case, Rhodes. You too, Tidwell." He slammed his hands on his desk. The little cubicle shook, and the sound thundered across the office. "You two waiting for an invitation? Get out of here."

He didn't have to tell me again. I beat Sam to the parking lot.

He tossed me the key. "You drive."

The silence was deafening as we drove to the hospital. The criticism truly shook him. To me, it was a return to the Army. People in command barked, and those of us under them moved. Sometimes, it didn't even matter what we did as a response as long as we did something.

"Do we know if he's talking?" I asked.

Sam said nothing.

"I'm sorry I dragged you into this."

"You didn't twist my arm."

"Yes, but I kind of implied I needed your help."

I pulled into the parking garage. "If we can get the name of the person who tipped Tito off to the Bentley, we'll have a viable lead as to the other shooters."

He nodded.

The elevator door opened, and we rang the intercom for the intensive care unit.

"May I help you?" a young woman's voice asked.

"Detectives Tidwell and Rhodes. We're here for Tito Ruiz in room 4402."

The door clicked, and we pushed through. No one stood in the hall. "Hey Sam, isn't there supposed to be an officer outside his room?"

"He must be inside." Sam opened the door and stepped in. No one. "Call it in and see what happened to the detail."

As Sam moved to Tito's side and scanned the monitors, I called dispatch and inquired about the missing officer. An Officer Daniel Watson was supposed to be here on duty. They would track him down and send another officer to stand guard.

"Mister Ruiz." Sam shook his right arm. His eyes fluttered open. "I'm Detective Sam Tidwell. We have a few questions?"

"No hablo ingles." He coughed and began to wheeze.

Sam looked at me. I introduced us in Spanish. He nodded. I told him we knew he was in the Bentley and shot the owner. His eyes widened. I told him about our proof and the raid on his gang's warehouse. He pretended not to know what I was talking about. I could see fear in his eyes. He coughed again.

"His blood pressure is rising."

"That's because he's scared, Sam."

"Good. Ask him who tipped him off."

I asked Tito who called about the Bentley. He shook his head and said they would kill him. I told Tito they already tried. His entire body began to seize. He coughed repeatedly and struggled to breathe.

"Give us a name, Tito."

"Ch...Ch...Cha..." His eyes suddenly rolled back in his head, and his body spasmed. I watched as his blood pressure skyrocketed and his pulse doubled.

Sam hit the nurse's button and shouted, "We need help in here."

Within seconds, Tito's BP bottomed out, and his pulse

flatlined. "What's happening?" I cried. The next thing I knew, Sam and I were standing outside the room looking in.

A nurse pushed past us with a crash cart and called, "Clear." We watched as the hospital staff tried to resuscitate Tito Ruiz.

"Clear."

Tito's body jumped with the surge of electricity. His arms fell to the side.

"Clear."

His body jumped again, but the heart monitor remained flat and sang that monotonous tone telling everyone Tito was dead.

"I'm calling it," the doctor said. "Time of death—8:32."

"I don't understand," I said, opening the door. "We were talking with him, and his eyes rolled back, and his body shook."

As the rest of the team performed their respective tasks, a nurse met us at the door. "I'm sorry. Who are you?"

We flashed our badges. "Detectives Tidwell and Rhodes," Sam said.

"Like I said, we were told we could talk with him—that he was awake."

"Yes. An agent left ten minutes ago. He dismissed the officer, spoke with the patient, and left."

"You mean a detective? From our office?" I asked. "Can you describe him?"

"I think he was like FBI or something. He was dressed like those guys in *Men in Black*. He even kept his sunglasses on inside the room."

"Did he show his credentials?" Sam asked. She shrugged her shoulders. Looking around, Sam asked, "Where did the officer on duty go?"

"I'm sorry. I don't know. I didn't think much of it at the time."

Sam and I looked at each other. This case was going sideways. Why would the Feds be involved? "Do you have cameras in intensive care?" She shook her head. "What about the hallway?" I asked. Surely, a hospital would need cameras.

"I think so," she said. "You'll have to check with hospital

security on the first floor." She looked over her shoulder at the rest of her team. "I need to get back to it."

As we walked to the hallway to see if we could spot cameras, Sam asked, "What do you make of this?"

It was a good question. My mind was sorting the details. "It's more than a little fishy. The timing is too perfect to be a coincidence. We're missing something. A rich kid gets killed in a setup that injures his would-be carjacker. We get a call that Tito is conscious. Then someone looking like a Federal agent dismisses the officer and talks with Tito. Shortly afterward, Tito dies. That about sums it up."

"I don't believe in coincidence," Sam said flatly.

"Me either. This case is about more than a carjacking, Sam. And it certainly involves more than a chop-shop local gang." Then it hit me. "Did you hear what he was saying? Ch…Ch…Cha. That has to be Chase Martin. I knew he was behind this."

"I don't know, Abbey. He used a short vowel sound for 'a,' not a long one."

"Come on, Sam. He didn't speak English. 'Cha' in his final breath. We have his fingerprints and his cigar in the car. He even admitted he was between jobs."

"Abbey, this is the work of a professional, not some drop-out cop trying to become private security."

"I've got a feeling, Sam." My gut was telling me Chase Martin was involved in this case somehow. I didn't know the level of his involvement, but he was guilty of something.

"Pardon me for saying this, kid, but you want it to be him." I let the *kid* comment fly. He was accusing me of bias—another word for disrespect.

"I do not. I'm just following the clues, Sam. Why are you so certain it's *not* Chase?"

"This entire case is beyond his reach. Think for a minute. Who do we know who has that kind of pull or money?"

I only knew of one person that fit that bill. "We better be sure before we go there."

Sam winked and said, "That's my line." His phone buzzed. "Tidwell. Yes, Mayor. No, I haven't forgotten. Right now? Well, we're in the middle of a case. I don't think…" He sighed. "He hung up on me."

"Talk about timing. What was that about?"

"I have to pick up my suit, and you're supposed to go for a dress fitting."

"I was hoping they'd given up on the notion of having us attend the fundraiser tomorrow night."

They hadn't.

"I didn't order a suit," Sam said.

"They bought you one. Remember? We're supposed to meet Mr. Thomas's seamstress and tailor in his presidential suite at the Four Seasons for final fittings."

"I told him we were busy, but he said to drop everything. Can you believe it?" Sam asked.

"Of course, Sam. He's doing this to please his friend, Jonathan Thomas, hoping he'll revitalize the east side of the river." We both knew what that meant. All the mayor and his buddy seemed to care about was finding the murderer of Dean Swain. I'm sure the mayor didn't care if we discovered the cause of Tito Ruiz's death. His priority was Jonathan Lee Thomas, even if that meant having his two *star* detectives fitted for their fundraiser dress and tux. As much as we hated doing so, Sam and I headed to the Four Seasons in downtown Nashville. Whatever happened to Tito would have to wait. It bothered me to no end knowing two gunmen were still on the loose and our key witness just died mysteriously—possibly at the hands of the FBI. How deep were Jonathan Thomas's pockets? But why would he want his stepson dead? Why would he use a Mexican gang member to steal the Bentley and have a crew waiting behind a semi-trailer to kill Tito? Nothing in this crazy case made sense.

Chapter Seventeen

Saturday, March 29, 8:00 PM—Loews Nashville Hotel

The rain came down in sheets. Thankfully, they sent a limo for me, which pulled under the cover of my apartment's canopy and dropped me off at the front door of the Loews Nashville Hotel. I didn't know whether to feel like a princess arriving at the ball or a prostitute here to please the donors. The driver pulled to a stop, and a man in a black suit opened my door.

"Miss Rhodes, my name is Buck Pader. I'm the head of security for JLT Enterprises." He extended his hand, which was a good thing. There was no way I was getting out of the back seat of this limo by myself. "You look magnificent." He was a stocky man of average height. His voice was rough and grave—the sound of a lifetime smoker.

"It's Detective Rhodes," I said, putting a stop to the awkward exchange. He walked me to the door and allowed the bellman to open it for us both. "Mr. Thomas has a table reserved for you and your partner." I caught him looking at my figure. "You'll see four other security team members milling about the fundraiser tonight." He mentioned their names, but I was concentrating on my entrance, trying not to embarrass myself. "We're all dressed alike."

My dress was something you'd see on Hollywood's Red Carpet, only nobody famous was in it—just me. I'd never worn anything this exotic. It was made entirely of taffeta and velvet—not the kind of dress you want to wear on a rainy day. It wasn't the kind of dress I'd choose. It did, however, accentuate my figure. I struggled to walk. Thankfully, the seamstress made a slit in the side, allowing my leg a little freedom. It was the only part of my body allowed any freedom in this dress. It was so snug that I couldn't hide a square of toilet paper underneath. I was uncomfortable for two reasons. First, the candy-apple red material drew all eyes to me, and I'm not too fond of attention. Second, I couldn't draw in a full breath of air.

"Abbey, you look stunning."

"Sam, don't you dare leave my side tonight." I clung to his arm. Sam was my security blanket for the evening. What was the saying? Misery loves company? "Sam, I'm serious. Please stay with me."

"Okay, but I should have brought a bat."

Everyone in the lobby was dressed to the hilt. "A bat? I don't get it."

"To beat away all the men tonight."

"Not funny." I couldn't tell if he was teasing me or not. I didn't want someone to like me because of my looks or shape. I wanted someone to like me for who I am. I didn't want to be reduced to an object of someone's affection. Why couldn't I be the subject of it? I'd been in situations where men never looked above my shoulders. They didn't care.

Sam stood poised with his arm ready for my hand, so I took it. The nice thing about Sam, other than the differences in our ages, was that I reminded him of his daughter, and he would respect me as such. When we were on the job, I was his partner. Off the job, like tonight, and he was the best of gentlemen. I took his arm, and we walked confidently through the lobby straight to the elevator.

As soon as the doors shut, Sam said, "I hate these things." He looked into his reflection and added, "I look like a penguin." I couldn't help but laugh. I needed to laugh, but it reminded me of the tightness of my dress. We composed ourselves before the doors opened on the fourth floor.

Mayor O'Reilly made eye contact, and his aide, Larry Barter, rushed to our side. "The mayor has seats reserved for you both. You'll be dining with Mr. Thomas."

"Oh, that's not necessary," Sam said. "We'll find a less conspicuous table in the back."

"I'm afraid they both insisted. It's in honor of his son Dean and your ability to close the case so quickly."

"But the case isn't closed," I said. "We still have two or three more people to find." He ignored my comment and pointed to our seats.

"You'll be introduced before the meal." He saw someone else and darted off with a grand smile. He ran like the Energizer bunny, from one person to the next, making sure we were all in our proper place for the show.

"Working the room for the mayor," Sam said. "Let's just take our places, smile, and get through the night. Agreed?"

"Agreed, but I feel like a hooker. I keep getting nods and winks from men with someone else—probably their wives. I feel cheap."

"You don't look cheap," Sam said with a laugh. "I couldn't afford you."

A dagger in my heart. I know he didn't mean it, but that's how I felt. So much for being a princess at the ball. The band played "String of Pearls," by Glen Miller Band. I only knew it because Mr. Morales, my benefactor in Guatemala, played it all the time. He wanted to endow me with culture. Ironic.

A hand tapped my shoulder, "May I have the honor of a dance?"

I couldn't help but flinch. I turned to see Jonathan Thomas. "I'm not very good at dancing," I said. It was a lie. Mr. Morales trained me for years.

"Good. Then I won't look so bad," he answered with a faint smile. "You look elegant, my dear."

I wasn't his dear, and I had no plans of becoming it. I wanted to establish the boundaries right off the bat, so I said, "It's Detective Rhodes."

"Oh, I see." He took a step back. "I didn't mean to offend you, Detective Rhodes." He bowed and extended his hand. "It would be a great honor if you would favor me with a dance. If that makes you too uncomfortable, I will release you to wander on your own."

It seemed to hurt his feelings that I was denying a man who'd lost his stepson last week of one innocent dance. I took his right hand in my left, and I put my other hand on his shoulder. "Lead the way, Mr. Thomas." There. Another hint that this was a formal acceptance to dance. Thankfully, he didn't try to have me call him Jonathan. That would be too weird. He was Sam's age, and his wife was sitting at the table looking our way.

It was a familiar song. I followed just how Mr. Morales taught me to. I didn't expect the flurry of flashes as photographers followed us across the dance floor. Great, I would be in print in this ridiculous dress. My muscles tightened as everyone looked our way. The mayor smiled and said something to Mrs. Thomas. She didn't smile back. I knew what she was thinking about me. The song ended, and the band struck up, "In the Mood."

The mayor tapped my shoulder. "Mind if I cut in?" Mr. Thomas backed away and smiled. "I didn't realize you could dance to the oldies. In fact, I didn't know you danced so well."

The song was faster, so I was able to keep a little distance between us. "An old friend taught me. He loved Glenn Miller's Orchestra." The flashes followed us. I needed to get off the dance floor before I had another PTSD episode. My muscle memory was taking over. Even in the tight dress, I was moving smoothly. Thankfully, it was a short song.

As the mayor let go of my hand, another person grabbed my hand and spun me around. "Well, look who's on parade with all the rich and powerful men drooling and lining up for a dance."

Chase Martin!

"Let go," I said, trying to pull free from his grip. "I don't want to dance with you."

"Not rich enough for your dance card?" He pulled me close.

Dance card? Oh, no, not now. Thankfully, something caught my eye and distracted me from the pull of the past.

"You brought a gun to this event? I'm calling security."

"I *am* security, Abbey Rhodes." He released my hand and pulled his jacket back. It wasn't his forty-four.

"I thought you didn't have a nine-millimeter," I said, staring at the gun.

"You better keep dancing; you're drawing attention to us just standing here. People are going to wonder about us." I followed his lead and moved to "Moonlight Serenade." He nodded to the mayor and spun me. I nearly fell. "Mr. Thomas hired me as part of his security team."

"Mr. Thomas? You're kidding."

"No. Buck called to offer the job the night I visited the site with Dean. He was pleased that I was with Dean before—well, you know."

How did he know that? We didn't tell Mr. Thomas or the mayor about Chase. Sam didn't think it was pertinent.

"That's ironic, seeing as you abandoned Dean just moments before he was killed."

He bristled. *Good.*

"Did you know someone was waiting for him in the lot across the river?"

The song stopped, but Chase didn't. He kept dancing to the next song. Sam looked at me with his hands out to see if I wanted him to intervene. I smiled and shook my head. I wanted to see how much Chase Martin knew and why Jonathan Thomas would hire him.

"You dance well." His hand slid to my hip. "Professional?"

"Abbey! What happened?" I could hear the voice. It seemed eerily familiar. "Abbey! You're soaking wet and freezing. Let me get you inside." He tugged at my arm. He shook me. Why couldn't I wake up? I felt my body lifted from the ground. I could hear the thunder—feel the rain. Why couldn't I respond?

Whoever it was, he lifted me up and over his shoulder. I could feel the strength of his shoulders. That voice. I knew that voice.

"Sam?" My eyes fluttered open. Rain pelted my face. My dress—that beautiful dress was ruined. "What happened?"

"That's what I'm trying to find out. One moment you were dancing with Chase Martin. The next moment, you screamed and ran out of the room, tearing the dress so you could manage the steps. I called after you, but you ran out of the hotel and into the courtyard. By the time I found you, you were unconscious, lying in a fetal position in the storm. Took me forever to get the press out of here."

"I'm sorry." It was a storm—a storm of the past—a battle between who I was and who I am now.

"Who's Mr. Morales?"

"What?" I cringed. *What else did I say out loud?*

"You were calling for Mr. Morales. Then you kept saying, 'You promised to keep me safe. You promised to keep me safe.'" He set me down on a bench underneath the canopy of the hotel. "Who is he, Abbey? What happened to you?" Sam put his jacket around my shoulders. He knelt in front of me and pushed the wet hair out of my face.

"It was long time ago, Sam."

"I know PTSD when I see it, Abbey. Something horrible happened to you. Please, let me help."

"Can you take me home, Sam? Please, just take me home."

"Okay, girl, but we're going to talk about this next week. You understand?" I nodded.

Sam called an Uber and took me home. He got me settled into my apartment, but before he left, he said, "You need to talk with your counselor, but if you don't feel like you can, you need anyone to talk to or just to listen, no matter what time, you call me. Okay?"

I nodded, but I wasn't about to tell Sam what Chase triggered. I don't even think I could tell Susan—not yet. I was humiliated and vulnerable once again.

105

Chapter Eighteen

Ten years earlier, Morales' Dance House, Guatemala City, Guatemala

The humidity was thick, even for Guatemala. I had to peel off my shirt, which was soaked with sweat. I squeezed the pump twice, spraying the sweet perfume over my neck and chest. I changed into the nice dress Mr. Morales kept for me. He knew my situation. He knew my family had thrown me out to survive on my own. I was hungry—no, I was starving. I slept anywhere I could find shelter for the night. I begged for food. I begged for money. I hated it. I tried to go back home. I even groveled at my father's feet—begged for mercy. His friend raped me, and they believed his story over mine—which was the truth. Fifteen years old, the daughter of a missionary with a compound for the homeless, and he wouldn't let me in. I wasn't the kind of homeless person he wanted to help. I picked through the neighborhood garbage cans for edible items. Sometimes I lowered myself to the ground and drank muddy water from the puddles. Anything to survive. This was a step up from that.

"Here's your ticket belt, Hannah," Mr. Morales said. "It's going to be a good night to make money. It's payday at the factory." I nodded shyly. I hated the thought of renting myself out for a dance. The young men danced and rubbed against me. They smelled of sweet cologne. They brought flowers. The old men smelled of alcohol and cigarettes. Their hands wandered all over me while we *danced* to the music. Mr. Morales let them have their way with the young girls as long as their hands were on the outside of our dresses. Men thirty to fifty years my senior made crude comments. They called them offers. I called it filth.

I had just turned fifteen but had the body of a twenty-year-old. For some reason, they loved my baby face and womanly body. Creepy, but it was a good income. I could eat for the week as long as no one stole my money bag. Yung Xi and I got most of the attention because we were both unique. She was Chinese, and I was American—at least by birth. The rest of the girls were Guatemalan. They were just like the girls they could get off the street. We were special. We got two to three times as many tickets as the other girls. I danced twenty times that evening with little to no issue. On dance twenty-one, my luck changed for the worse.

"Mi dulce pequeno." Oh God, not him—not the man with rotten egg breath and wandering hands. He handed me three tickets. It was his way of keeping me to himself for three songs. His way of making certain he could rub his body against mine and grab my butt or breasts. He pulled me tight and smiled. His teeth, what few were left in his mouth, were rotten. It was probably the source of his bad breath. That and it was soured by alcohol. He pulled me in tight and rubbed my back.

I could tell he was getting excited and tried to pull away. He was too strong. I tried to convince myself that I could make it through the night. Each dance was worth ten Quetzal, the equivalent of a dollar thirty. I'd have to dance all night—put up with all sorts of comments and gestures. If I was lucky, I could get one hundred and fifty dances on a Saturday night. It would take about ten hours, but I could force myself to do it. I needed the money.

Something went terribly wrong the moment Mr. Morales left to check on one of his other businesses. The nasty old man pulled my dress up in the front. He backed me into a corner of the room. His hands were inside—where they didn't belong.

"Mr. Morales—"

"He's gone." The man shoved his dirty hand over my mouth and told me to shut up. His other hand moved hard and fast against me. I tried to scream. I tried to pull away, but he was too strong. Where was Mr. Morales? He had rules. Why didn't they obey his rules? I came to my senses and kneed the dirty man in the groin. He released me, and I ran. I ran until I couldn't run anymore. The sky lit up with lightning. The thunder rattled my chest. I ran. I fell. I got up and ran until I couldn't breathe. I fell. This time I didn't get up.

I swung at the shadows and hit something hard. I swung at another, and the rattle startled me. I suddenly came to and tried to orient myself. It was hard and wet all around me. The water pelted my face and chest. It wasn't rainwater. It was hot. I forced my eyes to open. Steam filled the air. I wasn't in Guatemala City. I was lying in the safety of my shower, back in my apartment in Nashville. I pushed up to my feet and turned the water off. I dropped my soaking-wet pajamas to the floor and wrapped a towel around my body. With my right hand, I wiped the mirror. I thought I left little, helpless Hannah Leah Abelard back in Guatemala, but there she was staring back at me with a desperate cry for help.

Chapter Nineteen

Sunday, March 30, 10:15 AM—Easter morning, Living Water Church

I needed a respite from the haunting memories. I needed the strength of a friend. Today, unfortunately, was the Sunday I'd promised Susan I would attend church, and I was a woman of my word. It was Easter Sunday, and the church was packed. I was already feeling claustrophobic. People were in front of me and behind me. I tried to hesitate, but the stream of humanity pushed me forward. I walked through the foyer of the little church, and recalled the first time I'd done so. It was Mark Ripley's death that brought me here. The first time I stood here, I struggled to cross the threshold. I had stared at the empty cross, and that's how my soul felt—empty. I wandered through the church that fateful day, building a case—one that led me to a dark place of similarity. Somehow, during my investigation, I struck up a friendship with Ripley's widow. I don't remember how it happened, but it did. Susan was my rock. She said I was hers, but I knew better.

Hannah Ripley waved for me to come to the front and sit with her family. Waves of nausea wafted over me as I took each step down the middle aisle of that place they called a sanctuary. It wasn't mine, but the only person who knew me and welcomed me anyway was here. I sat by Susan and quickly latched on to her arm so I wouldn't slip back into the past. Danny and Hannah insisted I sit between them. Reluctantly, I let go of Susan and sat between the children. They held on to me as if I were a safe haven. Today, they would have to be mine.

The front of the stage was filled with Easter lilies. The cross was blanketed with a white cloth. I suppose it was to signify the resurrection of Jesus. I'd heard it all before. *White for the cleansing of our sins. White for hope.* It reminded me of Mark Ripley's plaque in his pastor's office of Jeremiah, the prophet, quoting God's promises of hope and a future. Another of God's many lies.

The worship band led the congregation in two songs I'd never heard before. They were beautiful, but I had to resign myself to the role of spectator, not knowing the words or melody. They were new songs of praise, written after my departure from the church. After a prayer, they played a familiar song, "Up From the Grave He Arose." I knew it and caught myself singing along. I quickly stopped singing. He wasn't pulling me back that easily. It wasn't so much that I doubted the facts of His resurrection. I just didn't think God cared about me. He abandoned me, and I resented His representatives here on earth. They spoke of truth, but whispered lies—they professed His great love while spitting words of hate out of the other side of their mouths. I thought of my mother playing the piano, singing this song. I had a bad taste in my mouth and wanted desperately to get up and leave, but Hannah latched on to my arms and leaned into me.

We sat after the last song. One of the elders rose and said, "As most of you know, we are still in the process of searching for a full-time pastor. Our guest today has agreed to not only fill the pulpit today but also to preach for the month of April. He is a professor of English and Religion at Belmont University. Please help me in welcoming Dallas Gatlin."

The cute young man sitting in the pew directly behind us rose. He stepped onto the stage and set his Bible on the podium. He was actually more than cute; he was quite handsome. In his late twenties, six-two with dark brown hair and eyes. When he smiled, he exposed a dimple on his right cheek. He stood with authority and grace.

"Thank you, Stephen. If you have your Bible with you this

morning, I encourage you to turn to the eighth chapter of the Gospel of John. I know you came here this morning expecting your typical Easter message dealing with the resurrection of Jesus Christ. I hate to disappoint you, but that won't happen."

I liked him already. He didn't do the expected—the easy thing. He broke a simple, yet profound expectation on one of the most sacred days in the church calendar. Suddenly, I wanted to hear what he had to say.

"Instead, I want to show you a powerful illustration of God's love and grace. In other words, I want to give you the reason for the crucifixion and resurrection. This is a story about a woman—a woman caught in the act of adultery."

Oh well, my praise was misdirected. I'd heard my father preach this sermon multiple times. I heard him bash her for her sinful life and use the story to criticize all others who were living an evil life. As he cast me out of his house, I heard him use it as grounds for his actions. I cringed at the thought of his voice, "You Jezabel!"

"I always wondered why they didn't bring the man as well. If she was caught in the act of adultery, surely there was a second party to the crime." A few people laughed. I returned to the present. Laughter in church? He smiled. "No, they excused the man of his sin and focused on hers. In fact, I would argue they didn't care about the woman or her sin. They brought her to the public square not to judge the woman but to trap Jesus. What would He do? Would Jesus crumble under the pressure of the ruling class and agree to the law that demanded a stoning for such an offense? Or would Jesus publicly break the law and excuse the woman?"

Where was he going with this? That's not how the passage is supposed to be read. That's not how my father explained it. Who was this man, and how could he get away with this? I looked around for scowls and red faces. There were none. Even Duke Stearns, the cranky old deacon, was smiling.

"So the scribes and the Pharisees, the leaders of the local religion, presented the woman and the law condemning her. Then

111

they asked Jesus in front of the crowd, *What do you say?* Don't you just hate smug people—people who think they know everything?"

What?

"Oh, I know, we're not supposed to *hate* them. But I have to confess; they sure tick me off. Anyway. Jesus was in the middle of the court, presented with a judicial decision. Every eye was on Him. Condemn her or break the law and let her go."

The preacher who looked like a young Josh Duhamel, paused, scratched his chin, and paced back and forth. The silence was deafening.

What is he doing? Did he lose his train of thought? I was getting embarrassed for him.

Then that smile returned. He knelt on the left side of the stage and started drawing something with his finger. I stretched to see around the pulpit. It looked like he was writing words. I looked back at the congregation. Everyone was leaning forward, wondering the same thing as me.

He stood.

"Did I get your attention?" Several people laughed. "You see. That's exactly what Jesus did. In verses six and seven, John writes, 'They were saying this, testing Him, so that they might have ground for accusing Him. But Jesus stooped down and, with His finger, wrote on the ground.' That didn't affect them, and they asked Jesus a second time."

The preacher leaned into the acrylic podium and carefully made eye contact with everyone before continuing. "Get this, folks. Please pay attention to His next act. When the scribes and Pharisees pressed Jesus on the issue, He made this profound statement—a statement the church of today needs to hear. 'He who is without sin among you, let him be the first to throw a stone at her.' Can you imagine the thoughts running through their minds? I know the Pharisees considered themselves pure and obedient to the letter of the law. I'm sure some of them were bending down, reaching for the nearest rock. But Jesus stooped once more and

112

wrote on the ground. When he did, people began to leave. Why? Because no one was without sin."

He continued, listing a series of sins. By the time he was finished, I was certain he'd covered us all. Then he did the unimaginable. "I have to confess. My greatest sin is pride. Sometimes I get too full of myself, and I stumble. God must let me fall on my face before He is able to get my attention once again. That's probably because I'm hard-headed and proud. Maybe that's because I'm a man."

The women in the room laughed and elbowed the men sitting next to them.

"I don't stand up here casting stones. I'm not worthy of judging any of you. I'm just a messenger of God's word." He paused again. He looked down at his Bible and sighed. "But, by the grace of God, I am saved." A few hearty amens sounded out behind me.

"I got sidetracked. Let's continue the story. Everyone left. Only Jesus and the woman remained. Can you imagine her emotional ride? She expected them to stone her. She expected the teacher to agree with her accusers. But there she was, alive and alone with this strange teacher. Now, hear me out, folks. This is why I chose this passage for Easter Sunday. Jesus asked the woman where her accusers were. He asked her, 'Did no one condemn you?' Of course, He knew the answer. He wanted to hear it from her lips. She said, 'No.'"

Dallas came around the pulpit and sat on the edge of the step right in front of us. He took a deep breath and let it out. Then the smile returned. "You know what Jesus said to her? These are His exact words. 'I do not condemn you, either.' How powerful is that? He knew she'd sinned. He knew her sin was a stoning offense. And yet, Jesus, God in the flesh, refused to condemn her. Why? He didn't come to condemn but to save."

I let that sink in and felt the walls rising. If it were only true. Unfortunately, it went against everything my father taught about the Bible. "Christians today are soft," he'd say. "They've watered down the word of God to make themselves feel better." My father loved the Old Testament God—the God of justice and vengeance.

"But there's a caveat." He pulled me back to the present again. Dallas paused and looked my way. "Jesus forgave the woman, but He added this. 'Go. From now on, sin no more.'"

Impossible. Who could do that?

"Now, what Jesus said was, 'Leave your life of sin.' He doesn't forgive us just so we can return to our sinful ways. He forgives us to free us from the shackles of our sins. He empowers us to be free." He continued to look at me. "If you've sinned in your past, lay it at the feet of Jesus and leave it there. Confess your sins, and He will cleanse you of your past and free you." Did he know? He smiled. Did Susan tell him? She was smiling, too.

Everyone closed their eyes and bowed their heads—everyone but me. He led them in a prayer of confession, forgiveness, and freedom. I sat there with my eyes wide open, wishing it could be true. Even when everyone else was standing and singing the final song, I sat and stared at the wooden cross, the empty cross. Could I trust this man to deliver God's truth? He was the antithesis of my father. Where my father was condemning, Dallas was forgiving. Where my father preached from a seat of judgment, Dallas preached from the confessional booth of a sinner. Where my father spoke of obedience, Dallas spoke of love and grace. It sounded wonderful, but I'd learned from experience, if something sounds too good to be true, it usually is.

Chapter Twenty

Sunday, March 30, 12:05 PM—Home of Susan Ripley

"What did you think of our preacher today?" Susan asked as we set the kitchen table for lunch.

"Did you tell that man what happened to me?"

"What? No, Abbey, of course not. I'd never tell a soul. I'll take that to my grave."

"Well, it sure sounded like he knew my past. He stared right at me when he talked about the adulterous woman."

"Maybe God was trying to reach you and say He wasn't condemning you for your past."

"God? Don't start that again, Susan."

The doorbell rang. "Hannah, can you get that? It's probably Mr. Gatlin."

"The preacher? He's coming here?" A mixture of emotions flooded over me: anger, curiosity, shame, and interest. "Why?"

"I invited him to lunch. I thought you two should meet." Susan winked and finished setting the last spot. She smoothed out her dress and smiled as Hannah returned with him, wearing the same blue suit, minus the tie. "Mr. Gatlin, I'm so glad you could join us. Please, have a seat."

"I appreciate the invitation. But please, just call me Dallas. You saved me from a fast-food lunch." He looked at me and extended his hand. "I'm Dallas Gatlin."

I stared at his hand. He let it drop to his side. "Oh, I'm sorry. I'm Abbey Rhodes." He sat in the chair directly opposite mine. "I

115

must say, that was a very different Easter Sunday sermon." I still didn't know what to think. My mind, conditioned to years of heavy doctrine and abandonment, I rejected his Pollyana interpretation, even though I longed for it to be true. How could it be? God wouldn't let people get away with sinning against Him. He would punish them. Like my father would say, "God's heating up the caldron so He can burn away your iniquity." This man didn't know what I had done—the sins that hung over me. Besides, what did I care what he thought? He was a preacher.

"I'm not exactly your typical preacher," he admitted. "I teach English Literature and the Bible. I know I'm not an expert on the subject, but I'm convinced the church isn't growing because we act more like the Pharisees than Jesus." He watched as Susan put the food on the table and asked Hannah to get Danny. "It smells amazing, Mrs. Ripley."

"If I'm going to call you Dallas, you must call me Susan." She put serving spoons in each of the bowls. As soon as the kids joined us, she asked Danny to say the prayer. It was simple and short—my favorite kind. As soon as he finished, Danny reached for a chicken leg. "Danny! Let our guest go first."

"Oh, that's quite all right. The little guy looks hungry." He had a disarming demeanor. Even though he was a preacher, I felt at ease. Well, I suppose he wasn't a *real* preacher. Like he said, he was a college professor.

"Please, Abbey, explain what made it so different."

I took a bite of the broccoli casserole.

"Nice move," he said. "That's one way to get out of a discussion." His smile faded. "I guess different wasn't good."

"Oh, no, Dallas," Susan chimed in. "It was very interesting and challenging. Don't you agree, Abbey?"

I looked at Susan and nodded. I could agree to that.

"I've never heard that passage taught that way. I've always agreed with grace, but connecting His forgiveness of the woman to the resurrection really made me think. Don't you agree, Abbey?"

Enough.

"Susan, let her speak for herself. I could tell she was processing my words throughout the sermon. I want to hear what impact it had on her." He looked deeply into my eyes.

My heart fluttered, and I looked away.

"Danny, could you pass me a roll, please?" I asked. Anything to stall. He tossed one across the table.

"Danny Ripley! Where are your manners?" Susan's face betrayed her embarrassment. "I am so sorry."

It was a nice diversion from the previous question. *Thanks, Danny, I owe you one.*

"Was it my delivery or the content that disappointed you?"

That didn't last long. Better to get it over with.

"Both were fine." *Just say it and disappoint him.* "My father used that passage to instill and enslave his congregation with guilt."

His eyes widened. Good. I could tell he was trying to read into my cryptic message.

"Was your father a pastor?"

"Kind of. He was a missionary."

"Really?" I could tell he had other questions. It was my turn to let the silence fall upon us. He took a bite of his potato and looked down at his plate. Susan gave me a pleading look, wanting me to be nice and follow etiquette.

"That's why I remain skeptical of religious people." Now, she was embarrassed. Might as well go all in. "They always want to know personal things, and then they try to find a Bible passage that matches the situation, so you'll feel guilty. Most of them don't use those verses for encouragement." I took a big bite of my chicken. I was proud of myself.

"I totally agree," he said.

I admit I was disappointed. I wanted the comment to sting him—to put him on the defensive.

"That's what I try to teach my religion students. The church has gotten such a bad reputation with the world, which only sees the negative headlines. We need to do a better job showing the love of Christ."

"You know that includes you, don't you?" I asked, leaving no doubt of my intentions.

"Like Paul said, I too am chief among sinners." He had no idea who he was talking to. "You'll find no stones in my hands, Abbey." Then he leaned into the table and locked onto my eyes. "I don't know who hurt you, but I'm sorry—deeply sorry."

My heart fluttered again. I didn't know what to say. I wasn't used to this from any Christian but Susan. I certainly didn't expect humility and grace from a man. I'm sure the smug, confident look on my face faded away.

"I'm…I'm…" I looked to Susan for help. She was staring at Dallas. There was a twinkle in her eyes. She liked him. He was here for her—not me. I was so embarrassed. I should have known better. I thought she was trying to set us up. "Thank you for your apology, Professor Gatlin, but it isn't necessary. You did nothing to apologize for." I engaged in small talk with the kids while I finished my sandwich.

"Abbey is a homicide detective in Nashville," Susan said, returning the conversation to me.

"Oh, really? That's impressive." He looked at me and waited for a reply. I gave none. "Is it dangerous?" I gave him an indecisive look. "Are you working on anything now?"

Susan chimed in. "Oh, yes. They're investigating the murder of a very prominent man. In fact, the mayor invited Abbey to a big fundraiser to thank her for her performance."

"So, you caught the murderer?" he asked.

"It was a joint effort with homicide and auto theft," I said, trying desperately to avoid the attention. "But we still have a lot to solve before the case is closed."

"Beautiful and humble," he said. It excited me and terrified me. I welcomed the compliment but wished he hadn't led with my looks. Unfortunately, that's what men focus on. Now, it was my turn to turn his attention to Susan. "Did you know Susan works with the homeless on the banks of the Cumberland?"

His eyes lit up. "That's wonderful! I help with The Least of These ministries. I'm speaking at their next rally on the fifth of April in front of the courthouse."

"You work with the homeless ministries?" Susan asked. He nodded, and the two of them were so engaged with their discussion that they never noticed the kids and me putting our dishes in the dishwasher and going outside to play.

I knew he was too good to be true. Susan deserved Dallas more than I did. Being attracted to a preacher felt wrong. I had too much baggage anyway. I'm not sure he could have handled that. Still, he gave me a lot to think about.

As Hannah, Danny, and I kicked the soccer ball around, I wondered what other passages he and my father would disagree about. Maybe there was hope. Maybe God wasn't the hard-nosed vengeful judge my father made Him out to be. As much as it bothered me to do so, I'd have to attend another service and see what Dallas Gatlin had to say. I wasn't paying attention and hit the ball too hard to Danny. It smacked him in the face.

He was bawling. I knelt down on one knee and put him on my other leg. I held him to my chest and apologized. Susan came running to us, asking what happened. I explained that I kicked it too hard and hit him. She pulled Danny to her, but he clung to my neck.

"Don't let me go, Aunt Abbey. I won't cry anymore. I promise."

"It's okay to cry, Danny. I'm sure that hurt."

Dallas and Susan stood over us until Danny finally let go of me and begged me to keep playing. Dallas put out his hand and helped me up. "You're really good with kids. I'm impressed."

"I guess I like playing with the kids because I don't feel judged."

"Oh. Sorry. I hope I don't put on an air of judgment," Dallas said.

"I wasn't talking about you. I just feel like I'm walking on eggshells around church people."

"That must be exhausting," he said. "Please know that I've been impressed with your honesty today. I'm glad I came."

"Me too." It was honest. I looked over at Susan. She was smiling. Was that a good thing?

Chapter Twenty-one

Monday, March 31, 8:30 AM—Homeless Camp

I got a call from the Chief's office to come in at seven and spent nearly an hour shrinking into the seat in his office. The mayor cornered him and screamed about the embarrassment I'd cause the department and the city by fleeing the dance and the dinner. Captain Harris used every name in the book and some I'd never heard before to tell me how despicable and humiliating I was to the department. Then, he brought the lieutenant and Sergeant McNally in and chewed them out in my presence. He told them if I screwed up one more thing, I would be busted down to a school crossing guard by the end of the day.

I was humiliated.

Now, despite the Sergeant's emphatic warning to stay away from the homeless camp, Sam wanted to get another crack at our only possible witness to the shooting. "We have to find that soldier," he said.

"Sam, if they catch me here, I'll get demoted for sure."

Sam ignored the plea and said, "I think he saw everything. Even if there's just a slim chance he was lucid at that moment, we have to take it."

Oh, well. All or nothing. Right? "Yeah, but Christy said he was in another world." I glanced up at the tents on our left as we drove down the hill to the fenced-in lot. "Sam, wait." He stopped the car. "Why don't we park back up the hill and walk down? He'll probably still see us anyway, but we won't be as obvious as our car."

"I'm game. But if he's as sharp an observer as we think, it won't matter." He backed up and parked at the beginning of the access road. We walked down the road to the tracks. "Let's split up and approach from two sides—no guns pulled. Maybe we can keep him from running if he's here."

"Sounds good." I pointed to the east, the direction of the interstate, and said I would swing wide to the other side and work my way back. Sam would follow the tracks past the edge of the trees and work back along the river. We hoped one of us would find him and show ourselves to be harmless.

It was a chilly Spring morning. The clouds looked heavy with rain. The brush was dense. It ripped at my clothing. I pushed through, and the closer I came to the pillars of the interstate, the more trash I had to wade through. I made so much noise, that only a deaf person would be unaware of my presence. I pushed through the heavy underbrush and trash and curled to my left. The Cumberland River came into view. The wind picked up, and I pulled my jacket tightly around my chest.

When I looked up, I saw Lance Corporal Rushing standing on the hill above me, holding a hunting knife.

"Friend or foe?"

"Friend," I said, holding my empty hands to the sky.

"Why are you here?" he asked. I noticed something moving in his left hand. It was Christy's jacket blowing in the wind. I'd made a huge mistake. "Who are you, and why are you following me?" he demanded, now pointing the knife at me.

"Lance Corporal, stand down." I paused as I noticed him snapping to attention. I decided to take a chance. I'd dealt with similar situations back in Germany as an MP. "I'm Sergeant First Class, Abbey Rhodes."

He hesitated, looked me over, and sheathed his knife. "Yes, Sergeant."

"What's that in your hand, Lance Corporal?"

He looked down at his left hand. "A jacket, Sergeant."

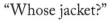

"Whose jacket?"

I watched as he studied the jacket and searched for recognition. His body slumped, and he fell to his knees. He looked up with water-filled eyes. "It's Christy's."

I didn't know whether to continue in army mode or to meet him in reality. I chose the latter. "Mr. Rushing, what happened to Christy?" He continued to stare at the jacket. After a few moments of silence, I asked him again.

"They got her. I tried to protect her, but they got to her."

"Who took her?"

"They did," he said, pointing over his shoulder toward her tent. His body stiffened, and he popped up to his feet. He'd made the switch back to soldier. He turned and glared at me before running down the steep slope and diving into the water. I watched for any sign of him downriver. Nothing. A noise caught my attention, and I turned.

"Any sign of him?" Sam asked. "I didn't have any luck."

"You just missed him, Sam. He dove into the river when he heard you coming." Sam turned to look at the river. "I didn't see him come up." I climbed the hill and picked up Christy's jacket. "Sam, look. He had Christy's jacket in his hands. There's blood on it."

"Do you think he killed her?"

"No, I don't." I was really confused now. I told Sam about our strange conversation and how he responded to me as an MP. "He went back and forth from soldier to homeless man. He pointed to her tent and said, 'They took her.'"

"They who?"

"I don't know. He was pointing to her tent. It could mean anybody, or it could be a delusion."

"Let's head back to Homicide. There's nothing more we can do here."

Chapter Twenty-two

Monday, March 31, 10:00 AM—Homicide offices

"**B**ut Sergeant," Sam implored, "I need more resources to capture that soldier." He held up Christy's jacket. "He had her jacket in his hand and pulled a knife on Detective Rhodes. It's bloody. That means she's hurt or possibly dead."

"How many times have I told you two? No body, no homicide."

"But what about Dean Swain's murder?" I asked. "He's our only witness to the crime. He's the only one who may have seen what happened that night."

"*May* have. That's the key to all of this. I'm not going to authorize a manhunt for a possible witness—a witness who, by your own admission, may not even be mentally stable. Besides, you caught Dean Swain's murderer, but you let him slip through your fingers."

"That wasn't our fault, Sergeant," Sam defended. "We left for the hospital the moment you told us Tito Ruiz was awake. When we got there, someone had already spoken to him. The man presented himself to the hospital staff as a federal agent. Tito died before we could get his statement. Honest, Sergeant, we looked through the hospital surveillance videos, and he had his back turned to every camera. That soldier is our only viable lead at the moment."

Sergeant McNally's veins bulged. He paused to run his hands over his thick mustache. "Stay on task and come up with another plan. The answer's no. Dismissed." Sam grunted and left the two of us standing there.

"Sergeant?"

"Dismissed, Rhodes." He glared at me and added, "Get out of my office before I throw you out."

I turned on my heels and followed Sam, who was already throwing things at the walls of our cubicle. He mumbled as he threw his stapler across the heads of other homicide detectives and into the far wall. "Of all the idiotic, bullheaded—"

"Tidwell! If I hear another word out of you—"

"You won't, Sergeant," I said, wrapping my arms around Sam. "For goodness sake, Sam, calm down." This was a reversal of roles. "What's gotten into you? You're usually the calm one."

He took a deep breath and sat down. As he straightened the mess on his desk, he said in a low voice, "This whole thing stinks. Somebody's playing us, and I don't like it."

Spence reached over the side of the cubical and handed Sam his stapler. "Roger said thanks, but he already has one." Spence looked at me and signaled that I needed to get Sam out of here.

"Hey, Sam, let's go get some air." He didn't fight me as I took him by the arm and led him to the courtyard out back. "Looks like rain." He looked up and shrugged his shoulders. "Sam, what's eating at you?"

He pulled a chair out from under a small table and sat down. "Abbey. None of this makes sense."

"For instance?" I asked. I had my own problems with this case. I wanted to hear what bothered him.

"First of all, we have a Bentley parked in a scrap metal yard."

"Okay, Sam. That's an easy one. Dean was planning on a pedestrian bridge landing there."

He looked up at me. "According to?"

"Chase Martin." I hated that man. I couldn't believe Sam was making me say his name again.

"Chase Martin, whose prints and cigar were both found inside the Bentley. Chase Martin who was seen leaving with Dean Swain—the last person to see him alive." He paused. I suppose

125

he was waiting for me to join in. I didn't. "Chase Martin, who, according to you, now works for the deceased man's stepfather as a member of his security team. Who was hired even though he left Dean on the other side of the river. Chase Martin, who caused you to experience a severe case of PTSD. So severe that you bolted outside and sat in the cold rain sobbing and calling out for someone named Mr. Morales." He ran his hands through his salt and pepper hair. "How am I doing so far?"

"Right on all accounts, Sam. Go on." We were of one accord so far. What else did Sam suspect?

"Then we have someone who tipped off Tito Ruiz, telling him when and where to find the Bentley." I nodded. "But as Tito was trying to steal the car, two mystery gunmen shot him while a third man watched."

"Why were they there, and why did they want Dean killed?"

"Exactly! Who would benefit from Dean's death?" Sam asked. "No one got the Bentley, so they obviously weren't after the car. His mother is his next of kin, but she's got all the money she could ever want." He ran his fingers through his beard several times as he stared into space. "And who took the time to turn the car off? I checked with Adams, and he confirmed the car still had half a tank of gas."

I hadn't thought of this. I'd been so busy running Susan's errands that I wasn't focused on our case. Sarge was right. *This* case was my priority. This was a true homicide. As far as we knew, the homeless cases were disappearances, which could be people moving from one camp to another. The blood on Christy's jacket could be from a bloody nose. "Who would benefit from Dean's death?" I was asking it more to myself than Sam, but he chimed in.

"Someone wanting his idea."

"What idea? That crazy garage?"

"Yes. To buy that site and make it a mega parking structure. Someone interested in landing the East Bank project might need to add a fix to the parking problem."

"The main person is his stepfather," I said.

"But he's not the only one. Did you see all of the investors and developers at the fundraiser?" I didn't. I was too busy dancing. "Two main groups were competing with JLT Enterprises. What if they killed Dean to divert Jonathan Thomas's attention?"

"How would they know of Dean's plan? Who else did he tell besides Chase Martin?"

"There he is again. That man is a bigger part of this than I thought," Sam said. "And his sudden employment with JLT Enterprises can mean one of two things. Either he earned his position by tipping someone off, or he is a plant for another investor. Either way, he's dirty."

"I agree, but we have no evidence."

"His evidence is all over that car. We bring him in like you wanted to and squeeze him for information. Let's see if anyone comes to his rescue." It was good seeing Sam back in the game. He had forgotten the rebuke from Sarge and was fully invested, once again, in the case.

My phone rang. It was Susan Ripley. "Good morning, Susan."

"Hey, Abbey. I owe you an apology."

"For what?"

"I didn't even see you leave yesterday."

I smiled. "I guess you were deep in a discussion with Dallas Gatlin."

"I was. We talked for several hours about ministries, especially the homeless in Nashville. He's an intriguing man."

"I bet he is," I said with a teasing tone. She didn't catch it.

"Oh, I called to see if you found out anything else about Christy."

"No. We're deep in a case right now." I didn't want to tell her about the bloody coat and the soldier until I had something solid. She would panic and do something stupid.

"Abbey, this is important to me."

"I know it is Susan. I'm sorry, but my job is my priority right now, and my job is homicide, not missing persons. My superiors have made that abundantly clear to me." Before she could say anything else, I told her goodbye and hung up.

"What did she want?" Sam asked.

"It doesn't matter. We need to dig into the motives for Dean's death. First order of business is to see who knew of his parking garage plans."

"I'll ask around and see if anyone has made a bid on those two plots of land," Sam said.

"Stay with the basics," I said for the benefit of both of us. "Motive, method, and opportunity. Let's list everyone that qualifies."

Chapter Twenty-three

Ten Years Earlier, 3:06 AM—Outskirts of Guatemala City, Guatemala

"Get off of me!" I pushed the boy away and hit the other with my left fist. They weren't laughing anymore. I went after them, but they all ran. I looked at the torn sleeve on the dress. Mr. Morales would kill me. I had been running for two days with a pouch full of wet dance tickets. I was tired of men thinking they owned me and could do anything they wanted. If I had to kill to keep it from happening, I was ready. This wasn't how I imagined my teenage years going. I had plans—plans for a soccer scholarship and college—plans to get out of Guatemala for good.

"Hannah, is that you?" It was Mr. Morales in his red Thunderbird. "I heard what happened." He got out. I shrunk back into the tin structure. He knelt and held his hand out to me like I was a timid animal in a zoo. "It's okay, Hannah. He won't do that to you ever again. I made sure of that."

He inched forward, and I inched back. What did he mean by, *I made sure of that?* Did he threaten the old man, or did he kill him? I hoped he'd killed the man. That way I'd never have to face him again.

"Let me help you, Hannah."

What did he care? His business was built on girls like me—girls who were homeless, who needed money, and who were willing to *entertain* his clients. Did he want me back because I brought in business for him?

"I had no choice, Mr. Morales."

I could take care of myself. I could find a way to live without having to do those things.

"That's okay, Hannah. He got what he deserved." He looked at me and shook his head. "You don't have to live like this, Hannah."

"I don't have any other choice." I shrank back once again.

"Yes, you do. If you come with me, I promise no man will ever lay his hands on you again."

What did that mean? They had to touch me to dance with me.

"I want to make you an offer to make up for your recent struggles."

I shrunk back into the farthest corner of the little shelter. "What kind of offer?"

"Come live with me, Hannah. I'll provide for all your needs. I'll see that you get back into school and finish with a diploma. You can play soccer. That's what you always talk about. I'll even pay for college if that's what you want."

"Why? Why would you help me, Mr. Morales?"

"You're special, Hannah. You're smart as well as beautiful."

"What do you get out of it, Mr. Morales?" There had to be a catch. There was always a catch when someone offered to help me—especially men.

"I get to see you every day, and I get to help you not only survive, but thrive." He inched forward and kept his hand extended. "I'll teach you about my other businesses. You decide what you want to do."

"Like dancing?"

"No, Hannah. No more dancing for you, at least not like that." He lowered his hand. "I'm sorry he hurt you."

I inched out of the shelter and looked into his eyes. I could tell if he was lying. The eyes always told if someone was lying. "And if I agree to come with you, what do I have to do?"

"Just live there. You have my word that I will never touch you. No man will ever touch you again."

I was skeptical, but I didn't have many options. I took the ticket pouch off and handed it to him. "Can I still get paid for these?"

"Yes, but you won't need those, Hannah. I'll pay for anything you need or want."

"Just for living with you? I won't have to sleep with you, will I?"

He laughed and shook his head. "No, girl. You'll have your own room, complete with a bathroom."

A bathroom? Of my own? "Okay, Mr. Morales. I accept."

At first, it was just as he said. His house was huge, surrounded by a stone wall. He had workers for everything. They tended his lawn and garden, cooked, and cleaned. The food was wonderful, and his cook made anything I wanted. He bought an entire wardrobe for me. He got me into a private school. He even got me into a soccer camp so I could catch up on my skills. I couldn't understand why he would do it.

Then, one morning, as I was getting a shower before school, I saw him staring at me. I grabbed the towel to cover myself. I screamed, but he didn't run away. He simply said, "It's all right, Hannah. You're safe."

"Why are you in my bathroom? You said you wouldn't lay a hand on me."

"Oh, dear, I won't. I promise. I told you all I want is to see you every day."

"See me? I thought you meant to see me in the house—see me walking around."

He stood. "I'll leave, Hannah. But you need to reconsider my offer. I thought I was clear. I want to see you every day—see all of you. I'll never touch you. I just want to look. You're a beautiful girl, Hannah. Let me continue to look, and you can have everything you want. If you don't want me watching, you're free to leave."

He shut the door behind him. I shrunk down in the shower, the water still pouring over my head, and cried. I cried for so long that I fell asleep in the running water. When I woke, I was dressed and lying in my bed. I'd missed school. I heard him walking on the hard tile floor. He was coming my way.

†††

I jumped up and fell out of bed. I was back in Nashville again. I had to call someone. If I called my counselor, she may have suspended me from active duty. If I called Susan, she'd want to know the details. She'd pry until she found out more about Mr. Morales. I couldn't go there, not right now. I looked at the clock: 4:25 a.m. I dialed the only other number I knew and listened to the ring—once…twice…three times.

"Abbey, do you know what time it is?" The voice was groggy and held a sense of irritation.

I squeaked out a timid, "Yes, Lieutenant Daniels, but I had no one else I could call."

"All right, Abbey. Spill it. What's Going on."

I recounted my last few episodes of PTSD, including the dreams and the details. He was the only one I could trust to keep the confidence without going crazy on me.

"Have you talked with your counselor?"

"I can't. Not right now."

"What about Susan?"

"No."

"Well, I guess I should be honored. What can I do for you?"

"Just listen. I need to tell someone, but I don't want you to try to solve it."

"I can do that." And he did. For the next thirty minutes, Lieutenant Daniels listened quietly to my nightmares and fears. It felt good to share—to get it off my chest. I wasn't alone, not any longer.

I took his advice and called work to take a personal day. Maybe I could sleep. Maybe I could process what was happening and why it was coming back so intensely. Maybe, after I sorted it all out, I could schedule an appointment with my counselor.

Chapter Twenty-four

Tuesday, April 1, 6:25 PM—Harmony Apartments

I woke up around two in the afternoon, ate lunch, and grabbed a shower. I pulled down all of my photo albums and worked my way backward in time. I couldn't begin with the pictures Mr. Morales took. I started in happier times—my time in the army—the point in which I became Abbey Rhodes. Although I chose the name to spite my father, I'd grown fond of it. I was Abbey Rhodes, a fearless, competent detective. People counted on me. I was nothing like the little girl from Guatemala.

After I turned eighteen, I legally changed my name from Hannah Leah Abelard to Abbey Rhodes. I enlisted in the army and requested a post as far away from Guatemala as possible. I ended up in Grafenwöhr, Germany, as part of the 709th Battalion, a unit of the 18th Military Police Brigade. Nobody knew Hannah Abelard. She no longer existed. I was just one of a new crop of soldiers hoping to become Military Police. I chose this because it gave me power, and I hoped to use it one day to help people like me. I excelled on every test, succeeded in every challenge, and rose to the rank of Sergeant before I fulfilled my time of service.

It was great having a fresh start with a new name. Nobody knew my past. To them, I was Abbey Rhodes, a part of the crew. My fellow recruits and I did everything together, but while they spent their money, I saved mine. I wasn't thinking of the moment, I was thinking of the future. If Mr. Morales taught me anything it was money is power.

I perused the photo albums and reminisced. The images pulled me back—back to the rigorous basic combat training, the struggles of memorizing the law book, and numerous hours at the shooting range. I rose to the challenge, even surprising myself. I smiled, thinking of the times with close friends, on base and off. Germany was a wonderful change from the heat of Guatemala. At first, I hated the cold and the snow, but I came to love it. Everything was different—exactly what I needed for a fresh start and a new life.

After spending hours sorting through photos and letters from the army, I set them aside and took a deep breath. I opened my album from Guatemala. I needed to know why these images were haunting me.

There he was, Mr. Morales. A short man of strong Mayan heritage with silver-rimmed glasses standing in front of his three cars. He loved his cars. When I first met him, I was begging for food. He fed me and offered me the opportunity to dance on Fridays and Saturdays to make money. I thought it was his only business. I was wrong. It was his first, one he held on to for sentimental reasons. Everything changed when he took me in and allowed me to live with him. In one way, I became his daughter. In another, I became his obsession. He loved me both ways: for my character and my body. He kept his promise and never touched me. Nobody ever touched me again. And as long as I allowed him to watch me bathe and dress, I could stay. I felt cheap, but I also felt safe. No more worrying about food, money, shelter, or safety. I was bought and paid for. No wonder Chase Martin's comment threw me into a tailspin.

Mr. Morales gave me the equivalent of five hundred dollars a week for spending money. I saved most of it. He enrolled me in a private high school under the name of Hannah Morales and got me on the school's soccer team. That's why my sister never knew how to find me—that was until my picture appeared in the paper for a special soccer award my senior year. But I'd let the Abelard family go. They didn't want me, and I no longer wanted them.

Mr. Morales did everything for me. He even made sure I got my driver's license and taught me how to drive his precious cars. He complimented me all the time, and not only on my looks. Where my father had torn me down, Mr. Morales built me up. He introduced me as his daughter, Hannah, when we were out in public. I found that I had a knack for languages, and with a dark summer tan, I could pass myself off easily as Guatemalan. One negative thing he did was further my distance from God and the church. He said Christians were fools, giving their money and time to an imaginary deity. "What a waste," he would say. Then he would add, "The church people will never fool us, will they, Hannah? We're too smart for such things." I would nod, but somewhere deep inside, I knew I still believed in a God. How could I be angry with God if He didn't exist? I knew He did because I hated Him for putting me in this position. I believed wholeheartedly what my father said—that God couldn't possibly care for me.

I turned page after page. I never realized how many pictures Mr. Morales took of me. When we were together, his chest puffed up like a rooster's. Finally, someone was proud of me. So, why did I remember him with such disdain? As I studied the pictures, I realized I didn't hate him. In every picture together, I was smiling and looking up at him with pride. There were several pictures of the two of us at professional soccer games. He also took many of me playing on the school team. He was proud of me. I wasn't an embarrassment, a leech, or even a corrupted sinner to Mr. Morales. I was the daughter he never had. I suppose I was happy for the most part. That was until…

My phone rang. I didn't recognize the number. "This is Han… Abbey."

"Abbey, thank God! This is Maggie. Can you come to the hospital?"

It was Sam's sister. What could she possibly want? "Is Sam okay?"

"No, Sweetie. He's been shot."

135

"What? Where?" This was my worst nightmare, losing some-one close to me. I didn't have many friends. Sam was my partner, mentor, father-figure, and friend.

"They found his body near a homeless camp by the river. He's been shot three times in his chest. He's in surgery now. I need you."

Shot? By whom? What was he doing by the river? All these questions flooded my mind. "Maggie, how did they find him?"

"An anonymous caller reported the body. Abbey, please come to the hospital, and I'll tell you all I know when you get here."

"Of course. Vanderbilt?"

"Yes. They took him straight through the emergency room to surgery. He's lost a lot of blood."

"I'm on my way, Maggie. I'll be there as soon as I can."

I rushed to the hospital and found Maggie in an empty hospi-tal room waiting for Sam to come out of surgery. She didn't know much more about the shooting than she told me on the phone. Sarge showed up moments later and explained that Sam was shot twice in the chest with a nine-millimeter. A third shot grazed his right shoulder. "We'll put a rush on the ballistics when the doctor removes the bullets. I have a gut feeling they will match the ones in Tito Ruiz." I could tell Sarge was toning it down because Maggie was in the room.

"I should've been there. I'm sorry." I apologized to Maggie and Sarge. The one I wanted to tell was Sam. I shouldn't have taken the personal day. "If I'd been there…"

"I'd be chewing your butt out," Sarge said. "Why was Sam back at the homeless site? I told you two to stay away from there."

"I don't know, Sarge. I suppose he wanted another crack at Lance Corporal Rushing."

"That soldier?" I nodded. "I hear he's as looney as a bird. Not a reliable witness. Why are you two wasting your time on him? They wouldn't accept his testimony."

"Not in court, maybe, but if we could get a lead out of him, it would be worth it."

Maggie's head shot up, and she lit into me. "Worth it? Worth Sam's life? How could a lead be worth my brother's life?"

"I didn't mean it that way, Maggie." I touched her shoulder, but she pulled away from my touch.

"Well, that's what you said." She folded her arms over her chest and huffed at me.

They rolled Sam into the room and gave us the update. The surgery went well. The bullets were close to his heart. Luckily, they missed. "We're going to keep him sedated a few days so he can heal faster." After answering our questions, they left.

Sarge encouraged Maggie to go home and get a good night's sleep. He said Sam would need her more once he was awake. Sarge assured her Sam would pull out of it. He knew better than to make promises like that. I knew that for a fact because he'd lectured me on the subject a few times. Sarge excused himself and said, "Call me if anything changes."

When they left, I pulled a chair to the side of Sam's bed and fell apart. I couldn't lose Sam, especially when I should have been there to protect him. Who among the homeless would have possession of a gun? Not Damien or his henchmen. If they had guns, they wouldn't carry hatchets and machetes. Lance Corporal Rushing carried a knife, so he was off the suspect list. It had to be someone visiting the site—looking for the only witness to their crime. Why did Sarge think the ballistics would match the shooters of Tito Ruiz? Who was the mystery FBI agent, and why weren't they responding to our inquiry? Too many questions; not enough answers.

My mind was all over the place, running possible scenarios, including what I would have done had I been with Sam. It kept coming back to the homeless camp. Something about that place connected to the murder of Dean Swain and the shooting of Tito Ruiz. How was the FBI involved? And how did he manage to avoid facial recognition on any of the hospital cameras? I started to plan my next series of actions. I tried my best to steer my mind away from the desire for revenge, but it kept wandering back to the idea.

The staff encouraged me to go home and get some rest. I refused. I felt responsible for Sam's condition. The least I could do was stay with him until Maggie returned the next day. I talked with Sam as if he was awake and sitting with me. I'd heard that sedated people could still hear and understand.

Chapter Twenty-five

Wednesday, April 2, 5:57 AM—Vanderbilt Hospital

Getting a good night's sleep in a hospital is impossible. When I fell asleep in the recliner, something on Sam's monitor would beep, or a nurse would come into the room to check on Sam. His vitals were holding steady. He'd lost a lot of blood from the bullet wounds and the time it took for someone to find him. Thankfully, they found him in time, or he'd be in the morgue instead of the hospital. Sarge didn't know who called it in. Curious. Just one of many curiosities of Sam's shooting. He was now the third victim tied to the Dean Swain murder.

I gave up on sleep and moved my chair back to Sam's bedside. "Come on, Sam, you have to pull through." I took his hand in mine, hoping for any sign of consciousness. "Who shot you, Sam?" I knew nine-millimeter was a common caliber, but my gut said it was the same gunman. Sarge agreed. Ballistics would soon tell us whether or not we were right in our assumptions.

Why was Sam out there by himself? Who followed him? Who would want to shoot Sam? Surely, they knew that shooting a detective of Metro Police would bring the hammer down, much like the bombing of Pearl Harbor. Something else bothered me. Who called it in, and why didn't he stay with Sam? The paramedics had to search for the body, which lost more time. The caller used a burner phone. Could it be one of the many homeless? Could it have been someone passing by? No. Who passes by a dead-end road that leads to an abandoned loading dock amid homeless compounds? What homeless person can afford a cell phone? The government gives them to approved applicants for emergency use. Who would call without identifying themselves? Were they trying to hide something? Too many questions.

"Okay, Sam. Let's start back at the beginning." I discussed the case with him as if he could interact with me. It was therapeutic. At least it kept my mind off the past.

"It starts at the cigar bar where Dean Swain draws a lot of attention to himself and his money. Chase Martin, who happens to be at the same cigar bar, runs two men off by flashing his gun. Who were the two men? Apparently, Dean didn't know them. By some act of fate, Chase is looking for a security job, and Dean is looking for personal security." I shook my head and leaned over the bed railing. "Are we supposed to believe that was coincidence, Sam?"

Everything was too convenient. Someone had to be orchestrating the events. Chase rode with Dean from the cigar bar to the homeless camp. Dean laid out his grand plan for the parking garage and bridge to the East Bank.

"And we're supposed to believe Chase, desperate for a job, would reject Dean's offer because he thought Dean was intoxicated? No way, Sam. My money is still on Chase."

He'd have to take it if he was desperate for a job, and Dean handed him one on a silver platter. Chase didn't strike me as a man of deep integrity. Why wouldn't he go with Dean to the scrap yard and see the other side of the project? That wasn't committing him to the job. Did he know they were waiting for Dean?

"Maybe Chase was the setup man, Sam. That would fill a huge gap in the events. What did it mean that Dean's stepfather hired him if he was? That would mean Jonathan Thomas was behind it all. No. What motive would he have to kill his stepson? He would gain nothing. Besides, he was the driving force, pushing us to solve the case expeditiously."

I was debating myself mentally, taking Sam's typical responses to my thoughts. Why would Chase risk us following breadcrumbs to him? Okay, rule him out.

"Back to motive, Sam. Who benefits from Dean's death?" I asked aloud as if Sam would answer the question. "Maybe Dean's plan wasn't crazy. Maybe someone else heard it and took Dean out to have it for himself." Who else did Dean tell? That still leads me back to Chase. From there, we go to the scrap yard. "How did Tito Ruiz know the Bentley would be there?" I made a note to check with Spence and Baxter to see if any numbers were common between Dean's and Tito's phones.

"Where was I? The scrap lot. No way Tito just happened by it and saw a nice car. You couldn't see the Bentley from the road. It is possible he saw it and followed it. If that's the case, the two shooters were there to kill Dean. Tito got in the way, and they fired on him instead." No. If Tito did their job for them, they'd let it go. "Two shooters? Two men in the bar. Maybe that's the connection. Maybe they followed Dean and Chase to the homeless camp. If Chase had walked home from there, the two men could have followed Dean to the scrap yard, knowing he had no one to defend him. That's a lot of *ifs*, Sam." Okay, reboot.

"You agreed with Detective Underwood that we had a conspiracy, option three." That meant someone commissioned Tito Ruiz to steal the Bentley, knowing he would kill Dean to take it. That means they not only wanted Dean dead, but they wanted someone else to take the fall. But why be so obvious or careless if this was a conspiracy? Why not use the same caliber of pistol as Dean? Why not fire off several rounds from his gun? It was either purposely sloppy or inexperienced. And who turned off the Bentley? Again, I came back to the question of benefit. "Who would gain from Dean's death? Chase wouldn't—but he did. He got the job he wanted, working security for a multimillionaire. Sam, you said there was no way Chase Martin could have orchestrated all of this. Not enough influence or resources."

I'd have to see what other investment groups were interested in the other side of the river. "Maybe someone made an offer on the land. If so, that would connect the missing homeless, including Christy." They were silently clearing them out to make room for the parking garage. It instilled fear in those who still lived there. "Sam, we have a lot of theories but no solid evidence. What did you find that got you shot?" If he could only tell me who shot him, we'd have the connection. Tito knew, but they killed him to keep him silent. "What did you discover, Sam?"

A nurse came in, checked Sam's vitals, and replaced his saline bag. She scanned his wristband, made a note, and injected medicine into the port. "He's strong," she said. "I'm sure he'll be okay."

"Yes, he is. Any idea when he might wake up?"

"We're keeping him sedated right now, giving his body time to heal. He's lucky. The bullet came dangerously close to his heart. Half an inch to the left, he wouldn't be here."

"I appreciate your honesty." She left, and I got up to go to the bathroom. I splashed water on my face and ran my fingers through my hair to give it some volume. I was exhausted. Maggie would be back around eight, and then I could go to work and dig into the case. Sarge said Spence would help in Sam's absence.

When I came out of the bathroom, I noticed a male nurse putting a needle in Sam's IV port. "Wait. The other nurse gave his medicine a few minutes ago."

He was startled by my presence. "He needs another dose."

"I don't think so." I moved to Sam's side, slid my hand to the nurse's button, and pressed it. When she answered the call, the male nurse smiled and emptied the syringe in Sam's port. He ran out of the room. I ran after him and shouted, "Catch that man!" He was through the stairwell door before anyone could respond. I wanted to chase after him, but I had to keep that medicine from getting into Sam. I ran back to the room and pulled the needle from his arm.

Sam's nurse and a security officer rushed into the room. I told them what happened and moved away so the nurse could tend to

Sam. "I want to know what he injected into that port." I turned to the security guard and said, "I need to see all security footage from this room to the exits. We need to see who that man was." The plot thickened. Whoever shot Sam wanted to make sure he died. What did Sam see that made them so nervous? Why would they need him silenced?

It made me wonder about Tito's death. I'd have to order an autopsy on Tito Ruiz and see if his body contained the same liquid injected into Sam's port.

Chapter Twenty-six

Wednesday, April 2, 5:45 PM—Homicide

Spence and I poured over the security video from the hospital and found no clear image of the imposter. I met with a police sketch artist and described the man to the best of my ability. She made a wonderful rendering of him. We gave it to Sarge, who moved it up the chain of command. By six o'clock, we received confirmation from ballistics that the nine millimeters matched the ones used on Tito. That meant Sam and Lance Corporal Rushing were probably both in danger.

Our administrative assistant, Deborah, buzzed and said, "The toxicology report is in your email. Tito's autopsy report is as well."

"Already?"

"Yes. The Chief put a rush on it."

I opened the first file, Sam's IV. "Ricin. He was going to kill Sam with Ricin."

"Why would someone risk getting caught to poison Sam?" Spence asked.

"Because he could identify the shooter or shooters. Whoever it was used the same gun that shot Tito Ruiz, which puts him or them at the murder scene." I was convinced there were still two shooters. Now, this supported my suspicions. Why would they be at the homeless camp? Were they looking for Lance Corporal Rushing, too? They must have seen him watching that night. Or did they, somehow, know we were looking for him? Did Sam discover something else?

"Why leave Sam alive?" Spence asked. "Why not kill him with another shot? He was down with two in the chest. Putting one in his head would have been child's play."

"Maybe they thought he was dead already. There was a lot of blood. Or maybe someone interfered with the job. Maybe they put him down and took off before someone else identified them. Unless they used silencers, those shots could be heard for a mile. There's no way the people in those camps didn't hear them."

"You keep saying *them*. What makes you think there were two shooters? All we know is that the bullets matched the slugs taken from the car. One person could have had two guns. You also hypothesized there was a third person at the murder scene. Where's the evidence, Abbey? We need hard facts to make our case." While we continued to debate the number of shooters, Spence opened the autopsy report and scanned the document. "I bet it's—Ricin. Tito didn't die of the gunshot wounds. They poisoned him, too."

I rolled my chair out into the walkway between our cubicle and those of the sergeants. "Hey, Sergeant McNally? Did the FBI ever confirm they had an agent relieve our officer?"

"They neither confirm or deny the presence of an agent there. Let me go up the chain of command and see if we can get a firm answer one way or the other."

Ugh! Bureaucracy. I hate it. "Shooting is one thing. Lots of people have access to nine-millimeter handguns. But Ricin? Using it on both Tito and Sam—that connects both the FBI agent and the nurse. We know the nurse was an imposter. I bet the FBI agent was, too."

"I agree, Abbey, but we need proof."

"Come on, Spence. This is a coordinated attempt to remove all the witnesses. Something big is going on here." Something else was bothering me. "Doesn't Ricin take several days to kill someone?"

"Depends on the dosage," Spence said. "Injected directly into the bloodstream with a massive amount of Ricin—it could kill in minutes or hours."

"The Fed in Tito's room." Everything was falling into place. "Someone poisoned Tito disguised as a federal officer. He used that guise to relieve the officer on duty. Freeing himself to inject Tito with the poison."

"But someone came in as a nurse to kill Sam. Thankfully, you were there to stop him."

"We need to show Tito's nurse the sketch of the man who attempted to poison Sam and see if it's the same guy. If not, have her describe him to a sketch artist. This may be the break we've been looking for."

We alerted Sergeant McNally to the newly discovered evidence. He ordered a second officer to guard Sam's room and shouted over the cubicles, "All hands on deck! Everyone to the conference room."

Once we assembled, he said, "As you all know, Sam Tidwell was shot twice in the chest and once in the arm while searching for a witness. This morning, someone attempted to inject poison into his IV. We also recently discovered that the same poison killed Tito Ruiz. We're going to find this idiot and whoever he's trying to protect. I want everyone to set his present case aside and hop on this. Is that understood?" He said it with such a thunderous voice that no one responded immediately. "Understand?" he shouted again.

"Yes, Sargeant!" came the response in unison.

"Good. Now listen to Rhodes as she gets everyone up to speed."

I discussed the facts we knew, the unknowns we were searching for, and our theories so far. Spence distributed copies of the sketch based on my recollection. "We need someone to take this to Tito's hospital staff and see if this is the same man who presented himself as a federal officer. The Chief just heard back from the feds. They deny having any agent in the area." Two detectives said they would investigate it. "In each case, he knew exactly where the cameras were placed. He avoided facial identification at each hospital."

Spence said, "We're looking for at least two men. One is this guy." He held up the sketch. "Another person of interest is Chase Martin." I showed the picture of Chase. "We don't know how deeply he is involved in the case, but his prints and DNA were in Dean Swain's car, and he was the last person to see Dean alive."

"Any questions?" Sarge asked. "They made this personal by hitting our family. Captain Harris will hold a press conference today to show the sketch of our primary suspect and the picture of Chase Martin." Sarge looked my way and said, "Rhodes, you and Spencer head over to Martin's apartment and bring him in for questioning. Baxter and Hawley, get down to JLT temporary offices and look there. I'm sure as soon as they get wind of our interest, they'll be on the run. Let's get them before they get away!"

I was angry and had to stuff it down. Someone tried twice to kill my partner and friend. More than likely, they would try again. I knew what he looked like, which put my life in jeopardy, too. I had to find him and beat him to the punch. Guilt was weighing heavy on me, threatening to push me back down into the deep, dark pit. I couldn't let it. I had to stay focused on Sam and finding his would-be murderer before he struck again. Spence was good, but, like me, he lacked Sam Tidwell's experience. We'd have to be on our A-game. I was up for the challenge. Whoever *they* were, they woke a sleeping giant and would regret it. Sergeant McNalley was taking this personally. He wouldn't rest until we solved the case and put them behind bars.

Chapter Twenty-seven

Friday, April 4, 8:45 AM—Riverfront Park, Nashville

Chase was not at his apartment, but Spence had a great idea since we were close. We parked at Riverfront Park at the end of Broadway and approached the homeless camps from there. Spence walked along the edge of the Cumberland, and I walked on the railroad tracks. That way, he could flush our soldier out, and I could watch for him on the tracks—assuming he returned to the area after diving in the river. We were now convinced he knew something. Even if we couldn't catch him and talk with him, we could find some way to warn him—tell him he was in danger.

When I came to the road leading to the abandoned loading dock, I followed it to the main camp run by Damien. Spence was already there, showing the sketch and the picture of Chase. He said, "I've had several hits on your sketch, but no one recognizes the photo."

"I see you've met Damien."

Damien nodded and smiled.

"Yes. He's been very helpful in bringing people together to look at the images." Spence shook his hand and said, "He says there are three other camps we should check out."

"I know where they are," I said. "Let's see if they can help."

We walked back up the road to the next camp. On the way, I filled Spence in on Damien and his men. Several people in the other camps recognized the man in the sketch. Some saw him with one other man. Others said three men were walking around the camps.

"He and another man were here twice, looking around," one woman said.

The consistent story was that at least two men were looking for someone on this side of the river. Once they were confronted, they left. This didn't agree with Damien's testimony that the men argued about their right to walk through public land, but he could have been more aggressive and gotten a different response. I know I tend to push back when bullies threaten me.

Finally, at the last camp, the one furthest from the river, an older man pointed to Chase Martin's photo. "I saw that man a couple of weeks ago. He and another guy drove down here in some fancy car. They parked in the lot down there," the man said, pointing to the empty parking lot by the loading dock.

"What did they do?" I asked.

"Nothing. They just stood in the middle of the lot."

"Did you notice if they left together?" I asked. This was my chance to break Chase Martin's alibi.

He thought for a moment before saying, "No. That guy walked out of here, but the other guy left in his car." Crap. That meant Chase was telling the truth. That still didn't clear him from telling someone about Dean's intentions and whereabouts. That still didn't clear him of the conspiracy to kill Dean and Tito.

"He was talking on his phone. He sounded pretty upset."

Really? "Did you happen to hear what he said?"

"No, but I asked him for some change. He yelled at me and said he didn't have any money. Those rich people are all the same." The man cleared his throat and spit away from us.

We thanked him and started back down the hill. "Hey, Spence, let's head over to that pillar under the interstate. I want to see if there's any sign of our soldier."

We trudged our way through the thicket and up the small rise to the edge of the pillar. I bent down and put my hand over

149

the ashes of an old fire. "It's still warm. Look. There are fish bones. They weren't here the other day."

"All that means is someone cooked fish. That's not proof your soldier is back," Spence said, dampening my mood. He wasn't encouraging like Sam. Spence thought it would be best if he tried to poke holes in a theory, saying, "If it can stand up to my challenge, it's a good theory." He followed the sound of buzzing flies. "These guts are fresh." He stood up and turned around. "That him?"

My eyes followed Spence's finger. Someone was running along the edge of the river to the east. "Yes. That's him." I whistled as loud as I could. He stopped and looked my way. "Lance Corporal Rushing!"

He saluted me before resuming his run along the river's edge. Within seconds, he disappeared into the thicket. "You weren't kidding. He's like a ghost," Spence said. "Let's head back and see what everyone else found. Someone must know the man in the sketch."

"We have a witness who says Chase was on his phone right after he left Dean Swain. Spence, I'm telling you; he's involved in this somehow."

"All we have is a phone call, Abbey. Besides, why would Jonathan Thomas hire Chase if he was in on his stepson's death?"

"You're assuming he was aware of Chase's involvement." We finally reached the car after a long walk back along the tracks. When I got in, I added, "We know this is a coordinated effort. The two gunmen had to be in place before Dean arrived at the lot. I know I'm reaching, but they both had nine-millimeter handguns and wore the same brand and style of shoe—like a part of a uniform."

"I agree that this seems coordinated." He put his hand to his chin. "You may have something with the shoes."

"I'll look into the shoes—see who sells them. Spence, don't you think it's odd that no one heard the gunshots when Dean Swain was killed or when Sam was hit? They could hear Dean talking on his phone, but they couldn't hear gunshots?" Like I believed that.

"I think it has more to do with fear than the ability to hear the shots," he said. "If they admit to hearing the shots, then they become witnesses. I think even they know what happens to people with knowledge around here. They tend to disappear like Dean, Tito, and Sam."

Spence had a point. Ignorance was safety. Hearing a man on a phone is not the same as admitting you heard gunshots.

Chapter Twenty-eight

Friday, April 4, 11:02 AM—Homicide Offices

Spence and I barely entered the door to our homicide offices when Sergeant McNally barked out, "Rhodes and Spencer, Captain Harris's office, now."

Great. What did I do now? We went immediately to see Captain Harris. I was shocked to see Jonathan Lee Thomas sitting across from the Captain's desk. He rose as we knocked on the door. Captain Harris waved us in and pointed to two empty chairs at the back of his office. "Pull up a seat."

"Captain?" I asked. "Is something wrong?" Spence and I pulled up our chairs next to Mr. Thomas's and sat down.

"Mr. Thomas identified your two suspects."

Mr. Thomas said, "I'm rather embarrassed to say they're both on my payroll. The man in the photograph is Chase Martin. I recently hired him as a part of my security team. The one in the sketch is Chad Cole. He's been with me for three years. I can't imagine he'd do anything like this."

"Do you know where we can find them?" I asked.

"I'm afraid not. You can contact the head of my security team. His name is Buck Pader. He's looking for them now. Neither man showed up for his work detail today."

That's convenient. "When did you see them last?" I asked.

"The morning of Captain Harris's press conference."

"By any chance, do these men carry nine-millimeter weapons?" Spence asked.

He raised an eyebrow and said, "You'd be better off asking Buck."

"Do you have his number?" Spence asked.

"I've already given the numbers of my entire security team to Captain Harris." He paused for a moment. "Do you think they had anything to do with Dean's death?"

"We're still looking into that," I said. "It would help to speak with both men and track their whereabouts the past week and a half."

He nodded. "Buck said they've both ditched their phones, so we can't trace them now. What about tracing their activity through phone records."

"We'll need to get a warrant," Captain Harris chimed in.

"Not if I give consent," Mr. Thomas said. "I pay for the phones and the plans as a part of my business. Unfortunately, Mr. Martin only recently joined my team. You won't have much to track his whereabouts."

Captain Harris nodded at Spence, who rose and said, "I'm on it." The captain handed a list of the security team's names and numbers to Spence as he walked by.

"And get a warrant for Chase Martin's personal cell so we can track his movements on the night of the murder."

"That would be helpful, Captain," I said. "We have witnesses who place him at the homeless camp with Dean the night of the murder. They say he walked out of there talking to someone by phone. He was agitated. I'd like to know who was on the other end of that conversation." I did my best to read Mr. Thomas's body language to see if he was in on this or was innocently connected to all parties. He was hard to read. I guess a man of his stature doesn't get to the top without having some kind of poker face.

Captain Harris dismissed me. He continued to talk with Mr. Thomas as I left. I had no problem getting a search warrant for his phone now that Chase Martin was in the wind and was the last person to see Dean Swain alive. Spence contacted the carrier with Mr. Thomas's blessing and obtained the tracking report for Chad Cole's phone. I worked on getting the same for Chase Martin. We both decided to get printouts of each man's texts for the same period.

As we studied the report for Chad's phone, Spence spread out a map of Nashville and marked each location. He used different colors to represent each day of Chad's travel. We noticed immediately that Chad was present in the scrap lot on the night of Dean's murder. Strike one. I called Buck Pader, the head of Mr. Thomas's security team, and confirmed that all their team members used standard Glock nine-millimeter handguns. Strike two. Spence marked the day of Sam's shooting, and Chad's phone revealed he was there at the same time. Strike Three. We had him—now if we could only find him.

Spence completed the same process for Chase Martin using his personal and business phones. I was sad to see that his personal phone confirmed Chase's story. That night, he went from the cigar bar to the homeless camps. Then, he walked directly to his apartment. I knew in my gut that Chase was involved somehow. Why couldn't we prove it?

Once Spence traced Chase's business phone, we had him. He was with Chad Cole at the homeless camp the night of Sam's shooting. "We have him!"

"He was there, Abbey, but remember the ballistic reports showed the same two guns were used in the shootings of Sam and Tito," Spence said. "We have no proof of Chase Martin firing at either man."

"Are you trying to prove him innocent?" I snapped. "This shows he was there when Sam was shot. Whether or not he pulled the trigger, he allowed it to happen. Guilty by association."

"Calm down, Abbey. I'm just…"

"No one calms down when someone tells you to calm down, Spence. It only makes it worse." I got up and walked a few laps around the cubicles. This was getting personal, and I needed to take a step away. When I finished my third lap, I eased back into the cubicle. There it was. I'd seen it before, but I didn't realize the significance. "Spence, what day is this?" I asked, pointing to a mark at Shelby Park. "Thursday, March twenty-seven. Why?"

"That's the rally for Clean Up Nashville. Chad Cole was at that rally. This ties him to Stacey Hopkins."

"What does she have to do with Dean's or Sam's cases?"

"Nothing. But it may tie Chad to the homeless camp disappearances, too."

"I don't mean to butt in, but I heard Sergeant McNally tell you to let that go. We have no proof any of those people are dead. Besides, this case is our priority. We've got to nail Sam's shooter with solid evidence."

Stay in your lane, Abbey. He was right. Sam's case was number one on the docket, Dean's conspiracy was second, and the disappearances at the homeless camp were a distant third. It was then that I realized we were still missing the second shooter. "Okay, let's say, for all practical purposes, we've found Sam's shooter. It's the same man who tried to poison him in the hospital. But the nursing staff said that wasn't the same man who presented himself as a federal officer at Tito's hospital. Even though we have the same MO, we have two different people."

"Chad Cole is one, but we're still missing the other. And we can rule Chase Martin out for that, at least."

"Right. So who's the missing shooter?"

"Abbey, do you think it's another member of his security team?" Spence asked. "Do you think he ordered the hit on his own stepson?"

"I don't know, Spence. I've been wondering that myself. Maybe we should visit Buck Pader. Let's see if he willingly submits his team's guns for a ballistics check."

"We could get a warrant. We have probable cause to suspect one more person from the team."

Spence and I ran through the sequence of events, beginning with Music City Cigar Bar. Chad's phone was never there. "So, who were the two men at the bar?" I asked.

155

"Let's look over that video once more. You and Sam focused on Dean and Chase, right?" I nodded. "We need to focus on the two men at the bar. First, let's get a photo ID for each man on Jonathan Thomas's security team. That way, we know whether or not we have a deeper issue if we can match any of them with the two men."

"Then let's show them to Tito's nurse and see if she identifies the man impersonating the federal officer."

From the cigar bar, we traced Dean's movement to the parking lot in the center of all four homeless camps on the southwest bank of the Cumberland. Chase Martin received a call and then left for his apartment. "Do his phone records say who he called?"

Spence looked at the call record and scrolled down to the date and time he was with Dean Swain. "There aren't any outbound calls. He did, however, receive a call that night."

"What's the number?" I asked. Spence gave me the number, and I called it.

"This is Buck." I put him on the speakerphone.

"Buck, this is Detective Abbey Rhodes."

"Yes, Detective. Mr. Thomas said you might call."

I introduced Spence and started with the tedious business of gathering ballistics for their weapons. He agreed. I asked if he had any luck contacting Chad and Chase. He didn't. Then, as best I could, I eased into the conversation concerning his call to Chase Martin on the night of Dean's death.

He was quiet for a moment. Then he said, "Wednesday, March nineteen?"

"Yes, sir. Do you remember that call?" I asked.

"Of course," Buck said. "That was the night I scheduled his interview for the security team at JLT Enterprises."

"You scheduled his interview the night of Dean's death?" Spence asked.

"Wow! I never put the two together," Buck said. "I guess in hindsight, that looks bad."

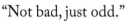

"Not bad, just odd."

"I'm curious," I said. "Listen, Buck; an eyewitness said Chase sounded angry on that call. Do you remember what he might have said?"

"Let me think. Oh, yes. It was about a red flag I had on his resume. I asked why he dropped out of Metro Police after he'd made it through the academy."

"And that made him angry?" Spence asked.

"He said he'd already answered that question multiple times. He wanted to know why we were harping on it."

"And that didn't knock him out of contention?" I asked. "Even with an attitude like that?"

"No. I like a man with a little spunk. He had great scores on our aptitude and firearm tests."

"So he'd interviewed with you before that night?"

"Yes. He had two meetings with our team. I called that night for his sit down with me. It was the final part of the process."

"Did he know your connection with Dean Swain? That you ran his father's security detail?"

Buck said, "I'm not sure. How was I to know Chase even knew Dean?"

"When did he start working for you?" I asked.

"Saturday, March the twenty-ninth—the night of the fundraiser."

The night of the fundraiser. My big disaster. I wouldn't forget that conversation which catapulted me into a full-blown PTSD event. "And five days later, he's on the run, suspected in the shooting of a homicide detective?"

"Seems so," Buck said with sadness. "I'm a better trainer than a recruiter."

"Don't you think it's odd that two members of your team are suspected in that case?" Spence asked.

"Odd? It pisses me off," Buck snapped. "I want to catch them myself and strap them to a chair. I'll get the truth out of 'em." He was humiliated and planned on exacting some revenge for the embarrassment they caused. "I'll get to the bottom of this. I promise you that."

"I think you better let us handle that," I cautioned. "You don't want your involvement jeopardizing your innocence. If you talk to them before we do, it might appear as if you're controlling their testimonies."

"No, Detective. I would never do that."

"Just to be on the safe side, let us handle it from here. Oh, before I forget it, can we get photos of each person on your team?"

I hung up, and we returned to the evidence we had. Spence started sifting through the pages upon pages of texts from Chad's phone. I was surprised that Chase didn't text from his personal phone. Either he preferred talking to texting, or he didn't want to leave a trail of evidence for others to find. Whatever his motive, I was left with no proof that tied him to Dean's death.

Forty-five minutes later, Spence called me to his desk and said, "Look at this." There were a series of texts between Chad Cole, Doug Ackerman, and Zach Clement that could address Dean's death. Although it was spoken with ambiguous language and code, the telling comment was sent from Chad to the other two saying, "U hrd hm. Hes liblty."

Doug Ackerman replied, "Think he meant it?"

"crs he did," Chad answered.

If Chad's comment referred to Dean Swain as a liability, someone possibly suggested or implied they should get rid of him. They never mentioned shooting or hurting him.

"Can we track their phones and see if Ackerman or Clement was at that scrap yard?"

"Might take some time, but I can do that," Spence assured me. "Trying to find the second shooter?"

"I think I'm going to attend The Least of These rally tomorrow and ask if anyone on their staff or volunteer list ever visited the homeless camps on the southwest side. If someone did, maybe they can identify another man from the security team."

"Sounds like a plan. I'll run the photos over to Tito's nurse. Let's see if she identifies anyone else."

Chapter Twenty-nine

Saturday, April 5, 11:00 AM—War Memorial Plaza

The Least of These rally was much larger than the estimated count of those opposed to the homeless at the Clean Up Nashville rally in Shelby Park. By mere attendance alone, it seemed more people were interested in helping the *disenfranchised* than forcing them out of town. Lyndsey Franklin was a gifted speaker. She was passionate about her cause. I listened as she wove facts with figurative language. "Is one person's life worth more than another's?" she asked.

The crowd shouted, "No!"

"Then why is it teachers barely get by when our athletes live in mansions? Why do we cry to defund the police but spend over a thousand dollars for a Taylor Swift concert? Why do we block interstates for presidents but sweep the homeless into the gutter? Why? Because we do value one life over another." No doubt she was eloquent. She finished her speech and introduced Professor Dallas Gatlin.

Even though I saw him just this last Sunday, he looked taller and more handsome than I remembered. He, too, had a way with words. I found myself mesmerized by his looks and speech. "If you will graciously grant me ten minutes of your time, I will share the humble origin of our ministry."

They shouted. "Go ahead," "We want to hear," and "Dallas... Dallas...Dallas."

"Please, my friends, I don't want your attention focused on

160

me, but rather this critical ministry." It only served to fire them up even more. "We call our ministry, *The Least of These*, to remind us that all life has value, especially those cast away by our society. You may think our title is unique—a creation of our imagination. It is not. It comes straight from the mouth of Jesus Christ, our Lord and Savior." People cheered. "He should get the credit, not me, Lyndsey, staff, or volunteers, no matter how hard we work. We work as if working for Jesus, following His will in our lives." They cheered again—obviously, a religious crowd. He was pushing all the right buttons.

I tried to imagine what it would be like in one of his classes. Would he be as commanding? As eloquent? Would the young women in his class feel the way I did? I'd already tuned out twice watching him. I'm not sure I would do well in his classroom. I'd spend too much time looking at him and too little taking notes. But he seemed so intelligent and charismatic, yet genuinely humble— so eloquent without sounding condescending. He was everything my father wasn't.

"We do what He commanded us to do as the true sheep of His fold. In the twenty-fifth chapter of the gospel of Matthew, Jesus tells of the final judgment, when He will separate His sheep from the goats of this world. Now, don't be confused. When our culture hears the word Goat, we think it means the greatest of all time. That's not the goat to which Jesus refers. Jesus says these goats *will go away into eternal punishment.*"

There it was, the condemnation.

They booed and shouted several comments like, "We're not goats," and "Not us."

"Of course not. Jesus wasn't speaking of us, His true sheep. He was warning those who called themselves good, but their fruit showed otherwise. Some choose to act only when it affects them directly." I knew he was speaking of people like Stacey Hopkins. It was evident when she wanted to rid their neighborhoods of the homeless while caring nothing about those by the interstate.

I hoped Dallas was not like that. I was torn. I'd seen my share of gifted speakers with shallow hearts. "We aren't like that. We care about all people regardless of their social status, the color of their skin, or the way they look."

"That's right," someone shouted.

Dallas smiled. I could tell he had them right where he wanted them. He spoke of godly living—selfless living. He championed those who gave of their time and resources to make such things possible. "Love requires sacrifice."

My heart fluttered. *Get a grip!* I quickly pushed the emotions down—down so far they couldn't weaken me. I'd had years of practice.

Then Dallas said, "Jesus describes our ministry with references to feeding the hungry, giving water to the thirsty, greeting strangers, clothing the less fortunate, and visiting the prisoners." They cheered again. "All of these things we do with love and humility." He smiled and allowed the crowd time to shout their comments of affirmation. "Here's the kicker. Jesus told His sheep, 'Truly I say to you, to the extent that you did it to one of these brothers of Mine, even the least of these, you did it to Me.'"

I thought they were going to break out in revival. I waited for the offering plates to pass and for the speeches to mark the power of the donation. I could feel my back bristle with the familiar comments. But Dallas threw me a curve. He called for volunteers. He called for legislation that would treat the homeless with courtesy and value. He turned their attention away from himself to the volunteers and workers of the ministry. My father would never have done that.

"And that, my friends, is why we call our ministry The Least of These." He bowed to the crowd and quietly took his seat on the stage.

Lyndsey rose and took her time getting to the podium. I couldn't tell for certain, but it looked like she was crying. She tried to speak but couldn't form words. Finally, after regaining her composure, she said, "Thank you, Professor Gatlin, for those moving words." She pointed to two tables before the stage and said, "Our volunteers are seated at each table with brochures and sign-up lists. Please complete a volunteer sheet if our ministry appeals to you and you want to help.

I made eye contact with Dallas, who waved and worked his way through the crowd toward me. It took a while. Many people in the crowd wanted to say something to him. He was very gracious and gave each a portion of his time. Finally making it back to me, he said, "You did make it out to see me."

"Well, not *just* to see you," I said with a smile. *What a stupid thing to say.* I sounded like a schoolgirl with a crush. Was I? No, I was here on business. This was not a personal call.

Dallas turned to Spence and said, "And you are?" He held out his hand to shake Spence's.

"Detective David Spencer. Most people call me Spence." Spence gave me the eye and pretended to have something important to say to someone by the stage.

"Hate to disappoint you, Professor, but we're in the middle of an investigation."

"Detective Rhodes, I didn't realize we were being so formal." He winked. I wasn't sure if it was in sarcasm or as a means of flirting. I secretly hoped the latter. "Can I be of any assistance to your investigation?"

"That depends. How well do you know the staff and volunteers?"

"Very well. I work with Lyndsey to recruit, enlist, and screen both."

"Well, then, Professor Gatlin, you could help us. We need to see if anyone in your organization…"

"Ministry," he corrected.

"Yes, ministry. Has anyone worked with the homeless on the southwest bank of the Cumberland?" He inquired as to the specific site, and I gave him the location.

"Let's see." He took me to the stage and asked Lyndsey and

her staff. One of her staff members said he was just there Friday distributing food packets. We took his information and said we would follow up with him. Dallas and Lyndsey gathered the volunteers and asked them the same question. One young woman said she went with the staff member Friday to hand out food. We also got her contact information and set a time for the two of them to come to Homicide. When we were through, I asked Lyndsey if she was ready for our lunch appointment.

She nodded and said, "I hope you don't mind, but I asked Dallas if he would join us."

Mind? I was hoping he'd be included. "Of course not. He can talk with Detective Spencer while you and I review our case's details."

We walked over to the Frothy Monkey, what I call a girly-girl place with all the fancy sandwiches. I was so embarrassed. Lyndsey, Dallas, and even Spence ordered without a menu, a sign of being frequent customers. I couldn't focus on the menu, so I ordered a regular cheeseburger and corn chips off the kids' menu. I felt stupid, but I loved this kind of food. It was always a great treat after years of Army food. They all pretended not to notice, but I caught Dallas smiling.

That smile turned me upside down. Why?

Lyndsey and I discussed Lance Corporal Rushing, which only served to solidify Christy's account of the man. Once I realized there was nothing more to learn about him, I moved the discussion to her history with Stacey Hopkins. "We both graduated from Lipscomb University. We were in several classes together, but she was a year ahead of me."

"Were you friends?" I asked.

She took a sip of her water and thought for a moment. "I'd say we were friendly, but we've never been friends." She smiled and said, "We've always had different filters."

"Filters? I don't understand." I knew the reference, but what made theirs different?

"You know, lenses through which we see the world. She came

164

from money—never had to worry about tuition, books, or entertainment. I worked two jobs, fought for every scholarship, and had no one else to fall back on."

"I'm sorry." I knew the feeling. I could see how she deeply resented Stacey, Stacey's money, and her cause. "Were you ever homeless yourself?"

"Yes." She said it with no hesitation. It was almost a badge of honor for her. When she spoke about homelessness, she didn't simply research the subject. She lived it. Lyndsey was an authority on it.

"How'd you get out?"

"Get out? You say that as if it is a prison, and I escaped."

Did I dare say it aloud? I could hear the conversation between Dallas and Spence. Surely, they could hear ours. Well, let's see what he thinks about a woman with a tainted past. Easy to preach on it. Did he live it? "It was for me." Lyndsey's eyes widened. Yes. I did understand. "I was kicked out of my home when I was fourteen."

"I didn't know," she said. Both Spence and Dallas paused their conversation and looked our way. "So, we're sisters of a sort."

"Of a sort," I said. "Right, boys?" They fumbled with their glasses and tried to resume their conversation. "So, Lyndsey, what do you do for a living?"

"Thanks to Professor Gatlin, I have a scholarship that pays for my master's studies and room and board. He also helped me obtain a grant for the ministry with a part-time salary."

"Oh, so you live off the homeless?" It was out before I could stop it, and it sounded worse than originally intended. I was blessed and cursed with sarcasm. This was not the positive version. Unfortunately, I wasn't blessed with the wisdom of timing.

"Lyndsey lives off kind and generous donors who admire her heart for the homeless," Dallas said. "The recipients of our ministry pay nothing. I assure you. This allows her to focus on them."

"I'm so sorry. Sometimes, my mouth gets ahead of my mind."

"Peter had the same issue," Dallas said.

165

"Peter who?" Spence asked.

"I think he's referring to the Apostle Peter, who suffered from foot-in-mouth disease," I said. My face was burning. I knew it had to be blushing red. "He often spoke without thinking—or at least before he thought about what he was saying."

"You keep surprising me, Detective Rhodes. Now, you reveal your deep understanding of the Bible. What's next?" Dallas said it with another wink. I think that was the friendly wink, not the sarcastic one.

"I'm really sorry, Lyndsey. I have a quick wit and a wicked tongue."

"I understand more than you can imagine," she said. "Apology accepted." She paused as the server brought our meals, and Dallas asked a blessing on the food. When he finished and said, "Amen," he addressed the table. "I believe Stacey Hopkins sees homelessness as a thing—like a plague—to be irradicated by cutting it away from the body."

"I know homelessness as a people," Lyndsey said. "I don't know who coined the original phrase, but we're all one disaster away from homelessness." She turned to me. "For you, it was getting kicked out of the house. For me, it was two parents who OD'd on cocaine. For others, it's inflation, poor investments, a string of bad choices, loss of job—you name it." I nodded. I'd never thought of myself that way before. "Some of us make it out—as you so aptly put it— and some don't." She paused once again to make eye contact with each of us. "I desire to help as many as I can. We don't just hand out fish," she said. "We also teach others to fish for themselves."

"That's why I got involved as well," Dallas said. "I'm one of the blessed few who made it without significant crises. The biggest decisions I've made dealt with education and a career. I've always been blessed with options. I want to provide those for others who never knew opportunities existed for them."

I took a drink of water. I wasn't thirsty, but I was so moved I couldn't speak. Spence may have noticed, or he may have just tired of all the emotional talk. "Back to our case," he said. "Is there any reason we should suspect a member of Clean Up Nashville for the disappearances?"

"Not without a television crew behind her," Lyndsey said. "Stacey would make a grand spectacle out of it. Honestly, unless it touches her property or playground, Stacey doesn't care."

That's the same conclusion I came to upon meeting Stacey Hopkins. "So her movement is a personal tool, not a political one?" I asked.

"So to speak. Yes." Dallas looked into my eyes and said something. I couldn't hear him over the sound of my heartbeat. This was getting ridiculous. I had to get a grip on myself. Spence tossed some money on the table and pulled on my arm. He thanked them for their time and said we needed to go see a friend.

Once we were outside the restaurant, Spence said, "Abbey Rhodes, you've got it bad, girl."

"Huh? Got what?"

"Yeah, right! That man put a spell on you, Abbey." Spence elbowed me in the ribs and said, "Let's check on Sam."

Sam! What a friend I was. I'd gotten so wrapped up in the case and Susan's new friend that I'd forgotten to check in on Sam.

Chapter Thirty

Saturday, April 5, 3:17 PM—Homicide

W e spent half an hour with Sam at the hospital. Nothing changed. They were still keeping him sedated to heal. Maggie was pleasant. She must have forgotten or forgiven me for my careless comment. I talked to Sam for a little while, updating him on the case. Spence told him about Dallas Gatlin. I think he did it to get on my last nerve. We spoke to the two guards outside Sam's room to see if anything suspicious happened. Nothing.

After we left Vanderbilt, we drove to St. Thomas Mid-Town Hospital to see Tito's nurse. Spence tried the day before, but she was off duty. As soon as we showed the photos of Jonathon Thomas's security team, she positively identified the second man, Zach Clement, as the FBI impostor. Spence called Buck Pader but had to leave a message.

We returned to Homicide at 3:17. Someone was waiting for us in the conference room. Deborah said our visitor wanted to give us information on our soldier. The stench smacked us in the face when we opened the door. A filthy, homeless man stood and held out his hand. Against my better judgment, I shook it. "Detectives Rhodes and Spencer. What can we do for you, Mr..."

"Javy Perez," he said before sitting back down.

"Okay, Mr. Perez," I continued. "Wait. I've seen you before."

"I recognized you from the camp," he said. "I saw you interacting with Denzel."

I didn't know who Denzel was, but that's where I saw him. He

168

had a tent near the soldier. "What can Detective Spencer and I do for you?" I put my hands in my purse and found the hand-sanitizer by touch, while keeping eye-contact with our guest.

"You don't have to hide it," he said. "I don't blame you."

"Okay." I put my hands above the table and rubbed them with the sanitizing lotion. I also put a dab under my nose. "Why are we here?"

He took a deep breath, reached into his back pocket, and pulled out his identification. "I'm a journalist doing an undercover piece on Lance Corporal Denzel Rushing."

I looked at his ID. That's his Denzel. "So, you're not homeless?"

"Only until I get enough on him for the story."

"Why him?" Spence asked. "What's so special about a homeless vet? There's got to be hundreds of them."

"There are—probably thousands. He was in the Afghanistan withdrawal—one of the men who was handed a baby for safe-keeping."

"I remember seeing that on the news," I said, covering my mouth in shock. "He almost fell into the barbed wire."

"I was there, covering the withdrawal," Javy said. "When I discovered more of his background and experience, I pitched the story. My editor said it was a nice idea, but ideas aren't stories. She said when I had something to impress her, give her a call."

Spence leaned in. "So, you've been living like a homeless man? So that you can watch an ex-soldier?"

"He's not just any ex-soldier," Javy said. "He's a Bronze Star recipient for heroic actions. He saved two other soldiers while taking enemy fire. He dragged them over a mile to safety. Then, he was stationed at Kabul Airport. He was nearly killed in the suicide bombing. He made it home, but his mind is still there."

"Why are you telling us this now?" I asked. "If you recognized me earlier, why didn't you identify yourself then?"

"I couldn't blow my cover. I've been working on this a long time—earning his trust, eating with him, and listening to his stories."

"He talks to you?" Spence asked. "Like a normal conversation?" Spence grabbed a pad and pen from the center of the conference table. "What does he say?"

"He thinks I'm a fellow soldier. He reviews our orders."

"Are you here to tell us his story?" I asked. We could hear his report all day, but I wanted to know why he suddenly broke cover and walked to the homicide offices.

"I've seen some things—dark things. I knew this would be a dangerous task, but I didn't think I'd have to hide from cop killers."

"Cop killers?" That got my attention. "What cop?"

"The other detective that was with you the first time you came to the camps."

I dove over the table and grabbed him by the shirt. "You saw them shoot Sam, and you're just now coming here?"

If it weren't for Spence's quick actions, I'd probably have committed assault. Technically, I'd violated point two already: "A person commits assault who: (2) Intentionally or knowingly causes another to reasonably fear imminent bodily injury." I could see it in his eyes. He was terrified. Spence moved me back to my seat and calmed Javy.

"Yes. I'm ashamed of it, but my story was more important to me." I about launched myself again, but he said, "I'm sorry. I can't change what I did or didn't do, but I can identify the men if you have any photos of suspects."

Spence said, "Wait here while Detective Rhodes brings us some pictures."

"Me? Why me? This is my case."

Spence glared at me and looked at the door. He was right; I needed a moment. I went to my cubby and retrieved the pictures of the security team. I handed them to Spence and stood in the back corner, giving the man some space. I needed him to focus on the pictures, not me.

"Yeah, that's them."

"Which ones?" Spence asked. "Point to each one."

He pointed to three men.

"You sure?" Spence asked.

"Absolutely! They came looking for Denzel but ran into your detective instead."

"How do you know they were looking for Lance Corporal Rushing?"

"They came to our camp and asked me if I knew him. I played dumb like I didn't know what they were asking."

I looked at the three men. "You've identified Chad Cole, Zach Clements, and Chase Martin." I pointed to Chase's photo. "He was there too?"

"Yes. The other two came another time without him, but he was there the night your detective was shot."

"How did it happen?" I asked. I was about to break down in tears as he described the events leading to Sam's injuries. Although he couldn't hear what they said, he clearly saw what happened from the hill under the interstate. The three men were looking for Denzel. Just as he had done with us, Denzel looped around and lost them. As the men were doubling back, they ran into Sam. One of the men pulled a gun on Sam and shot him. Sam staggered back and reached for his weapon. The other man shot twice. He hit Sam in the chest, and when he tried to get off a second shot, Chase Martin pushed him. That shot just grazed Sam's arm. Sam went to the ground, clutching his wounds. The three men argued and then ran to their car. They sped away, leaving Sam to die.

"I had to walk quite a distance to find a phone and call it in," Javy said.

"Why didn't you identify yourself?" Spence asked.

"I panicked. I worried about being accused of the crime. I also needed to protect my work. I thought I could at least call for an ambulance. I didn't expect him to live."

I was angry with his selfishness—and yet thankful for his call. I wanted to review his testimony one more time for consistency. "Which men shot Sam?"

He pointed to Chad and Zach.

"What about the other one?"

"He drew his gun, but he didn't shoot. He knocked the second shooter to the side, making him miss his second shot."

That made Chase an accessory. He was there. He was with the shooters, and he brandished his weapon. "Are you willing to testify to this?" I asked.

"Yes. I'll write a statement. Just let me go back to the camp to finish my story. You know where to find me, and I promise I won't resist."

"I don't know if we can do that," Spence said. "I can't knowingly put you back in harm's way. They may come back for you."

"Have you seen anything else that may interest us?" I asked.

He spoke of suspicious activity in the main camp, Damien's camp. When asked about the disappearances of the four women, he said he heard screams but didn't see anything. I asked where the screams came from, and he said on the bank just below the camp, where people fill their water jugs and pots.

"Did you say their water pots?" I asked.

"Yes. Why?"

I turned to Spence. "Christy's water pot was missing. I think the woman from the top of the hill was missing her water bucket, too."

"Did you say 'scream' or 'screams'?" Spence asked.

"Screams. Two different distinct screams."

"The same night?" Spence asked.

"Yes. It was early in the morning, just before light."

"They must have been attacked while filling their water buckets. I wonder why?"

"I think a boat interrupted them," Javy said. "Everything went quiet after a boat pulled near the site. They must not have found anything because the boat drove off shortly after." He also gave details about Damien's operation, which sounded like he and his men were serving as mules. A car with the same three men would come to the camp every week. The people would meet Damien and his henchmen in the parking lot and exchange something. I made a note to contact South Precinct and inform them about Damien's operation. They could look into that while we searched for the three men from Jonathan Thomas's security team. I convinced Spence to take the statement and let Javy return to the camp. I said Javy could serve as our eyes and ears until we needed him to testify. The way the courts worked, it would be months before they needed him anyway.

Three out of eight men on the security team were involved in the shootings of Tito and Sam. Now I knew why they wanted them both dead and followed them to the hospital to finish the job. Both Tito and Sam could identify the killers. Who else was involved? How high did this go? Was Buck Pader involved? Surely, the head of a security team knew where his men were at any given moment. Did Jonathon Thomas know about it? And if he did, was he the one who put the hit on Dean? He was a personal friend of the mayor. We had to walk delicately from that point on.

I decided to call Buck and let him know we had a witness who could identify three of his men. That would test his knowledge and involvement.

"We have a witness who saw Chad Cole and Zach Clement shoot Detective Tidwell and leave him for dead. Chase Martin was with them."

Buck repeated the names of the three and said they were all missing now. He said he tracked Zach's phone until it was ditched at the corner of 4th and Division in Nashville. That was two blocks from Chase Martin's apartment. Surely they weren't that stupid. They wouldn't go to any of their own apartments knowing the police were looking for them. *Would they?* I had to rule it out.

Chapter Thirty-one

Saturday, April 5, 5:23 PM—Chase Martin's Apartment

Spence and I returned to Chase Martin's apartment to see if there was any evidence of Chase having come back since our last search. The same woman from our last visit opened the door for us, and we could immediately see a difference. The place was a mess—not the kind when someone tosses the place looking for something. It was more like a college freshman's dorm after a long weekend. Knowing what it looked like before and seeing the terror on Chase's face when we touched anything, I suspected someone else messed up the place, wanting us to think Chase was panicking. Maybe it was Chad and Zach that came looking for something. Maybe they were after Chase for messing up the third shot, especially now that it had been broadcast that Sam was alive.

We went in with weapons drawn, just in case. "Metro Homicide," I announced. "We have a search warrant for the premises. If anyone is present, show yourself now." No one answered. I explained to Spence how Chase Martin's apartment normally looked with his OCD. We made a quick sweep of the apartment. Finding no one, we holstered our weapons.

I went directly to his bathroom. The medicine was missing. Then I checked the closet. His gun, ammunition, and climbing bag were all missing as well. He'd been back. I still wasn't convinced he'd made the mess. Even though he would be in a hurry to grab his things and go, his OCD would not allow him to leave the apartment in this condition.

"We need to dust the place for any prints that aren't Chase's," I said. I didn't touch anything without having my gloves in place. Spence either.

Spence called for a CSI team to scour Chase's apartment to see if we missed anything. While they were here, they could dust for additional prints. We continued a detailed search with our gloves on. Several things were missing from the apartment. Sarge was right. Chase was in the wind.

"Abbey, look here." I went to the bedroom. Spence was standing there holding a nine-millimeter Glock.

"Where did you find that?"

"Under the mattress near the nightstand."

"I've been here twice now. Once with Sam and once with you. That gun was not here either time. Let's take it back and have them run ballistics on the gun. I have a feeling it's the other murder weapon."

"So Chase was the other shooter?" Spence asked.

"No, but that's what someone wants us to believe. Remember, Javy Perez said Chase didn't shoot." I looked around. "Now, I'm wondering if the person who left it is the one who took the other stuff from here. If so, Chase will be reeling without his meds. That will make him very unstable."

"If you're going to go to the trouble of planting evidence, at least make it look good," Spence said. "This person is sloppy."

"Just like the crime scene," I said. "They weren't very thorough there either." I sat at the table. "Let's review the evidence and the timeline while we wait for CSI to arrive."

Spence and I reviewed the facts, seeing if we could figure out what we were missing. Was I reading too much into this case? Was it simply three young, inexperienced men conspiring to kill Dean Swain and have Tito Ruiz take the fall? Were they jealous? Were they acting on someone else's orders? Maybe they set up the carjacking but had to intervene when Tito jumped the gun and tried to take off early before Dean was down by the river.

"Chad Cole's text: 'You heard him; he's a liability.' Who is 'him,' and what did that mean?" Spence asked.

"I assume Dean Swain was the liability."

"Who's liability, though?" Spence asked.

"The only person that makes sense to me is Jonathan Thomas. Dean was a social media icon. Most of his stuff was juvenile behavior or womanizing. He had to be a drag on Jonathan's reputation and his business."

"Do you think Jonathan Thomas put the hit on his stepson?" Spence asked. "Would he be dumb enough to have his own security team do the deed?"

"I wouldn't think so. Someone with his money could have hired it done." I thought for a moment. "Maybe they took that off-the-cuff comment to mean they should act on it. Maybe Mr. Thomas said it flippantly, but his security team took it literally. People misinterpreted my sarcasm all the time."

"What was the date on that stream of texts?" Spence asked. I searched through copies of the paperwork on my phone until I found them.

"Tuesday, March eighteenth. That's the day before Dean's death. Did they have any contact with Tito Ruiz?" I asked. I don't know why we didn't look for that connection earlier. We had to find Tito's number again. Then we searched Zach Clement's phone log—no calls or texts to Tito.

"What about the other two?" Spence asked. "Chad Cole and Doug Ackerman."

"So far, Doug Ackerman isn't connected to anything other than that earlier text from Chad. His phone tracking had him on the other side of town during the murder."

Spence focused on Chad's log. "Here it is. Two calls to Tito Ruiz. One on the eighteenth, and the other two hours before Dean's death."

"Two hours? How would they know Dean would be there?" I asked. "Do you think Chad was at the Cigar Bar?" Then it dawned on me. "Tito tried to tell us who set him up. He kept saying, *Cha*, which made me think he was saying Chase. He was trying to say, *Chad*."

"Even if Chad was at the bar, how would he know Dean would leave when he did and go to the site?"

"What are we missing, Spence?" Did Dean have a pattern of behavior? Did he do this regularly? "Did someone set him up and ask him to go there?" We searched the call logs for any connection between these men and Dean. We found none. We were missing a critical link. How did they orchestrate Dean's movements that night?

"What about Chase Martin?" Spence asked. "Didn't he have contact with Dean and then get up to leave? Maybe he was the setup man. Maybe he initiated contact at the right time, enticed Dean to follow, and manipulated him into showing the plot for the garage."

"Even if he did, Chase didn't follow him to the recycling lot. And he never called anyone. The only call he had was from Buck Pader offering the job."

"Okay, let's review what we know for certain," Spence said.

"We've done this a hundred times, Spence."

"Well, let's do it again. Chad Cole coordinated the contact with Tito Ruiz. Tito shows up to steal the Bentley. He shoots Dean three times. Dean dies. Chad Cole and Zach Clement are on-site during the murder. Two men shoot Tito Ruiz. Tito escapes. Zach shows up at the hospital disguised as a Federal agent and kills Tito. Sam stumbles into Chad, Zach, and Chase near the homeless camps. Chad and Zach shoot him. Chad, disguised as a nurse, attempts to kill Sam."

"Wait a minute. The four disappearances from the homeless camps. Maybe they saw or heard something they shouldn't have and were killed as well."

"I don't know, Abbey. I don't think they're related to our case," Spence argued. "Why do you keep trying to connect them? Is it for your friend?"

I had to admit I wanted to help Susan. I knew we couldn't work the case without a body. Sarge and Captain Harris made that perfectly clear. Maybe I was grasping at straws. Maybe I subconsciously linked it to our case for Susan's sake. Whatever the reason, something didn't set well in my gut. There was more to that camp than met the eye. "I guess, Spence."

"We have warrants out on Chad, Zach, and Chase already. Their images are on social media and in the news. Someone will find them and call it in soon. Then, we'll get our answers."

"I've got to clear my head. Let's call it a night and get a fresh start on Monday."

Chapter Thirty-two

Sunday, April 6, 10:45 AM—Living Water Church

I attended services at Living Water Church again, which made Susan and the kids as happy as larks in the morning. Dallas Gatlin sat on the same pew as the Ripley family this time. I found myself sitting between Dallas and Susan. I could smell his cologne and leaned his way. I could tell the kids were upset, but Susan insisted. I was so confused. Did Susan like Dallas, or did she want me to?

As the service progressed, I caught myself listening to the Scripture reading and the congregation's singing. I couldn't remember a time when I felt good in church—not like this. I almost felt guilty. Why was I here? I tried to dismiss the questions and doubts—to be in the moment and take everything in. That's what my counselor advised me to do: be in the moment.

I even closed my eyes when one of the elders stood and led in prayer. I listened to his words and wished I could believe like he did—believe that God was listening and ready to answer the prayer—that He even cared. It wasn't the God I knew. The elder expressed love and thankfulness in his prayer. I wished I could feel that way. I didn't feel anger or resentment, which was new for me. But I didn't feel close to God either.

They sang two more songs, one about loving their enemies. Who'd do that? Dallas would offer the answer shortly. Once again, he chose a strange passage to preach.

He stood, walked to the pulpit, looked down at me, and

179

smiled. Then he turned to the congregation and said, "It's good to be with you again this Sunday. If you have your Bible with you this morning, turn to Matthew chapter five. I'll begin with verse thirty-eight. If you don't have a Bible, there's one in the pew rack in front of you." He paused for a moment and then began reading, "'You have heard that it was said, 'An eye for an eye, and a tooth for a tooth.'"

Yep. I'd heard that before. My father loved that verse. He used it whenever he wanted to exact punishment or shun someone. Punishment was to fit the crime—tit for tat, whatever that meant. Who makes up sayings like that anyway?

Dallas continued. "'But I say to you, do not resist an evil person...'"

What? So, I'm just supposed to be a doormat and let murderers go? Rapists, too? Let the criminals run free, just like in California. No thanks.

"...whoever slaps you on your right cheek, turn the other to him also..."

That was stupid. Dallas was losing me. I'd been touched before, and I had to resist. It was the only way I survived. Did Dallas want me to turn the other cheek to the men who shot Sam? I began to regret coming to church. I didn't need this garbage. I came to hear him speak, but his Bible was wrong. No one could survive living like he was telling us to. People would walk all over you and take advantage of you at every turn. I knew that for a fact.

"'...if anyone wants to sue you and take your shirt, let him have your coat also. Whoever forces you to go one mile, go with him two...'"

Maybe this worked in Jesus's time, but people today would abuse you. He was saying that Christians should be weaklings— pushovers. I wasn't into that. They could do that if they wanted to, but they'd regret it. I, for one, was going to stand up for myself and defend against anyone who thought he could abuse me. I became a cop to defend others, so don't tell me to let people run rampant.

"'You have heard that it was said, 'You shall love your neighbor and hate your enemy.' But I say to you, love your enemies and pray for those who persecute you...'"

I was losing all confidence in Dallas. His earlier sermons were powerful and unique. This preached weakness. It was stupid. I wasn't sure I wanted to listen to his explanation of the verses. It was totally impractical.

"'If you love those who love you, what reward do you have? Do not even the tax collectors do the same?'"

Susan said, "Amen." Tax collectors? What did the IRS have to do with it? Did they even have that in Jesus's time?

Dallas walked to our side of the pulpit and looked at us. "It sounds like terrible advice, doesn't it?" I wanted to say, "Amen." He stared at me. "How chaotic would the world be if we did that?" Then he walked to the other side of the pulpit and looked at them. "Then again, how chaotic is the world now? How's our present plan working for us?" Where was he going with this?

"I want you to think about your kitchen table, social club, and Sunday School classroom for a moment this morning." He paused, allowing everyone time to put the image in his mind. "Is everyone like you? Do they like the same things you do? Are they from the same side of town as you? Do you feel comfortable around them?" There were no Amens, but I turned and watched as heads lowered. Why was he making us feel guilty? I thought he was different than my father. I suppose all preachers are the same at heart. I looked around. The church was nearly full again. It hadn't been this full since Mark Ripley's time. If he kept this up, they may leave again.

"We've lost our power, our influence because we hide in this box we call a church." He paused to let that hit. It hit hard. "I would wager the church has lost its power because it has let the world influence us more than we influence the world. Why? Because we go out into the world not to share Jesus and His truths but to share in the world. We love worldly things. I'd bet if we took a close look at the world, we'd be hard-pressed to identify Christians because we look the same—do the same things—value the same things. We are no different. We've become social and religious chameleons, blending into the image of the world. Instead of working to make everyone more like Christ, the church has become more like the world and its ways." Just like my father.

Dallas suddenly took a shift. He began confessing his short-comings, flaws, and failures. He spoke of his prayers at the end of the day, confessing missed opportunities and easy choices. "Being a Christian in this world is hard, and I work at a Christian univer-sity. It's easy for me to follow Christ there because I'm expected to. But what about those who work in secular jobs? Being authentic in a world of critics is next to impossible. Forgiving your enemies, the people who have wronged you is unreasonable. Why would Jesus ask that of us?" He waited for responses. He got none. Dallas returned to the pulpit.

"Jesus told us to love others as He loved us. Well, I ask you, how did He love us? Did He love only those who were like Him? Who was like Him? Did He only love those who earned it? No one has earned His love. Did Jesus only love when it was convenient? No!" He almost screamed that last word. It caught us all off guard.

He looked sad. Was Dallas disappointed in us? "His love was sacrificial. How much are we willing to sacrifice, to give up, in order to love?" He looked right at me. Was that a sign? A signal? Did he think of me when he thought of love? If so, was he making a sacrifice to love someone like me. I was so confused. I turned to Susan and she was staring at him smiling.

"If we are to be like Jesus, we too must learn to forgive our enemies." Still no Amens. "Did you know, Christians, that we were once enemies of God? Did you know how we became allies? Friends with God?" A few heads nodded. Sheepishly. "Jesus died to make that possible."

He continued to give examples of Jesus, who forgave a tax collector, an adulterous woman, Peter, who denied Him three times, and the soldiers who nailed Him to the cross. "In the midst of His crucifixion, Jesus prayed, 'Father, forgive them, for they know not what they do.' How difficult was that?" Dallas paused to let the weight of that moment sink in. "We can come here every week and listen to wonderful songs and have sermons that make us all feel good about ourselves. We can come here to socialize with our friends. Or, we can come here to learn how to be like Christ."

"Amen." It was Susan again. He smiled. She smiled back. Susan did like him, and by the look on his face, Dallas liked her, too. I suddenly felt like a third wheel, and I was sitting between them earlier. As a detective, I was sure I was missing all of the clues. Who was I to think someone like Dallas could ever love someone like me?

"I want to make a difference in this world. Do you?" Several heads nodded. "If we want to influence our world, we must learn to love the people in it. Did you know the Lord's Prayer includes the line, 'And forgive us our debts, as we also have forgiven our debtors'? How generous are you with your forgiveness? What if God forgave you the same way you forgave your enemies?"

Ouch.

Dallas sat down on the edge of the stage. "I know by now you're wondering why you allowed me to preach a whole month. You're probably wondering what I might speak on next week. Don't worry about next week. Just sit there and listen to the voice of the Holy Spirit. I want you to focus on Him and His voice. I'm not here to convict you; that's His job."

That was interesting. My father always made it his job to convict, to make us feel guilty and ashamed. I suppose that was his way of having power over us. Dallas was a stark contrast to my father, after all. He was more like Mark Ripley. I also thought it was interesting that Dallas wasn't a full-time preacher. He said he preached because he loved the opportunity to challenge our faulty traditions and misconceptions of God. His first two sermons proved that. Today, I wasn't sure what he was trying to do, and yet something was happening with me—something was stirring.

Then, he looked directly at me. "God doesn't shame you or make you feel guilty to tear you down. That's what the devil does. God's Spirit convicts you so you will change for the better—so you'll improve yourself. The devil tears you down; God lifts you up."

He still stared at me. After another moment's pause, Dallas said, "We think a clenched fist makes us powerful. It doesn't. An open hand, a hand that reaches out and helps someone to his feet, is a true measure of strength. It takes more courage to forgive than to fight—to let go than to hold on to a grudge or a hurt. When we refuse to forgive, we hurt ourselves more than we could ever hurt the other person—the person who wronged us."

Did he know my past? Susan swore she told him nothing. Then how did he know about my anger? My desire for revenge?

"When God forgives, He forgets the wrong. We can't. It takes work to forgive. It takes courage to let go of the hate. It takes the power of the Holy Spirit to forgive and love those who don't deserve it."

I was beginning to understand what he meant. This anger toward my father ate my soul like cancer. I'm sure my father wasn't bothered a bit by it. He was free of the hurt he'd caused me—the life he forced me to live to survive. I, on the other hand, suffered in the depths of my very being. It clung to me like barnacles on a boat, crusting over my heart.

"You can't do it on your own. Will you surrender your will to God this morning? Will you ask Him to help you forgive—to help you let go? I offer the front of this stage as an altar of God. I want you to come today and symbolically lay your anger, hate, and revenge down at Jesus's feet. And here's the hard part. I want you to let go of your anger and leave it there. When you give it to Him, you give up the right to take it back. Let's pray."

He prayed, and they sang a song. Several people came down and prayed at the front of the stage. By the end of the song, more people were kneeling at the front of the sanctuary than were left standing in the pews. I was in a fog until Susan grabbed my arm and asked, "Are you coming for lunch?"

I nodded. Dallas came up to me and put out his hand. "Detective Rhodes, I'm so glad you could make time in your busy schedule to come this morning."

Surprising myself, I said, "Today, I came to see you." It was the truth. I still wasn't into church, but I was beginning to fall for him.

Then he said something that punched me in the gut. "Are you here personally or professionally?" he asked with a glint in his eye.

It stung my soul. I pulled away and turned to leave.

I could hear him calling out to me. "What did I say, Abbey? What did I do?"

Professional? Was he calling me a prostitute? A whore? Obviously, it applied. I didn't come here to see God. I came here to see an attractive man who truly impressed me with his kindness and intelligence. Still, I was cheap and selfish. I didn't come to church to meet God or be more like Jesus. I came to feel loved.

I ran to my car and took off. Susan called several times, but I refused to answer and let it go to voicemail. I thought of Dallas's question. Is that the only way men looked at me? Was that how I thought of myself? Was that all I was worth? Was I cursed to be merely an object? If so, my father was right about me. The old negative mental tapes began to play again. I listened and submitted to their control. If a man as nice and gracious as Dallas thought that way of me, there was no hope.

Chapter Thirty-three

Sunday, April 6, 1:17 PM—Vanderbilt Hospital

I gave Maggie a break from the hospital. I told her to go home and get some rest or to feel free to run errands. I would be happy to sit with Sam. I'm glad she took me up on the offer. I needed to talk with someone; he was the safest person I knew. He couldn't interrupt, and he couldn't even respond. I was praying Sam couldn't hear me either.

I told the officers outside I was going to mull over the case while I was visiting with my partner. "It helps if I say it aloud. Just ignore me." I shut the door and went back to Sam's side. If anything, it allowed me to vent my frustrations and confusion.

"I can't focus, Sam. My brain's running all over the place." I took his hand in mine. "I could sure use some of your wise fatherly advice right now." I turned to be sure the door was closed. I'd already checked it earlier, but I didn't want anyone to hear my rambling. Paranoia was setting in. To ease my anxiety, I turned the heavy chair, so it faced the door. That way I could see if someone came in. "I need to focus on the case, but my head's in the clouds. I feel something for Dallas, and it scares me. What if he doesn't like me? What if he does? Which is worse, Sam?"

At some point, the conversation switched to an internal dialogue as I sat with Sam, imagining his responses. Dallas was handsome, charming, and seemed to be all about forgiveness. God knew I needed it. But the theory and practice of forgiveness are two different animals. It's one thing to preach about

186

something—another to live it. My father taught me that. He was a living dichotomy, talking about Jesus and His love, but living a heartless and critical life with his family. He never said nice things about my mother, sister, or me, especially in private. I never felt love from him. But Dallas looked at me with loving eyes. He said nice things. That could be his natural charm. Maybe he gives everyone that same smile and says nice things to everyone. Maybe his look and smile don't mean what I think they do.

Susan wanted me to meet him, but he caught her eye, too. They had much more in common. They were both good people who were genuinely concerned about others. He was a lot like Mark—maybe too much. Which one of us did Dallas like? Assuming he liked either of us that way. "Oh, Sam, I'm about to burst. I can't risk getting hurt, but I don't want to be lonely forever, either. What should I do?" I paused as if he was going to answer. "I'm getting ahead of myself. Dallas hasn't even asked me out. But if he does, should I take a chance? What if he hurts me, too, like Aaron did? What if Susan likes him and my pursuit of Dallas ruins my friendship with her? I can't lose her. She's my anchor. I'd rather have her for a friend than him for a boyfriend. But I don't know if I could stand watching them together. I need you, Sam."

Did I admit that? My counselor had been pushing me to say it for months—that I needed someone, and Susan was important to my balance and stability. It was true, I needed them both. So why couldn't I bring myself to say it? Why was it so hard to lower my walls and accept help? "Why couldn't I ask you this before… well, you know, before you were hurt? I keep pushing people away. I don't want to push Dallas away, but I'm afraid all men are like my neighbor Aaron. He was charming, too, remember? He was also a selfish liar who used me, Sam. He called me damaged goods. I can't go through that again. But every time someone gets close to me I find something wrong—I push him away."

I chatted about Dallas and Susan for half an hour, discussing the pros and cons of such a relationship. Then, a critical voice reminded me that Dallas was a preacher and a minister even though his profession was teaching. That stopped the debate cold. I could never date a preacher. I suddenly had images of my father's face on Dallas's body—my father's voice coming out of Dallas's mouth. My stomach turned. Guilt and shame flooded over me like Niagara Falls. My past was a part of me I could never shed. I was anchored to it, and it refused to let go. I could no longer keep it to myself.

That did it. "Sam, I've got to confess something to you—something I've never told another soul. Not Susan, not Lieutenant Daniels, and not even my counselor. When I lived with Mr. Morales in Guatemala City, he used to watch me. He watched me dress, and he watched me shower. He got something out of it. But, worse than that, Sam, I knew he watched me, and I let it happen." I took a deep breath. I let the tears fall. No one was there to criticize me, anyway. "I let it continue because that was the price I had to pay for food and shelter. I had to survive, Sam, and I sold my soul to do it." I heard a noise and stared intently at the door handle. Was someone listening to me? After a minute passed with no other noises, I continued in a softer voice.

"I felt cheap and ashamed, but I let him do it. For over three years, from when I was fourteen and a half to my eighteenth birthday, I let him watch me, Sam. Somehow I grew accustomed to his presence. I told myself it was normal for an older man to lust after a young girl, that it was natural." I took another deep breath and let it out slowly. I could do it. I could say those words aloud and finally get it off my chest. "Just after my seventeenth birthday, I found a camera—and another—and another. He had five cameras hidden in my bathroom and bedroom, Sam. That's just the ones I could find. He'd not only been watching me, he was recording me." Suddenly, the tears turned into sobs. I couldn't utter another word. I couldn't stop my shoulders from shaking.

Get a grip on yourself, Abbey! But I couldn't. I couldn't bring myself to admit Mr. Morales was making and selling videos of me on the dark web, that other men were watching me too. Who knows where the videos went—who bought them—where they were now? I could never have a normal relationship, especially with a good man. As soon as I did, one of the videos would surely surface. I just knew it would. It would ruin my life once again. No. It was better to shut down mentally—to keep men at a safe distance. It was better to live alone than to risk being hurt again, to be embarrassed, shamed, and shunned. Susan deserved Dallas more than I did, and he deserved a good person like Susan. They would make a good couple.

My pocket vibrated with three short bursts. It did it twice before my mind cleared enough to realize my phone was ringing.

"Detective Rhodes."

"Detective Rhodes, this is Buck Pader. You're going to want to see this." He forwarded a photo from his cell phone. He was at the homeless camp. Two of his men were dead. Their necks had been cut with a hunting knife.

Chapter Thirty-four

Sunday, April 6, 5:07 PM—Homeless Camps

I called Spence, told him about Buck's call, and asked him to meet me at the gravel lot in the middle of the homeless camps.

I counted three vehicles when I pulled into the fenced lot. Buck wasn't the only one here. He stood next to his truck and waved his arms wildly. I parked next to him and got out. Looking at the other cars, I asked, "What is this, Buck?"

"Come on, Detective, I'll show you."

"No, Buck. Why are there three vehicles?"

"That one belongs to Chad. This one's mine," he said, pointing to a big black truck. "And that one belongs to the leader of my core team. I got my men looking for that SOB."

"Who?"

"Three of my most trusted men," he said proudly, thinking I was asking who he had looking in the woods.

"No, Buck. Who are they looking for?"

"He killed Chad and Zach."

"Buck, you and your men can't be here. You'll jeopardize the crime scene."

His face was red. "If it wasn't for me and my men, Detective, you wouldn't know there was a crime scene." He turned his back on me and started walking to the hole in the fence.

"Buck, stop! You have to call your men off. You called me for a reason, and I'm taking charge of the scene."

He turned and shouted back, "We're not stopping until he's dead."

Great! "Until who's dead, Buck? Everyone who might know something about Dean's death?" I know it sounded accusatory, but my patience was wearing thin, especially with Buck and his security team.

Thankfully, Spence pulled up just in time to help. "What's going on?"

"Two men from his security team are dead, and Buck and his men are walking all over the crime scene. He said they're looking for…" It dawned on me that I didn't know who he was looking for. "Buck, who are you hunting?"

"That soldier! He gutted my men like they were fish."

"He gutted them?" I asked, picturing the sight I was about to behold.

"Not gutted them," he said. "He slit their throats and bled 'em dry."

Spence was calmer than I was. "Why don't you start by showing us the crime scene?"

Buck led us through the hole in the fence and to the right. We headed up toward the four tents beside the pillar. "There!" he said, pointing to two bodies about four feet apart. They were face down, each in a pool of his blood. They must have been heading for his tent, but they only made it halfway.

"Have you touched them?" I asked.

"Not with my hands. I rolled them over to see who they were, but I rolled 'em back so you could see it like I found it."

"Where did you make contact with their bodies?" Spence asked, trying to make sense of what Buck was saying. Buck was highly agitated. His mind was flitting about—along with it, his mouth.

"I rolled them over with my foot," Buck said. "We need to get going."

"First, we need to check the bodies for any prints."

"I said I didn't touch 'em," Buck snapped. "For detectives, you don't listen very well."

"We're looking for the murderer's prints," I explained, taking some of the heat off Spence.

"Why? I told you who killed 'em. It's that blasted soldier. He cut them with that knife of his."

"What makes you think he did it?" Spence asked.

"Because Denzel is out of his mind," Buck snapped.

Denzel? "What did you just say?" I asked.

"He's out of his mind."

"You called him Denzel," I said. How did he know his name? We only learned it when Javy told us his story.

"That's his name, isn't it?" Buck asked.

"But how did *you* know that?" I asked as I watched his body language and face for any recognition of what he had just done.

"Know what?" Buck asked.

"His name? You said, *Denzel.*"

"You told me, I guess." Buck was looking back and forth between me and Spence. His body rocked forward and backward. This was not the rugged, confident, Buck Pader I'd seen before.

"No, Buck. I never mentioned his name."

He pointed to Spence. "Then I guess he did. Does it matter who told me? He killed my men, and we need to find him. He's got to answer for this."

I looked to Spence, and he signaled me to let it go for now. "Have you found anything else?" Spence asked.

"I was just heading toward his tent when you pulled up," Buck said.

How did he know about Denzel's name, knife, or tent? Was Buck in on this, too? Now, we really had to be careful. This wasn't so much the matter of upsetting Buck as it was watching our backs. If Buck were willing to kill his own men, he'd have no qualms about hurting us. "Who's out here with you, Buck?" I asked, hoping he wouldn't hear the nervousness in my voice.

"Peter, Lee, and Dan. They're my core group—been with me since the beginning. Not like these younger boys who went rogue."

"Would you mind rolling the bodies over again for us? Put your foot as close as you can to the same spot as before," Spence said. Buck did as he asked. "Is that Chad Cole and Zach Clement?"

"Yep. I told you that earlier. I'd hoped they would have come in peacefully," Buck said. "No chance of that now."

"What about Chase Martin?" I asked. "Any sign of him?" I could see the light going off in Buck's head.

"No, but we'll find him, and he'll pay for what he did."

This guy was a wild vigilante. "That's *our* job, Buck," Spence said.

"Well, you're not very good at it, Detective." This side of him reminded me a lot of Duke Stearns—hardnosed rough exterior. Cutting his opponent down to size gave him more power and control. It was all about control, and Buck was losing his.

This was a part of Buck I hadn't seen, and I didn't like it. We headed up to the tents and found another body. "That's…" I stopped myself before I said something I didn't need to, "…not our soldier." Why would someone kill Javy? Did Denzel go wild? Did he find out Javy was lying to him? Did he see the men who killed Sam and exact revenge on them? He had a large knife, and these men were killed with one. Spence called for backup. We had three fresh bodies and a rogue hunting party.

Buck said, "He probably got in the way, and the soldier killed him. If he's out here, my men will get him."

Got in the way? Maybe he got in Buck's way. I needed to think. We needed clarity to process the crime scene. I couldn't focus if I kept watching my back for Buck and his men. "You need to leave now! Get your men and go home."

"I don't think…"

"No, you *don't* think, so I'll do it for you, Buck. Call your men in and go home, or I'll have you arrested right now for conspiracy to commit murder." I'd had it with him and his so-called security team.

193

"You wouldn't dare."

I got my phone and called Sergeant McNally.

"You're bluffing."

"Sarge, this is Detective Rhodes. Buck Pader and his men are here at the site of three murders and are interfering with our investigation. They refuse to leave. Yes, he's standing right here, sir."

I handed the phone to Buck.

"I don't believe you." He grabbed the phone, "What do you want?" The color washed out of his face. "No, Sergeant McNally, I didn't know you were on the— Yes, sir. We were just leaving." He hung up and handed the phone back to me. "I thought you were bluffing."

"No, Buck. I knew you wouldn't respect me because I'm a woman, so I passed it up to my superior. Now, if you and your men will kindly leave, we have an investigation to conduct."

Buck got on the phone and called his men. He was angry and embarrassed. They were all gone within minutes, leaving us in peace to work alone.

"Wow. I thought you were kidding, too," Spence said. "Pardon the expression, but that took balls, Abbey."

I hated that saying—implying women didn't have the courage or fortitude to make tough decisions. "If it did, Spence, you would have done it for me." I knelt over the body and focused on Javy. "I'm just tired, Spence. I'm tired of the runarounds and the interference. Javy came to us to help, and it got him killed." Of course, we had to look into Denzel Rushing; he was the prime suspect. But my money was on Buck Pader and his team. I knew in my gut this was another staged scene to throw us off their scent. And after the stunt he pulled, I wanted it to be Buck.

"What do we do now?" Spence asked. He looked at Javy, and then his glance wandered down the hill toward the other two dead men.

"I'll examine Javy. You look at Chad and Zach. Take as many pictures as you can until CSI gets here." There were obvious signs of struggle with Javy. His throat was slit from ear to ear, but unlike the other two men, Javy was left face up. Two of his fingers on his right hand were bent backward. Someone tortured him. That meant they were looking for information—probably Denzel's location. If that was the case, Denzel was innocent—at least of Javy's murder. I bet that was how Buck knew the soldier's name; he tortured it out of Javy.

I examined the dirt and ash cast about in the struggle. I saw something familiar—prints from a Fast Tac Low brand shoe, just like the ones at Dean's crime scene. I called Spence. "What type of shoes are they wearing?" They wore the same kind. "What sizes?"

There was a long silence.

"Abbey?"

"Yeah, Spence?"

"We should have checked Buck and his men for blood splatter before they left."

He was right. By sending them away, we may have inadvertently lost pertinent evidence. "Check Chad's and Zach's hands."

"I already did. They're clean."

"Any signs of a struggle?"

"No, and the way their bodies are staggered, I think someone they knew was walking with them. He put one down easily and snuck up on the other. These bodies didn't fall; they were helped to the ground." Spence paused for a moment. "Abbey, if you ask me, this had to be someone they trusted."

I knew he meant Buck or one of his inner circle guys. "Do they have their phones on them?" I had taken Buck's word that their phones had been turned off and ditched. I couldn't remember checking the reality of his statement. How naïve.

"They both have phones. I don't know if these are the same ones they had before."

I called the number for Chase Martin. It went straight to message. I called his personal phone number—same thing. Then, I dialed Zach's phone. It rang. It rang again. Then Spence answered.

"So much for that," he said. "We've been duped, Abbey. Buck's been buffering for them."

I called Sergeant McNally and gave him the update. He put an all-points out on Buck and the rest of the team. I described their vehicles. I apologized for not getting their plates down, but Sarge said he would have the information in no time at all. He also said he would let Captain Harris tell the mayor what we'd discovered. We still didn't know if this conspiracy went all the way up to Jonathan Thomas or if his men acted on their own. Were they reacting to his comment about Dean, or had he given them the order?

We combed the Riverfront Park area to the Shelby Bottoms pedestrian bridge when reinforcements arrived. Still, there was no sign of Lance Corporal Denzel Rushing. Either they caught him and threw his body in the river, or he escaped once again. Either was a possible scenario. We let CSI have the crime scene to themselves. We called it a day just before dark. I was so tired I didn't bother with supper or a shower. I climbed into bed and fell fast asleep.

Chapter Thirty-five

Monday, April 7, 10:12 AM—Harmony Apartments

The buzzing sound droned in my head. I hit my alarm, knocking it to the floor. The buzzing continued. I reached for my phone.

"Hello."

No one was there.

Buzz…Buzz.

I forced open my eyes and looked at the phone. Twenty-five missed calls from four numbers. Two from an unknown caller. One from Maggie and twelve from Susan, along with a ton of texts. Ten from Spence. The buzzer sounded again. I finally realized it was my door intercom.

I shuffled from my bedroom to the front door and hit the button. "Who is it?"

"Abbey? Thank God you're alive! I thought they got to you." It was Spence. "I've been calling all morning."

"Sorry, I just woke up. Wait. Who got to me?" I was in a fog. My body was so heavy; it felt like it did when I had mono. I could barely summon enough energy to walk. "What are you talking about, Spence?"

"Buzz me in," Spence said.

I did, and within a minute or so, he knocked on the door. I opened it, and Spence shielded his eyes.

"Girl, put some clothes on."

I looked down and realized I was in my underwear and a

bra. "Oh, Spence. Sorry." I ran to the bedroom and threw on some sweats. At least there was one man who didn't ogle at my body. Spence did the gentlemanly thing and covered his eyes. It was a refreshing change.

"I can't believe you're still asleep. I've tried to call."

"You said that," I shouted from my bathroom. I pulled my hair into a ponytail, brushed my teeth, and smelled my breath. It was still sour. I swished some mouthwash and spit it in the sink. "What's so urgent?"

"Sam's awake."

"Spence! Why didn't you say that to begin with?" I grabbed a breakfast bar, my shoes, billfold, and keys and said, "You're driving." I never washed my face last night, so I still had some semblance of makeup. It didn't matter. Sam did. And he was conscious. We needed to update each other. I hoped he would remember his encounter with the three men from Jonathan Thomas's security team.

Thankfully, I only lived five minutes from Vanderbilt, at least after ten on a Monday morning. We rushed to the room. Maggie was sitting there brushing Sam's hair and getting him to drink some juice. "I called, but you never answered," she said.

"I know. I'm sorry, Maggie. I just now woke up. We had such a long day yesterday."

My phone buzzed. It was Susan. I silenced it and let it go to voicemail. I saw Maggie's look, as if I'd done that with her calls. "Honestly, Maggie, I was asleep when you called. That's a friend of mine. I'll call her as soon as we leave here."

Sam looked up. His eyes brightened. I gave him a hug. "Are there any new cases you need help with?"

Maggie gave him a hateful look.

"I need something to keep me occupied. I'm bored to tears," Sam said.

Maggie took the hint and went to the cafeteria for some coffee.

"Same case," I admitted. "It's finally beginning to unravel."

"I know who killed Tito," Sam said smugly. We knew, too,

but he seemed so proud of himself; Spence and I remained silent. "It was two members of Jonathan Thomas's security team. I think their names are Chad and Zach something."

"Chad Cole and Zach Clements," Spence said. Then he pursed his lips. I think he remembered we were going to let Sam have his moment.

"They shot me," he said. His demeanor suddenly changed. "Everything went black. I thought I was gone." He turned to the window. His face lost its color. Sam put his hand on his chest.

"We thought we'd lost you, Sam. When Maggie called and said you'd been shot, I thought the worst. I couldn't get here fast enough." I sat in the chair and took his hand.

He looked at our hands and smiled, then looked puzzled. "I had the strangest dream, Abbey. You were here, and you were telling me about Guatemala." My eyes widened. Could he possibly have heard me? "…some man by the name…"

I immediately cut him off before he said the name. "We'll talk about that later, Sam. Right now, we need to get you up to speed on the case. It's about to blow up." He nodded. "But first, I have to ask something. Did Chase Martin shoot you?"

He rubbed his beard. "No. I think he tried to stop the second shooter. After that, I don't remember anything."

That made me feel somewhat better. But Chase still let it happen and didn't do anything to resolve the issue. He could have called for an ambulance, called us, and let us know. Instead, he ran. He was still on the run. Spence and I filled Sam in on the case details from the beginning to now. "You're lucky, Sam."

"How did you find me?"

I wanted to tell him about Javy, who risked everything to save Sam, and tell us about the soldier. Sam didn't need to know the details yet. "We got an anonymous tip about the shooting and your whereabouts."

"Thank God," Sam said.

I let the *God* thing slide. I continued to fill in the details we had gathered since Sam was shot, including our encounter with Buck Pader and his men.

Spence added one detail that I hadn't connected. "I think it was Buck who turned off the Bentley. I think he was there coordinating everything. I don't think he called Chase to offer the job as he claimed but to let him know they were in position. I believe Chase had the job wrapped up the moment he accepted the role as the handler—making sure Dean left the cigar bar, went to the homeless camp, and continued on to the recycling lot."

"That makes sense to me," I admitted. "He didn't intervene with the two men in the bar to be nice to Dean, but to win his confidence and attention. I'm still wondering whether Chase Martin was in on the planning or was just the second patsy."

"Second patsy?" Sam asked.

"Tito was the first. He thought they would let him get away with the Bentley just for taking out Dean. Chase made the call thinking once the car was stolen, he'd have a legit job with JLT Enterprises as a security guard for the owner."

"It all fits," Spence said. "Now, we have to make sure it's not just our theory we're trying to prove, but where the evidence leads us."

Way to rain on my parade, Spence. He wasn't done.

"And we have enough evidence for the District Attorney's office to prosecute to the fullest extent of the law."

"I agree with you, young detectives." There it was. He had to comment on our ages. Sam was back. "A word of caution. I know you two are new to this. I'm not. You must know that a conspiracy is extremely difficult to prove; it's not a simple murder case. We're all taught to look for the motive, means, and opportunity. Well, that's not enough in a conspiracy case. For it, you must prove intent, corroboration, sequence, and evidence for each person involved." Sam put his hand on his chest again and took a slow breath. I watched as his blood pressure rose. "Are you sure you want to try for conspiracy? It's much easier to get each man for murder or manslaughter."

He was right. I looked at Spence, and we both nodded. Our work was cut out for us, but we were up for the challenge. "We still need to find Denzel and Chase. They're key parts of this investigation."

"What about the homeless disappearances?" Sam asked. "Are they connected in any way? Those men had to be there for some reason."

"They were there looking for Denzel. Somehow, they learned he was a possible witness. As far as the disappearances go, I turned them over to Central Precinct. The reporter who made the anonymous tip about your shooting came in later to follow up. He claimed they were making drug deals in Damien's camp. I think those women may have been caught watching a drop."

"Then we need to follow up on it," Sam said. He shifted in his bed. I could tell he was in pain.

"We can't. Captain Harris made it crystal clear that we were to steer clear of that issue—that there were competent officers who could take care of it."

"Have you heard an update from Central about it?" Sam asked.

"No, but I'm telling you, Sam. Cap and Sarge made it very clear I was to let go and focus on the homicide. You know, Sam—stay in my lane."

"What did he do, give you the no body—no homicide speech?" I tried to nod seriously, but I couldn't help but laugh at how well Sam imitated Sergeant McNally. "Who do they think they're dealing with?" Sam asked. "Abbey Rhodes doesn't know how to let go—or stay in her lane." Spence laughed at that. I didn't. The truth hurt. I often put my nose where it didn't belong.

"Very funny, Sam. I think I liked you better when you were sedated."

"Oh, girl, that really hurts. But seriously, you know That's what makes you special. You always see a bigger picture than the rest of us."

He reached for his juice and winced. I grabbed it for him

and gave him a sip from the straw. "You need to take it easy, Sam. I know you'd never admit it, but you're in pain. You're scaring someone. They've tried to kill you twice now. Take care, please."

On that cue, the nurse entered and said we needed to let him rest. Despite Sam's objections, the nurse scooted us out. We had work to do anyway, and we stayed longer than planned. I was happy Sam was going to make it. Then I had a twinge of fear, wondering how much of my story about Guatemala and Mr. Morales Sam remembered. I tried to review all I'd said to him. Maybe it was good that he heard and remembered some of my story. I needed to confide in someone. I knew Sam well enough to know he wouldn't let it drop. He didn't have dreams—at least, that's what he claimed. For Sam to remember a *dream*, especially with that much detail, he knew something wasn't right.

Chapter Thirty-six

Monday, April 7, 1:30 PM—Homicide

"**Y**ou're walking into dangerous waters, Rhodes. I hope you know how to swim," Captain Harris warned. He turned to Spence and asked. "You with her on this, Spencer?"

"Yes, sir. I think we have a solid case."

"Well, you better make one if you plan on putting all our heads on a chopping block," Sergeant McNally said in his gruff voice. "If you're going after a friend of the mayor, this case better be rock solid."

"It's solid up to Buck Pader, Sergeant," I said. Our cases on Chase Martin and Jonathan Thomas are still speculative."

"Make the cases you can, and let the others go. Don't jeopardize the case's power by trying to spread your net too thin," Captain Harris said. They were full of metaphors. "Go set it up, and we'll check in with you before the chief arrives tomorrow."

After we met with Sarge, Lieutenant, and Captain, Spence and I returned to the conference table to sort through and organize the evidence. We built a good case. Now, we had to present it before it could be sent to the DA. Our superiors would be here to review the evidence with the chief. The pressure was on. I started by putting the suspects on the wallboard. Spence would help by putting the facts sequentially on the opposite wall.

I put pictures of Chad Cole, Zach Clement, Tito Ruiz, Chase Martin, Buck Pader, and Jonathan Thomas on my wall. "What about Doug Ackerman, Spence? He was in on the initial text referring to Dean Swain as a problem."

He thought for a moment. "If you're putting Jonathan Thomas up there, you should include Doug Ackerman."

"I think our cases against them are circumstantial at best," I admitted.

"All the same, let's let Sarge and the others eliminate them." He put his first item on the wall. "Do we have anything before the texts about Dean?"

"I don't think so," I said as I assembled evidence under Chad's photo. Even though he was now dead, I needed to include his part in the conspiracy. Chad sent the initial text to Zach Clement and Doug Ackerman saying, "U hrd him. Hes liblty." After Doug Ackerman's question, "Do you think he meant it?" Chad answered, "y we nd 2 act." I put the photo of the plaster next to the other, showing the bottom of Chad's shoes. A perfect match. His gun matched half of the bullets pulled from Tito and the car. Sam's testimony had him for the attempted murder of a police officer. Those bullets also matched.

Deborah stepped in and said, "Ballistics called. They just sent over the last two reports."

Spence and I took a break from our task to check the email and files. "It's on the gun found in Chase Martin's apartment. Not surprised. It matches the gun used on Tito Ruiz. We know it's a plant because we have his phone tracked from the homeless camp to his apartment the night of Dean's murder."

"Abbey, look at that." Spence pointed to the second piece of information. I followed his finger to the paragraph, saying the gun had been wiped clean of all prints. However, the bullets all held Buck Pader's thumbprint.

"Gotcha!" We finally had Buck Pader dead to rights.

"Technically, Abbey, Buck could have loaded the clip before giving it to Chase as a part of his security team."

"You know he wouldn't do that."

"You and I do. A jury might not." I hated when Spence challenged something while we were brainstorming.

"What officer or guard allows someone else to load his gun?" I argued.

"Not many, Abbey, but again, he can say that Chase did since he's brand new to the team."

That made too much sense. A defense lawyer would eat that for lunch. I hated the court part of our jobs. Tracking down the guilty party was exciting and fulfilling. Building a case for the lawyers was not. "Spence, could we send officers to Chase's apartment complex and see if anyone on his hall has a doorbell camera?"

"I see where you're going with this," he said. "I'm on it." Spence got on the phone and arranged for officers of Central Precinct to canvass Chase's apartment to see if we could get images of Buck coming and going. Maybe we could also establish the last time Chase returned to the apartment. That would let me know if someone staged that scene as well. If he hadn't returned, Chase was more than likely off his meds. Not good.

While we waited for their search results, we continued to build our evidence walls. I had Chad Cole's case rock solid. Zach Clement's evidence didn't fall in line as easily as Chad's. Zach did have, however, an interesting text that said, "I might know somebody." That led to Tito Ruiz. Although the initial calls to Tito were from Chad's phone, we had evidence showing that Zach also made three. His shoe print was an exact match of the other plaster from the crime scene, style and size. Sam also testified that Zach was the second man who shot him. And we had them both identified as the men who came to the hospitals in disguise to kill Tito and Sam—Chad as the nurse and Zach as the federal agent.

Tito Ruiz left enough evidence in the Bentley that we really didn't need to look further to make a solid case against him. He also had a criminal history and violated his bond. He was a felon in possession of a firearm. That was all fine and well, but these three men were already dead. The other four were still alive as far as we knew. Theirs would be the cases we had to fight to win a conviction. I started with Buck Pader for no other reason than his interference and subterfuge ticked me off. He'd deflected our attempts to find his men, even lying about their phones. I still wasn't sure if the *he* referred to in the texts was Buck or Jonathan. I assumed it was Buck because no man other than Buck directly interacted with Jonathan Thomas—at least by phone evidence.

I should have seen him from the start. How often does the guilty party try to insert himself into the investigation to keep tabs on the case and misdirect the police? It's a classic, textbook mistake. Buck Pader did just that. He acted as if he was helping so he would be privy to our investigation and suspicions. He offered the men's names and photos to assist with our identification into the two men who went to finish off Tito and Sam, knowing that search would keep us busy while he cleaned up the evidence leading back to him. However, he messed up with a critical piece of evidence by handling and loading the clip of the nine-millimeter found later in Chase Martin's apartment. We still needed to find and apprehend Chase to corroborate the claim that Buck brought him in to arrange the theft of Dean's Bentley.

We also had Buck present in the deaths of Chad and Zach, where he and his men claimed to be avenging their deaths by the hand of Denzel. That's where Buck messed up. He had no way of knowing about the soldier's knife or name without previous contact with either Denzel or Javy. We were still awaiting fingerprint evidence from Javy's body or clothing. All we had was the imprint of the same shoes each of Jonathan's security team members wore. Buck's phone went straight to messages. We left one telling him we needed to ask a few more questions. In the meantime, the police were looking for Buck and any evidence that could tie him to their deaths—the knife or their blood. Without that, our case against Buck Pader was merely circumstantial. That irritated me because I knew he was guilty. Hopefully, he was cocky enough not to hide, but to come in and answer anything we could throw at him.

I stopped and looked at Spence's timeline. Chase Martin's story began with the *innocent* encounter with Dean Swain at the

Music City Cigar Bar. The two men on either side turned out to be regulars from the bar and didn't follow Dean or Chase. From there, he rode in the Bentley to the parking lot in the center of all four camps, creating numerous witnesses of him leaving Dean and the Bentley behind. He then received a phone call from Buck Pader. Their conversation was a mystery. We had versions from Buck and Chase that were virtually identical. I paused to look at the testimonies. They were too similar and used the same verbiage—sounding almost rehearsed. Then why was Chase agitated on the phone? The eyewitness said he was angry. Would you be openly angry with a potential employer who wanted clarification about your previous employment? Not if you wanted the job. Chase said he was desperate. What did Buck say? I located his response, where he said he liked Chase's spunk. *Right.*

As far as the evidence showing Chase was involved in the deaths of Dean or Tito, we had little. We had a partially smoked cigar and fingerprints on the passenger side of the Bentley. That only showed what he told us about riding in the car to the site of Dean's future parking garage. We had a gun, probably planted by Buck, in his apartment that was used to shoot Tito Ruiz. But the evidence showed Chase was on the opposite side of the river. Eyewitnesses supported that detail. Everything I could muster against Chase was sketchy. At best, we had him for criminal conspiracy.

Doug Ackerman never committed himself to the crime in a text or email. He never agreed to it and never showed knowledge of the actual crime. I had no case against him. I turned my attention to Jonathan Thomas. Everything on the surface showed he eagerly desired the perpetrators of his stepson's murder to be punished. He prodded Mayor O'Reilly to expedite the investigation. He praised Sam and me for tying the murder to Tito Ruiz and locating him in the El Comandantes' warehouse. Although all the men of the security team worked for Jonathan, and he paid their salaries and purchased their equipment, we had nothing that showed he had prior knowledge of the plan. By all respects and evidence, Jonathan

Lee Thomas was innocent. Then why did my gut tell me he was complicit in the death of his stepson, Dean Swain?

Spence and I sat at the end of the long conference table, perusing each other's walls. If we didn't understand or had a question, we each made sure the answer was readily available and on the respective board. We had a huge meeting tomorrow with the chief and wanted to impress him and provide him with solid evidence.

Chapter Thirty-seven

Tuesday, April 8, 9:30 AM—Homicide Conference Room

To say Spence and I were nervous would be a major understatement. We sat at the far end of the conference table as Captain Harris, Lieutenant Stallings, and Sergeant McNally studied our evidence walls. A moment later, Chief Clendenon entered the conference room. "Everyone take a seat," he said. "I've come directly from the mayor's office. My ass hurts." That didn't bode well for us. Usually, the chewing out goes in one direction—down, getting worse with each one, and I was at the bottom of the list.

"Mayor O'Reilly told me in no uncertain language that we better clear Jonathan Thomas of any and all charges, or heads would roll beginning with mine." Not good. He liked that expression. I didn't. "I gathered everyone together in one room because I don't want anything lost in translation."

"Chief…"

"Captain Harris, let me finish."

The captain obeyed. "I know I've gotten caught up in the political aspects of my job recently. When the mayor's happy with me, our budgets fair well. When he's not—well, you get the picture."

I wanted to address the elephant and declare we had nothing on Jonathan Thomas, but I valued my head. I wasn't going to speak out of turn again.

Chief Clendenon paused to study the walls. "I've been in your shoes." He looked at Spence and me. "Yes, even below your ranks."

He looked at the walls again. "And there's been one constant I could always rely on."

He scratched his head and took a deep breath. It seemed like forever before he let it out. "The law." His eyes looked distant—almost melancholy. "It's black and white, written in ink if not stone." I caught his reference, but where was he going with this? He looked directly at me. "Detective Rhodes, we're going wherever the evidence leads us. Is that clear?"

"Chief?"

Captain Harris bailed me out. He asked for clarification.

"Reggie, how would we have handled this if it wasn't a rich and powerful family?" Chief Clendenon asked.

"I'm not sure I follow." I knew he did. We all did. He was asking the question I'd asked from the beginning. Did every life have equal value? So far the answer was an emphatic, *no*.

"If he wasn't the stepson of Jonathan Lee Thomas, would any part of our investigation have changed?"

"Yes, Chief." It was out before I knew it. Oh well. Open mouth, insert foot. "Permission to speak freely?"

"Spit it out, Rhodes. Say what's on your mind."

"I know for a fact we would have done the same procedures…" I paused. Was I willing to say it?

"But, what, Rhodes," he asked.

"But we would never have gotten labs, prints, or ballistics this fast for anyone else." There. I said it. He needed to know, and I didn't need to carry that thought around anymore.

"You're right, Rhodes." He took his glasses off and pinched his nose. "I expedited that to keep the mayor off my back."

I was already in hot water; why not just jump in all the way? "If the victim was one of the homeless people, that case would be at the bottom of the list for labs. It shouldn't be that way. We should have some way of getting everyone's labs back in a timely manner, not just people connected to…"

"People of influence." Captain Harris threw in his two cents' worth. "If this were an issue of skin color, agencies are in place to look out for them. But people of a lower financial or social status have no one." That wasn't exactly true. The Least of These Ministries were lobbying for them. People like Susan Ripley spent out of their personal resources, even though she didn't have much. And, even though groups like Clean Up Nashville had it out for the homeless, countless others were fighting for them.

"Point taken," the chief said. "We'll see what we can do about that in the future."

"Chief, the fact that the four of you are sitting here reviewing our case before we send it to the DA is another sign of the privilege we're giving Mr. Thomas."

"Rhodes!" Captain Harris snapped at me.

"It's okay, Reggie. She speaks the truth. But, now that we are here, tell me what we have and who we can build solid cases for."

Someone knocked on the door. It was Deborah. "I hate to interrupt, but you're going to want this. Officer Langley from Central found Ring camera footage right across the hall from Chase Martin's apartment."

"Anything good?" I asked. *Please be about Buck.*

"They have Buck Pader on video picking the lock and bringing two handguns: one on his belt and one in his hand. The date matches your timeline to show he planted the evidence." She left, giving me a wink for support.

"All right let's start with Buck Pader," the chief said.

Spence and I laid out the case as thoroughly as possible, pausing to answer questions or comments. He ran the timeline, and I filled in the details for each individual involved. As I suspected, the best cases were made for Tito, Chad, Zach, and Buck. Chase Martin was still a person of interest, somehow guiding Dean to the site. Jonathan Thomas's case was purely circumstantial, only guilty by association.

"I want Buck Pader apprehended by the end of the week," Chief Clendenon said. "And somebody find Chase Martin. I want to hear what that young man has to say for himself. The longer it takes, the harder it will be. I'll see to it that you have whatever resources you need." He turned and smiled. "And, yes, Rhodes, under these circumstances with multiple deaths, I would have done this for anyone."

I smiled and nodded, accepting his comment. Then, the chief left. Only time would show if he were telling the truth.

Chapter Thirty-eight

Tuesday, April 8, 6:35 PM—Harmony Apartments

Due to backed-up traffic on the 265 loop, I took a new route home. Ironically, it led me past a billboard for Clean Up Nashville, touting their significant organization, which would *Secure The Lives Of Our Precious Children.* Plastered on the left side of the billboard was a huge image of Stacey Hopkins and her children, a poster family for wealth and influence.

I pulled into my parking spot at Harmony Apartments and headed to the lobby. I was thoroughly exhausted—physically and mentally. I pressed the up button. "You're avoiding me."

I knew that voice. "How'd you get in without a card?"

"By speaking very nicely to one of your fellow tenants."

"Come on up, Susan. I need to change into more comfortable clothes and kick off these shoes." She joined me on the elevator.

While we were waiting for the elevator to reach my floor, Spence texted me.

    The Security team is in custody. Only
    Buck and Chase are still missing. Doug
    Ackerman wants a deal for information.

I texted back.

    Thx, I trust U.

I hoped he would understand and make the call. I needed to explain my distance to Susan. She deserved my honesty and undivided attention. I owed her far more than that, but that was all I could offer at the moment.

I opened the apartment door and said, "Let me change first, and then we can talk."

She didn't let me return to the couch before saying, "What did I do, Abbey?"

"You didn't do anything, Susan. It's me." I hated that phrase, *It's not you, it's me.* So why did I give Susan a version of it?

"Of course I did, or you would have returned my calls and messages. Maybe I assume too much. Maybe I was wrong in thinking we were friends." *Ouch!* "Maybe you've only been kind to me because of Mark's death. I did put you in an awkward position and let the kids latch onto you."

"Would you chill?" I snapped. "You're giving me a headache."

"So it is true. My mother was right." She looked broken.

I didn't want to sound like her mother. "Wait. What? What did your mother say?"

"She said that I've been a leach, sucking the life out of you, forcing our family on you. You're a single woman with other things to do than play soccer with a teenager." She took out a Kleenex and blew her nose. "She said I'm using you as a babysitter and sounding board."

"Your mom is wrong, Susan. Your family is the best thing that's happened to me in…forever. I come to your house and play with Hannah because I want to. With Hannah it's easy and uncomplicated. When I'm there, I can be me with no other responsibilities hanging over me."

She slumped. That was not the reaction I was expecting. "If that's true, why are you pushing me away?"

"I'm not pushing *you* away. I'm withdrawing from everyone. There's a big difference." At least there was in my mind.

"I don't understand."

"My PTSD has come back with a vengeance."

"Did you speak to your counselor? Did she give you any exercises to help?"

I hemmed and hawed.

"Abbey?"

"I told her some of it. I'm still trying to process it all." It was true.

"That's what she's there for—to help you process it all." Susan acted like a big sister—at least how I had imagined my sister should have acted. She was involved and did not let me slough off important decisions because they were challenging. "You don't have to do everything by yourself anymore, Abbey." I knew she was right, but I still had major trust issues. "You need to tell someone before you break down and have…"

"I told Sam," I blurted out.

"Sam's in a coma," Susan said, folding her arms over her chest.

"No, he's not," I said. It was true. I knew I was technically lying to her, implying that he was out of the coma when I spoke to him. "Spence and I talked with him just the other day. And I told Sam everything the day before that."

"Really?" I could tell by the way she said it, she wasn't asking so much as she was calling me to prove it.

"Really." I said it spitefully. Then I gave her one of those middle school girl looks. I was acting like the younger sister—the much younger sister. "Spence was there with me. Go ahead. Call him." Well, Spence was there with me when Sam woke, not when I told him my past.

"What did Sam have to say about it?"

"You know Sam. He said we would have to talk more about it." Now, that was the truth. He did say that. "He didn't judge me." *Come on, Abbey. That was low.*

She looked away, pretending to look out my window. "I guess it's good you have someone like Sam in your life." I couldn't leave her with that—feeling like I trusted Sam more than I did her.

"I'm ashamed of my past, Susan. You know that." Now, I looked out the window; only I was looking into the past.

"Then why tell Sam and not me? You know I never tried to make you feel guilty for what happened to you." She looked sad. Why would she want to know my past? "I thought we were past all that."

"Past all what?" Did I miss something?

"Hiding things from each other," she said.

"Right. Like Susan Ripley has anything to hide. You're like the perfect sister no one can live up to." *Whoa. Where did that come from?* Was I blaming her for Miriam's actions? Was I subconsciously comparing Susan to my people-pleasing older sister? The one who took her fourteen-year-old sister to get an abortion so it didn't reflect poorly upon our father's ministry? That wasn't fair to Susan. She wasn't Miriam, and I shouldn't blame her for my past pain.

I turned to apologize, but Susan was smiling. "You think of me as your sister?" Before I could react, Susan had me in a death grip, squeezing the air out of my chest. "I love you too, Abbey." I tried to say *let me go*, but I couldn't get a breath. She suddenly realized what she was doing and let go. "Sorry. That was a little extreme." She held me at arm's length and looked into my eyes. "So, Sis, what's your new secret?"

It took forever for me to accept the tragedy I called a life in Guatemala. It took even longer to tell Sam, and I thought he couldn't hear me or remember what I'd said. Little did I know he'd remember it like a powerful dream.

"Have I ever told you about Mr. Morales?"

"The nice man who took care of you when your parents kicked you out of the house?" I nodded. I had portrayed him as a nice man. That way I never had to give the embarrassing details.

"He was. It's just—Mr. Morales had a problem, a fetish."

"A fetish? You mean like a dark obsession?" Susan leaned back and examined my face. "What are you trying to tell me, Abbey? Did he hurt you?"

Did he? He only touched me that once, but he didn't really hurt me. Did he?

"Abbey, why aren't you answering me?"

"I was thinking *how* to answer you." I was. How could I describe what Mr. Morales did? I said it to Sam because I knew

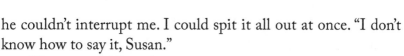

he couldn't interrupt me. I could spit it all out at once. "I don't know how to say it, Susan."

"But you told Sam."

"He was still unconscious. It's not the same."

She put her arm around me. "Oh, you poor girl. What did he do?" I started with that last dance and finished with me finding the cameras. Susan just stared at me with a solitary tear in her eye. She didn't say anything. "Did you find the tapes or videos?" I shook my head. "Where did you go from there?" she asked.

"Germany."

"I thought you said you were seventeen when you found the cameras. You didn't leave for the army until after you turned eighteen and changed your name." I nodded and started crying. I knew she was disappointed in me. Why wouldn't she be? I was disappointed in myself. Why had I stayed? Because my fear of the unknown was greater than my shame.

"That's why I changed my name. I wanted to leave that girl behind in Guatemala. I never wanted to see her again."

Susan took my hand and uttered the sweetest prayer for me. She prayed for healing, refreshing, and forgiveness. She prayed that God would help me forgive myself.

When she said, "Amen," I asked if she was hungry. I knew it was a bad segue, but I was starving. I didn't eat breakfast or lunch. I was so nervous about the meeting with my superiors, especially the police chief. "I haven't eaten today. I'm not trying to change the subject, although that would be nice."

"You go ahead and eat. I had something earlier," Susan said. "While you're making yourself something to eat, I want to ask something." She had more to ask? I did well to get through that conversation. I wasn't sure I could handle another. "What do you think about Dallas?"

"What do you think about him?" I asked, turning the tables on her.

"He's nice. He's smart."

"So, you do like him?" I asked. I was addressing a lot of elephants today. I suppose I was on a roll. Why stop now?

"Of course, I like him, Abbey, but not the way you think." She got up and joined me in the little kitchen. "He's a good man and reminds me a lot of Mark."

"I thought so," I said, not hearing what she said in the middle. "I can tell he likes you too."

Susan started laughing. "Are you kidding, girl? All he talks about is you."

"But you have him over all the time. You guys have so much in common. The other day, you two talked and laughed so much that you didn't even know I'd gone outside with the kids."

"That's because you got me talking about my favorite subject of ministry. You know I can't shut up when someone asks me about that. Besides, we did notice and watched you play. He was very impressed."

I ignored the comment about me. I wasn't prepared to open that Pandora's Box. "See, you two have that in common. You have so much in common."

"You said that already, Abbey. What's your point?" She grabbed my shoulder and turned me around. She studied my eyes. "What are you really thinking?"

I wasn't sure. I know it had to do with feeling unworthy. I didn't answer quickly enough for her.

"I'm waiting, Abbey. Do you not like Dallas?"

I laughed. Who wouldn't like him? "Of course, I like him, Stupid. He's perfect."

"No one is perfect, Abbey. I think that's part of your problem. You think everyone else is perfect, and you can't measure up."

She nailed it. She read me like a book.

"That's it. Isn't it?"

I couldn't answer. I felt like the little girl exposed in the shower, knowing someone was watching. I was vulnerable and weak. I despised the feeling of vulnerability. That's why I liked the mantra of Ever Vigilant so much. It always kept me on my guard. I slumped against the kitchen cabinets and slid to the floor. I started bawling.

I don't remember how long I cried, but Susan sat with me the whole time. She held me and let me cry. Then she did what she did best. She picked up all the pieces and put me back together again. She built me up and encouraged me, telling me all the things I did well—telling me how I saved Hannah's life—telling me her family loved me as their own, and making sure I knew, no matter what, God loved me. That snapped me out of my trance.

"No! He doesn't."

She wouldn't let me go. "Yes, Abbey, He does. He loved you so much…"

"Don't go there!" I glared at her and dared her to say His name. She didn't. She knew me well enough to know I was at a breaking point. If she pushed, I would shatter completely and irrevocably.

"Okay. Have your way. But I know the truth, and so do you. You have to delete those mental tapes of your father's criticisms. They're not true. That's not how Jesus is."

I screamed. I think I shocked us both. She let go, and I scampered to my feet. "I told you not to say it." She tried to hug me, but I pushed her away.

"I'm sorry, Abbey. I can't help it. I love you, and you need to know…" She didn't say it. She knew I'd finish the sentence in my head. That wasn't fair.

"I don't want to talk about it." The walls found their familiar place around my heart. The toaster oven chimed, but I'd lost my appetite.

Susan sat on the floor by herself. "I am sorry, Abbey."

I looked away. I was too adept at the mental games and the isolation. She could say anything she wanted now. It wouldn't matter. Her voice would not penetrate beyond the surface. I was impervious.

"I need help with Christy."

I said nothing.

"I still need you to look into her disappearance. I think something terrible happened to her."

I still said nothing.

"Will you do it for me?"

"I turned that over to the Central Precinct. You'll have to call them."

"I have, but it's not a high priority for them. I called, and they said they would look into it when they had a chance."

"There you go," I said as flatly as I could. "The fine men and women of Metro's Central Precinct have you covered. Go home and hug your kids, Susan. I can't help you." She tried to convince me, but she knew better. She knew that look. My "No" meant "Absolutely not." She apologized a few more times and then let herself out.

I went to the kitchen and threw my food in the trash. I'd have to go without food just like I would with relationships. I could survive without them. I knew I'd taken Susan from one extreme to the other. At the high, I called her sister. At the low, I pushed her out of my apartment and out of my life. So be it. My counselor was wrong. I didn't need anyone's help. I was an island—a self-sufficient island.

Yes, Captain. I will stay in my lane.

Chapter Thirty-nine

Tuesday, April 8, 10:30 PM—Harmony Apartments

It took two and a half hours, but I finally calmed down enough to eat supper. The food tasted like cardboard, but I forced it down. That's what survivors do. I'd let the second attempt at supper sit in the toaster oven for over an hour before trying to eat it. I'd run the conversation through my mind repeatedly, revising my part in multiple ways, but the outcome was the same. I stared blankly at the window, which was so dark I couldn't see out. It didn't matter. I wasn't looking for anything anyway. I was continuing to block out my emotions. Anything that surfaced was immediately stuffed down into the pit.

I considered looking through my photo albums, but I knew that would only exacerbate my problem, so I sat on my couch in silence. I needed a hot shower, but I couldn't move. I didn't want to change anything physically for fear my mental stability would shift and the emotions would overwhelm me.

I jumped when my phone rang. It rang again. I didn't recognize the number, so I let it go to voicemail. A few minutes later, it rang again. I let it go to voicemail once again. When the person called a third time, I reluctantly answered. "Yes."

"Is this Abbey—Abbey Rhodes?"

"Yes. Who is this?"

"It's Susan's mom. Is she there?"

I pulled the phone back and looked at the time. "She left two a half hours ago."

"Oh dear," she said. "She never came home. We've been trying to reach her, but she's not answering. I was hoping she was there talking with you. I'm afraid I wasn't very nice to her tonight." Did I dare tell her how my meeting with Susan ended? No. "You're a police officer. Can't you trace her phone or something?"

She didn't have the terminology correct, but I knew what she was asking for. "It's not that easy. I'd have to get a warrant and then search for the nearest cell tower."

Her voice betrayed her fear. "Isn't there anything you can do?" she asked. "I'm worried about her."

The news should have sent me into a tailspin, but I'd spent the last two hours withdrawing to my safe place—the dark place. "Let me talk to Hannah." I could hear her calling out for her. A minute later, Hannah grabbed the phone. "Hannah, do you still share your location with your mom?"

"Yes."

"Doesn't she share hers with you too?"

"Yes. That was part of her deal. Oh, I get it. Just a second." She put me on hold and checked her app. "It shows her between Interstate sixty-five and the river. Isn't that the homeless camp?"

"Yes. You keep an eye on your app and let me know if she changes location."

"What are you going to do?" I could hear the panic in her voice. Like me, Hannah ran scenarios—even the bad ones. It was our blessing and our curse to see all the possibilities.

"I'm going to call Detective Spencer and have him meet me there. We'll find your mom, and I'll bring her home. I promise."

I knew I wasn't supposed to make promises I couldn't keep, but she needed to hear something positive. Besides, I was determined to keep this one. I couldn't let our relationship end the way our meeting did, with my last ugly comment.

I called Spence, who promised to meet me there as soon as possible. What did Susan think she was doing, going to that place in the dead of night? Didn't she realize how dangerous it was, especially by herself? What did she hope to accomplish? I tried to block the scenarios from running through my thoughts—pictures of Susan dead or tossed into the water to fight the currents. With Christy gone, who did she know? Did she honestly think Damien would help her? All he wanted now was Christy's abandoned property. Find Christy alive, and he would lose it all. But he did see himself as a protector—a guardian—a master of the domain he called his little city. Still, I didn't trust him. According to Javy, Damien was dealing drugs, even if we found no sign of them. I hoped Susan would be cautious. But if she were cautious, she would have waited until daylight.

Chapter Forty

Tuesday, April 8, 10:49 PM—Homeless Camps

I flew down the crooked road and slid into the gravel parking lot, barely missing the edge of the gate. There was Susan's car. There was also another vehicle I recognized—Buck Pader's truck. This wasn't good. Did she reach out to him? Did Buck lure Susan here to trap me? I was torn. Should I call out to her and let her know I was on my way? If I did, would that alert Buck to my presence? Did he know Susan was here? If not, calling her name would jeopardize her safety. But why would Buck care about Susan in the first place? Maybe he thought she knew something about his conspiracy. What about Damien and his men? No time for debates.

I chose not to call out to her. No doubt everyone heard a car arriving, but at least they wouldn't know it was mine. She was my best friend, and I turned her away. She must have come here looking for answers about Christy. Who knows what she found?

I heard her scream. She was near the pillar. Change of plans. "Susan, I'm coming. Hang on!" I made no effort at stealth. Expediency was more critical. I had my flashlight in one hand and my Sig in the other. If he did anything to Susan, Buck Pader was a dead man. I ran as quickly as I could now. The wild Scotch Broom branches whipped at my face. It hurt, but I couldn't stop. The dense wildflower made running difficult. I pushed through. I could hear voices over the sound of my steps and breathing. Two men were arguing. I could hear muffled cries from Susan.

Thirty more feet, and I could save her. I shouted, letting Susan know I was almost there. The arguing continued; my shouts did not affect them. Twenty feet—ten feet—there. I slid into the clearing on the near side of the concrete pillar.

I couldn't believe my eyes. The moonlight reflecting off the water cast enough light that I could see clearly. Chase Martin had his hands over Susan's mouth, his .357 to her head. They stood at the edge of a small bluff that hung over a trash dump on the banks of the Cumberland. Buck Pader stood across the clearing at the far side of the long pillar with his nine-millimeter pointed at Susan. What had she done to anger both men? I listened to their conversation while I considered my options. I could see Susan's eyes wild with fear.

"You killed them and blamed everything on me," Chase shouted. "You set me up."

"Drop the gun, or I swear, I'll kill you both," Buck shouted back. He steadied his gun with his left hand.

So much for strategy. "Whoa! Nobody's shooting anybody," I said. "Let's take a breath." I took one step forward, shrinking the triangle.

"Stay out of this," Chase shouted. "You've screwed my life over enough already."

I wanted to argue my point—to let Chase know his mess was of his own making. *Okay. Focus.* He still held a gun to Susan's head. He was the immediate threat. I needed to calm Chase first. Then I'd deal with Buck.

"We know you didn't kill anyone, Chase," I said, hoping to lower his anxiety. Was he taking his meds? "Come on, Chase. Let Susan go, and we can work this out."

"I let her go, and he'll shoot me."

"I may shoot you anyway," Buck said.

"No, you won't."

It was a difficult balance. Chase needed peace and security, while Buck needed a stern and fierce opponent. Buck only respected power. I had to show him power while aligning with Chase and providing an ally.

"You killed my men," Buck said. "You cut them like they were pigs and left them to die."

"That's not true! Don't believe him."

Chase was frantic. I had a lot of work to do to earn Chase's trust.

"I thought you said Denzel did it, Buck."

He pointed his gun at me. Then he thought better of it and turned the gun back on Chase. "He did."

"Then tell me why you are upset with Chase?" I asked. The only reason I could figure was Chase knew too much.

"He's guilty," Buck said. "He ruined everything. Did you know he shot your partner?"

"No, I didn't. I tried to stop them," Chase said. "Believe me."

"I know. Sam told me."

I watched Chase and Susan as I tried to talk Buck down. "Tell me, Buck. What did he ruin? I need to know."

"Stay out of this! I knew you were trying to trick me," Chase shouted. "You've had it out for me from the start." He pressed the barrel of his gun into Susan's temple, and she screamed.

Where is Spence? "Chase. I know you didn't do it. I know you didn't kill anyone. Don't ruin your life by hurting her." He looked my way. "We have proof that Buck planted the gun in your apartment."

"I did not!" Buck pointed his gun back at me. "Don't lie to him." Chase moved a step to the west, and Buck turned the gun back on him. "Stay where you are, or I'll shoot." Chase stopped. Susan sobbed.

"Buck, we have you on video. Chase's neighbors have Ring Cams. And you were dumb enough to leave your thumbprints on the bullets."

He turned his gun back on me. His attention was divided.

Come on, Spence. Where are you? Was that a good move? I

hoped so. I was trying to build a rapport with Chase so he would let Susan go. "You have nowhere to go, Buck. If you shoot Chase in front of me, you're going down for a long time."

"Not if I shoot you first," he said with a smile.

I tried not to show fear. "You can't take both of us." I watched with my peripheral vision as Chase pulled the gun back from Susan's head. "You shoot me, and Chase will kill you. If you shoot Chase, I'll have no choice but to stop you by any means necessary. You can't win, Buck."

I was gambling on force and deterrence. I hoped I was right. He continued to divide his attention between us. He kept his gun aimed at me. I found myself wishing I had one of those hot, uncomfortable vests.

"Chase, everything we have on you is circumstantial—a phone call. Witnesses have you walking away from here at the time of Dean's death, which also clears you of Tito's murder." He was watching me now. At least I had him focused on me instead of Susan or Buck. "We know Denzel carries a knife, so he's the probable suspect for the deaths of Chad and Zach." I stole a glance at Buck to see if he showed any reaction. "You tell us what Buck did, and we can clear you of all charges." I didn't need his testimony to put Buck away, but Chase didn't know that.

"I don't trust you," he said. "Both of you switch sides with me—move over here with your backs to the river. When I get to my car, I'll let her go."

"You're not going anywhere," Buck said. "If I'm going down, you're coming with me."

"What did I ever do to you?" Chase asked. "I met Dean at the bar, and I got him down here. He took the bait just like you said he would. When I told him the plan wouldn't work, he went to measure the lot for the landing site of the bridge. I did my job. I even let you know he was heading to the lot. I did everything you asked. I told you I didn't want to be involved with anything illegal—anything that might hurt Dean."

There it was—his confession. We now had him for conspiracy. Maybe I could test the waters with Jonathan Thomas's role.

"You all had to shoot a cop and stir up the hornet's nest," Buck said. "I just told you to find that soldier and get rid of him."

"I tried to stop them." Chase turned to me. "I didn't shoot your partner. Chad and Zach did. I was there, but I didn't shoot him."

Confession number two. "But you left him to die, Chase. You left Sam to bleed out. You may as well have pulled the trigger."

"I panicked. I thought he was dead. I didn't know what to do."

"Shut up, you stupid idiot! You're giving her everything she needs to arrest you."

"You tricked me again," Chase said as he pressed the barrel once again into Susan's temple. Then he pointed the gun at Buck. "You said you were just going to steal his car, and I didn't even want that to happen. Why'd you kill him?" He swung the gun back to me and said, "I hate you!"

A blur from the darkness. Denzel jumped out of the shadows and slashed Chase's arm with his knife just as Chase fired. I heard the bullet whiz by my ear. I watched Susan fall to the ground. I steadied my gun on Chase. Was Susan hurt? Denzel grabbed Chase from behind and wrestled the gun from his hand. Another shot. Buck's bullet hit Chase in the right side of his chest, and both men tumbled off the bluff and into the Cumberland River.

Buck and I turned our guns on each other, but before either could fire, Spence tackled him from behind, knocking his gun away. Buck rolled and elbowed Spence in the face. He scrambled to get his gun, but Spence recovered and knocked Buck's hand away. He wrapped his arms around Buck and rolled away from the pistol. Buck tried to break free, but Spence tightened his grip. He wrapped his legs around Buck's and shifted his position. Spence, a former wrestler, quickly subdued Buck, securing both of his arms behind his back. "I'm good," he said. "Take care of her."

I holstered my Sig and ran to Susan. She sat on the ground. Her eyes were wide with terror. I spoke, but she didn't respond. I gently nudged her, but she continued to stare into the nothingness. I gave her a light slap on the cheek. She looked up through watery eyes.

"Abbey? You came."

"Of course I did." I could hear sirens approaching. "I'm here, Susan. Everything's going to be okay. Help is on its way." I sat on the ground with Susan and held her close. I eased her head to my shoulder and let her cry.

As Spence read Buck his rights, I noticed movement in the shadows. I pulled out my Sig. Was it Denzel or Chase? Who'd won the fight? I didn't hear a shot, I guessed that meant something. It moved again. I focused my Sig on the sounds. They moved closer. It was neither Chase nor Denzel. Damien and his henchmen stepped into the west side of the clearing and the light of the moon. "Can we help?"

"No. We're okay now. Thanks." I wanted to say, *Perfect timing*, or *About time*, but they did offer help. They could have stayed completely away from the danger.

"We heard shots."

"We've got it," I assured him. I wasn't in the mood to deal with Damien and his men. He nodded, and they disappeared back into the darkness of the night.

Several squad cars pulled into the lot and called out. We answered back, and they filled the clearing. An officer took Buck into custody. Spence followed the officer to his car and filled him in on the highlights of our case. I waited with Susan as the paramedics checked her vitals. They cleared her to go home, saying she was in shock and shouldn't be left alone. I left the officers to scour the banks of the Cumberland to see if either or both men survived. Even with the light from the moon, it was impossible to see into the shadows of either bank.

CSI would do their work overnight. Tomorrow, in the light of day, Spence and I could return to the site and get a better picture of the scene. I needed to get Susan home and in the care of her family.

We left her car at the site. Her father could pick it up tomorrow. Susan was in no condition to drive. I tried to talk with her all the way there, but Susan just broke down in tears. These types of events took their toll on me. I couldn't imagine how Susan was feeling.

Chapter Forty-one

Wednesday, April 9, 8:28 AM—Southwest Bank of the Cumberland River

Two teams of divers started at daylight. They alternated times in the water. Other boats tossed grappling hooks attached to ropes and dragged the bottom of the river for the bodies. I knew the chances of finding either man were slim. The river's current probably swept them toward Riverfront Park or Metro Center. But the divers started a systematic grid pattern beginning with the entry point under the interstate and combed the river for any sight of their bodies.

I turned my attention from the divers' boat to the scene from last night. Yellow crime scene markers were scattered about the clearing, including the point Denzel and Chase tumbled down the mounds of trash and into the river. Even without CSI's report, I could tell both men were injured by Buck's shot. The blood trail split right before it reached the water's edge. The police said there was no sign downriver on either bank where anyone climbed out, but they stopped their search of the banks this side of Riverfront Park.

My eyes followed the two blood trails up the bank, where they merged into one. At the edge of the bluff, a large splatter pattern marked the place where Chase and Denzel were shot. The bullet went through both men, meaning they should have had a high chance of surviving the shot. Chase's gun lay where Denzel cut his arms right after he shot. Denzel's knife lay in the grass a few feet away. It must have flipped out of his hand when he was shot. I watched the scene in reverse as my mind rewound the mental video. The grass was smashed down where Susan sat in shock hours ago. Two empty rounds sat at opposite ends of the circle. One belonged to Chase's .357, shot just inches from my head. The other was from Buck's 9 mm, the gun that wounded Denzel and Chase.

"Penny for your thoughts."

Without turning, I said, "They don't say that anymore, Sarge."

"Well, I'm old." He put his hand on my shoulder. "I've got to hand it to you, Rhodes. Your gut kept pulling you back to this site. Good work."

"I suppose."

All the evidence I needed was there, including the unintentional confessions of Chase and Buck. Somehow, it still didn't feel like a victory. Sam and Susan were both nearly killed in the process. Top it off, I lost two critical suspects in the river.

"Sarge, I need a course in hostage negotiations. I didn't do so well last night."

"Your hostage is alive and well." He took his hand from my shoulder and smoothed a wild hair in his mustache. "And so are you."

A whistle from the river's edge caught our attention.

"We got a body."

Sarge and I hustled down the riverbank past Damien's camp. One of the divers was pulling on a rope. I could hear him explaining that it had snagged on an old tree not more than three feet below the surface. "The other end's attached to her hand."

"Her?" Sarge asked. "I thought we were looking for two men."

"It's hard to tell nowadays," I added. We did have four missing women, though. Maybe it was one of them.

We watched as the diver handed off the rope to two other police officers standing on the bank. They pulled together and dragged the bloated body from the water onto the bank. A pot was attached to the other end of the rope. Could that be? I hollered down at the diver, "How long has it been under the water?"

"Hard to tell. I'll leave that to the ME's office."

"Best guess," Sergeant McNally said. "I won't hold you to it."

I could tell the diver didn't want to give an estimate, but the request came from a sergeant. "With the bloating, the loss of flesh in places due to abrasions, turtles, and fish—I guess a couple of weeks."

"Carry on." Sarge turned to me. "When were those disappearances you told me about?"

"Susan's friend, Christy, went missing the twenty-seventh of March, so fourteen days, Sarge." I looked at the body. "It's hard to tell if it's her with all the bloating, but that pot matches the set Susan gave her."

"Okay, Rhodes. You got your body. Now, this is an official homicide." Finally, I could focus on the four women. I'd have to wait for an official identification of the body, but I knew it was Christy. Where were the other three? Wasn't the woman on the hill missing her water bucket, too? I'd have to ask Sam. I'm sure he'd be delighted to have something important to do. His sister Maggie was smothering him with love and kindness. She was also shielding him from anything causing stress—except for her obsessive mothering. We represented stress, so she hesitated to leave us alone with Sam.

"Sergeant, you might want to see this," an officer said.

We made our way to the bank. Before we reached the officer, another diver, holding a second rope, surfaced. "Got something else."

It was less than two yards from Christy. Was it another body? One of the other missing women? No. It was a bucket covered with thick black plastic. Someone had drilled holes through the plastic and into the bucket so the water could pass through, decreasing the drag on the line. Two of the officers pulled the rope until the bucket reached dry land. Sarge pulled on some gloves.

"Take a picture before I open it."

I did. He cut the zip tie and opened the bag. The bag was stuffed full of smaller Ziplock bags containing white powder.

"Get CSI back out here," Sarge said. "We got drugs." He asked the diver, "Where did you find these?" He pointed back into the water. "See if there are any more just like it."

When they pulled the rope to the side, it exposed a section that had been buried beneath the ground's surface.

"Hey, Sarge?"

"What is it, Rhodes?"

"Look. The rope leads to that boxed structure over there."

It was Damien's home. Javy was right. They were moving drugs through here. They weren't only meeting with the people in the cars. They were also moving them by water. I wondered which way the drugs were going—boat to land or land to boat?

"The journalist said he saw them meeting up with cars on a regular basis—that bags were being exchanged. You think boats might pull up here to get or give a delivery, Sarge?"

"Either direction it was traveling, I bet that woman caught them, and they pushed her in. She probably got tangled up in the rope and drowned." He turned his attention back to the officer on the bank. "What were you going to show us earlier?"

"There's a wound in the back of the head. Looks like it came from a small ax or hatchet."

Damien's henchmen. I suddenly realized I hadn't seen Damien or his inner circle of men. Where were they?

"Sarge, there's a man in this camp who always carries a hatchet." I described him and gave Sergeant McNally a brief description of Damien as well. As I explained our various encounters with the members of this camp, one of the divers surfaced with another rope in his hands.

"We found another bucket." Once again, it was tethered to a rope that led to Damien's tent. Both ropes were buried inches below the surface. They took pictures and opened the black plastic bag. "Same as before."

This was no small operation. I remembered Sam's earlier comment. He'd questioned the camp's location—that it wasn't near the city's center where they could ask for money or food. It was isolated.

234

Now I knew why. They were making money transferring drugs for someone else. The divers resumed their search for bodies. I heard something behind us. It was Freeman, Millie's friend, another one of the missing women.

"Detective?" he asked sheepishly. "Did Rusty kill her?"

"Who's Rusty?" I asked. A handful of other people gathered nearby.

Freeman looked over his shoulder. Relieved it wasn't Damien or his men, he continued. "He's the man with the hatchet. The other man, the one with the machete, is Bruce. They do most of Damien's bidding." He turned and looked at the gathering crowd. "We're all afraid of them." He looked at Sarge. "Did they kill Millie, too?"

"Sir, we don't know what happened yet. As soon as we get the body to the Medical Examiner's office, we can figure that out. Detective Rhodes is on the case and won't quit until she has resolved it." I felt a warm flush fill my cheeks. "So far, they've only found one body."

"Freeman, has anyone here seen something he thinks we need to know?" I handed him my small pocket-sized notepad and a pen. "Would you feel safe gathering the information for me? Anything you find will help us get justice for Millie, Grace, Alice, and Christy."

He snatched them from my hand and walked toward the parking lot. A few people followed him.

"Sarge, should I take Rusty into custody when he returns?"

"Build your case first, Rhodes. They may play into your hands without endangering these people." He answered his phone. "Got it. Where? I'll send someone." He hung up and said, "Rhodes, go to the Social Security Administration office north of two-sixty-five. They found a man on the lawn who looked like he crawled out of the river. An ambulance is on its way. Beat it."

"Yes, Sergeant."

Chapter Forty-two

Wednesday, April 9, 11:07 AM—Social Security Administration parking lot

I didn't beat the ambulance, but I arrived as they were following the witness down to the river's edge. I flashed my badge and ran to the body. He was wearing fatigues and still lying on his stomach. His head was turned to the other side. All I could see was the back of his head. His left shoulder was a bloody mess. Buck must have loaded hollow points.

The paramedic took his pulse and announced the man was still alive. I could already see the rising and falling of his chest. She checked his vitals and said, "Vitals are weak but steady." They stabilized him on a gurney and carried him to the ambulance. Lance Corporal Denzel Rushing was alive.

The paramedic asked, "Which hospital?"

"Take him to the VA emergency room. He's a vet." I stepped into the back of the ambulance despite their suggestions to follow them in my car. "He has a mental condition, and I need to make sure he's taken care of."

"We'll take good care of him, Detective Rhodes," the paramedic said.

"I know you will, but I'm a familiar face. I want to keep him calm if he wakes." I gave them plenty of room to get an IV started. It was the first time I'd seen him up close. Denzel was covered with scars—some old and some new. Of course, the newest was the gunshot to his left shoulder. The bullet hit when he was lifting

Chase, so it went in just above the pectoral muscle and exited between his spine and shoulder blade. He was lucky. That also meant Chase's wound would have been about four inches lower. He probably didn't live. Denzel, however, was a strong man and battle-tested soldier. He was a survivor. Unfortunately, his mind was wounded much deeper than his flesh.

We arrived at the VA, and I followed them in. "He's Lance Corporal Denzel Rushing—a Bronze Star Recipient and an army honorable discharge." I didn't know that last part for sure, but based on the information from Javy, I assumed as much. That reminded me. I needed to find Javy's editor and break the news. So many bodies, all to get rid of a bratty kid that no one liked. They found his files and took him to surgery. I gave the nurse my card and asked to be notified when he was out.

"Hey, Spence. It was Denzel. He's still alive." I stepped outside to talk on the phone without disrupting anyone else. "How's it going there? Did they find any more women or Chase?"

"No, but they're still searching. By the way, somebody named Freeman gave me a list of complaints and names. He said they were willing to tell us anything we needed. Sergeant McNally said to tell you the three men are in custody. We were looking in their cabin when they returned to the camp. Instead of running, they tried to force us out, screaming all sorts of obscenities. Sergeant McNally was not happy when the man named Rusty pulled his hatchet out and tried to hit him."

"You're kidding! You'd have to be mental to fight with Sarge. He's a big man."

Spence laughed. "The battle was short-lived. Sergeant McNally blocked the man's swing and knocked him out with one blow. He wanted to personally book the one called Rusty." A siren screamed as an ambulance passed the VA on its way to Vanderbilt. "You want me to come get you?"

"Yeah. Maybe later, though. I want to see how he does in surgery. If he's conscious after recovery, I'm going to try to talk with him. I know his testimony is sketchy at best, but I'd like to see what he knows and remembers. If it's a lost cause, I'll leave after I talk with the doctor."

"Semper Fi," Spence said.

"We're army. That's marines."

"Oh."

"I think you were looking for *no man left behind.* That was an Army Ranger saying that we all adopted."

"Yeah. That's the one. It's the thought that counts. Right?"

"You got it, Spence. When you pick me up, let's see Sam." He agreed, saying he should have the crime scene wrapped up in two to three hours. "Hopefully, I'll know something by then."

Two hours later, the doctor entered the waiting room and said, "Detective Rhodes?" I stood. "Let's sit over here," he said, pointing to a table in the corner. "Denzel's a lucky man. The bullet missed his vital organs and bones. I notice by his records he's suffered from bomb shrapnel and an earlier gun wound." He paused and took the surgery hat off. "I also see that he has…"

"Mental wounds," I said, not knowing what diagnosis to use and not willing to embarrass myself in front of an educated man.

"Yes…well, that's a nice way of putting it." He smiled—or at least he tried.

"He's been homeless, doctor, so we both know he hasn't taken any meds for quite a while." I took a deep breath, looked out the window to my left, and let it out slowly. "What can we do for him?"

"We've already resumed his medicine through his IV, so it should help rather quickly. I don't know what's happened since the last time he was here or how advanced his condition has gotten."

"I think you're telling me he will need inpatient treatment." He nodded. "As a vet, that's covered, right?" Again, he nodded.

"I promise we'll take good care of him. The social worker is on her way to coordinate with us."

I took another deep breath. "So, doc, there's probably no use staying here and waiting to talk with him?"

"No. I'm afraid not."

"Will you do something for me, Doc?" I looked into his eyes. "Will you tell him he saved my friend's life—and mine?"

"I'll make sure he gets the message, Detective."

"Tell him Sargeant Rhodes said he performed admirably." He shook my hand before returning to the recovery room.

I texted Spence and told him to pick me up at Vanderbilt Hospital when he was done. I needed to walk. Besides, it was only around the corner. I'd missed three days of jogging, and my legs felt neglected. I'm sure Sam did, too. Now, if I could only convince Maggie to let us talk alone.

Chapter Forty-three

Wednesday, April 9, 4:22 PM—Vanderbilt Hospital

"I'm going crazy, Abbey. They gotta let me go home soon."

"Sam, Maggie said you're going home tomorrow after the doctor discharges you. You nearly died, Sam."

"Nearly isn't the same as dead." He looked around to make sure she was gone. "If I have to spend another hour with Maggie, I'm going to wish that bullet hit a little to the right."

"Don't even say that, Sam. It's not funny." I sat in the chair next to his bed. "Spence is a good partner, but he's not you."

"A little meticulous and letter-bound?"

"A little?"

"I'm bored to death, Abbey. Give me something to do. I don't care if it's organizing the facts or going over someone's testimony. Please."

"Want to know where we are with the case?"

"Yes. Please, before Maggie gets back. She'll say you're giving me stress—that it's bad for my heart."

"Is she going to let you go back to work, Sam?" He gave me a look that could kill.

I started back at the Music City Cigar Bar and gave Sam a detailed version with everything new we discovered. I told him of Buck's enlistment of Chase Martin, who had applied for a job with JLT Enterprises. How Chase thought he was just supposed to lead Dean Swain to the homeless camp and then tell him the idea would never work. Dean would take the bait and go to the other side to measure for his bridge.

Meanwhile, Tito Ruiz was hired to kill Dean, taking the car as his payment. Buck, Chad, and Zach waited for Dean to die and then shot Tito. Only Chad and Zach weren't lined up for clear shots, and Tito got away. Buck used his boss's connection with the mayor to keep tabs on our progress.

"Is Jonathan Thomas involved?" Sam asked, interrupting my summary.

"I think so, but we have no proof." I continued with the case all the way through the showdown with Chase and Buck. Then, I threw the twist on him. "Damien and his two goons killed Christy. She caught them accepting or shipping drugs, and Rusty—"

"Who's Rusty?"

"The tall ugly guy with the hatchet," I said.

"I knew there was something wrong with that guy. Did you catch Damien?"

I smiled and told Sam that Rusty picked a fight with Sergeant McNally. He laughed. "Yeah. Sarge booked him personally. I think he's questioning the three of them now."

"Why aren't you there?" Sam asked. "This is your case."

"It's an *all hands on deck* event. Everyone is in on the interviews. I went to the VA with Denzel. Spence stayed onsite to oversee the processing of the scene."

"Still, Abbey, this is your bust."

"To be honest, Sam, I don't want any more recognition. We may have to dance some more." We both laughed.

Sam had a goofy smile on his face. He folded his arms behind his head and winced in pain. "So, kid, you did it."

"No, Sam, we did it. Everybody played a critical role in the investigation. Even Sarge was on site." I took his hand in mine. "He did it for you, Sam. Everyone did it for you."

I know he'd never admit it, but Sam Tidwell's eyes teared up. "Proud of you, kid." His demeanor took a serious turn. "Now, that

I have you alone, Abbey, let's discuss that *dream* I had about you in Guatemala."

"I'd rather not, Sam. I'm sure your dream would stir up bad memories."

"I've been doing a lot of thinking, and I'm pretty sure it wasn't a dream. I think you were telling me about it."

"About what, Sam?" I tried to play it cool, hoping he would let me brush it off. He didn't.

"That kind of detail doesn't come from my dreams. I barely remember what I dream at night, if I have any." I started to protest, but he put his finger to my lips. "Spit it out, kid. I'm sure it's been eating at you for years. You know whatever you tell me will stay between us."

"I don't know, Sam." I was torn. I desperately wanted to free myself from the past, but I was terrified to expose myself and my past to anyone else. I'd already risked telling Susan. Keeping it to myself was eating me like a cancer, but once I told someone else, I lost my control over the truth or the pain. "I'm not sure I'm ready to do that."

"You'll never be ready. Trust me. A wise friend once told me *A burden shared is halved*, meaning two will now carry the load instead of just one. Let me help you with your burden, Abbey. You helped me so much with mine."

"Okay, but remember, you asked for it." I told Sam the very thing I'd said when he was sedated. I stopped to explain who Mr. Morales was, why I was out on my own—including the rape, and how I ended up with Mr. Morales as my benefactor. I took a deep breath and counted to ten. I could feel the anxiety rising. I told Sam about his voyeuristic tendencies and our deal. To Sam's credit, he let me talk. Susan interjected concern, questions, and wanted to stop and pray. Sam didn't say anything. His face didn't reflect pity, shame, or criticism.

I finally broke down and told him about the cameras and the videos that Mr. Morales sold of me bathing or changing. "Sam, those videos are still out there somewhere. What if they surface while I'm on the force?"

"Then we'll deal with it. More than likely, they won't. If they do, you won't be held accountable. You were a minor doing what you had to do to survive."

I'd tried to convince myself of that for years, hoping it would lighten some of the shame and guilt. It was nice to hear someone else say it. But still, it was my naked body on the videos. "I'd die of embarrassment."

"I'll stand with you when and if that moment arises. In the meantime, Abbey, give yourself some grace."

"I can't. I chose to stay there with him until I turned eighteen. That's when I joined the army and took off for Germany with a new name and a new start."

"A new name? Abbey's not your real name?" He seemed genuinely shocked.

"Don't you remember, Sam? When we were first interviewing Susan, and Hannah came into the room, I told her my name was Hannah too. You asked why I lied, and I told you it wasn't a lie, that my birth name was Hannah Leah Abelard, but I legally changed it to Abbey Rhodes when I turned eighteen, right before I left for the Army."

"Oh." It was all he said, but it was enough. He understood my pain. "I'm sure he didn't mean it that way when he named you."

"You don't know my father, Sam. He never did anything unintentionally. Everything had a purpose and a reason. He named my sister Miriam. Anyway, I wanted to make a break from Guatemala and all the pain, so I paid to have my name legally changed to Abbey Rhodes."

"What made you choose that?"

I smiled at the thought of my father. "My father hated the Beatles. He said they were responsible for the breakdown of society."

Sam laughed, and then he grabbed his chest. I could tell he was in pain. "After their best album, *Abbey Road*. That's awesome.

I'll never think of you the same when I call your name." Despite his pain, Sam laughed again. "You have a lot of spunk, Abbey Rhodes."

"Thanks." My phone buzzed. I looked down and read the text out loud. "The blood on Buck's knife was from Javy Perez."

"That's a good thing," Sam said. "So why are you making that face like you just lost your best friend?"

"Because they found three different blood types on Denzel's knife." I sighed and added, "Chase's, Chad's, and Zach's. Looks like Denzel murdered them."

"I understand Chase. He was saving Susan. But why would he kill the other two? Do you think he just went crazy and thought he was in battle?"

"Who knows?" I thought of how Spence said the bodies were laid on the ground and staggered. "I think he may have been avenging his friend Javy." They weren't put down softly out of care. He put the body down stealthily so he could surprise the next victim. He was a skilled soldier. That Afghanistan withdrawal must have caused him to snap. It's one thing to be in a war against your enemy. It's another to abandon people to the enemy under orders, knowing you're the only one they see. The administration didn't have to face those people. Soldiers like Denzel did.

"He's got a built-in insanity plea," Sam said. "No jury will convict him of murder without a mental clause. You said he was already heading to an inpatient facility."

"Yeah, but it breaks my heart that he has to go through it." I got another text. "Listen, Sam. They want me back at the station. I got to go."

"Let me know how it goes, Abbey. Please, keep me in the loop."

"You know I will, Sam." I kissed his forehead and left. I wondered how Buck would play it. Would he say someone planted the evidence in his truck? Or would he go the opposite direction and give up his boss, saying he acted on Jonathan's instructions? Maybe Buck was the kind who would take one for the team? No, he seemed more like the one to frame the team. Did this conspiracy really stop with Buck? I couldn't wait to interview him.

Chapter Forty-four

Wednesday, April 9, 7:27 PM—Homicide

I'd never seen the homicide offices so busy and full of people. Both the day and night homicide teams were there to sort through the people who had come forward to testify against Damien, Rusty, and Bruce. Even the Cold Case division was called in to help. The conference room was full, and detectives conducted interviews in their cubbies. When Sarge said, *All hands on deck*, he meant it. Captain Harris called out, "Rhodes, you're with me."

What did that mean? Did I do something wrong again? "On my way, Captain." I followed him to his office. "Yes, sir?"

"First, I wanted to tell you I'm proud of you. I didn't know how you'd respond when Detective Tidwell went down, but you stepped up."

"Thank you, Captain." That meant a lot, especially with all the ups and downs of this case.

"Secondly, I'm sure you wanted to interview Damien Jones yourself."

"Yes, sir. I'd like a piece of him—figuratively speaking."

"It's not going to happen, Rhodes. I had him and Bruce Wolowicz handed over to TBI's Drug Investigation Division. They have the resources and experience. We'll let them find out who they were running drugs for."

He had to see the disappointment in my face. I knew he was right, but I seriously wanted to be the one to wipe that smug look off Damien's face. "What about Rusty?"

"Rusty Gee is in the interrogation room with Sergeant McNally right now. Turns out the young man has a history of violence."

"I know this sounds horrible, Captain, but I'd love to see that interview."

"Watch Sergeant McNally's recording later." He gave the slightest hint of a smile, which was the only smile I'd seen from Captain Harris before. "Let's be perfectly clear, Rhodes. I know this is your case, but you will sit in on this interview to observe and write any questions or comments you wish to make. Slide the notebook to me if you wish me to pursue a certain angle or comment. I'm going to ask the questions. If you feel the need to chime at any time, do so on paper, but make it brief. I know this suspect will have the best lawyers, so we will do this by the book. I have more experience, and I want to see what we can get before he lawyers-up. No offense."

"Whatever you say, sir." I assumed he was speaking about Buck Pader. Even though he was suspected of orchestrating a conspiracy to kill Dean Swain, he was still a friend of Jonathan Lee Thomas, who had top lawyers at his beck and call. At some point, they would be activated, if just to minimize the embarrassment of having your private security team conspire to kill your stepson.

"You sit behind my desk and take notes of anything you hear that you believe is incorrect or significant. The camera will go on the moment he enters my office." Sitting behind the captain's desk while he sat in a side chair felt strange. "Bring him in."

Buck Pader was escorted into the captain's office in handcuffs. A Metro police officer gently pushed him into a far chair and took his position behind it.

"I've been set up," Buck said.

Captain Harris ignored the comment and began by explaining Buck's rights and informing him that the interview would be recorded. "Do you understand these rights as I have explained them?" Buck nodded. "I am Captain Harris, and this is Detective Rhodes. State your name for the record."

247

"Buck Pader."

"What is the nature of your relationship with Jonathan Lee Thomas?" the captain asked.

"I'm the head of his private security detail, but you know all that," Buck said in a voice full of frustration. "I know where you're going with this, but I tell you, I was set up."

"We'll get to that in a moment, Mr. Pader. Right now, I'm getting all the tedious details on record." Like Buck, I, too, wondered why Captain Harris didn't jump right into the pertinent information, especially if he thought Buck would ask for an attorney at some point. "How long have you worked for Mr. Thomas?"

"Twenty-three years this coming June."

"That's impressive, Mr. Pader."

"Thank you. You can call me Buck. Everybody does." Buck fidgeted in his chair. I could tell he was ready to finish this interview.

"How many people work in your security detail?"

"We started with just three: Peter, Lee, and Dan—and me, so that makes four. Then we hired another two men five years ago, and when Jonathan started traveling a lot, we added these last three: Chad, Zach, and Doug." He stopped, scratched his chin, and looked over his shoulder at the officer standing behind him. "Is he necessary?"

"Protocol. We want to do everything by the book, now don't we? Mr. Pader, please, continue."

"Then, you all know we added that traitor."

"Traitor?" Captain Harris asked.

"Chase Martin. I can see why you guys let him go," Buck said. Then, he looked directly at me and said, "You two have a history. Don't you?"

I wanted to shout at him, run at him, or throw something, but Captain Harris said, "We're not here to discuss Detective Rhodes. I want to get your side of the story."

"Okay." Buck sat up straight in his chair and puffed out his chest. I could tell he thought he'd won a major victory. He began his version with a history of Dean Swain and his embarrassing childish antics and social media life. "The kid thought he could do anything. His mom married money, and he took advantage of it. He did everything imaginable: alcohol, drugs, women—you name it. If you catch my drift, he went through women like other people watch tv, changing channels every minute. He'd use them up and then throw them away. I can't tell you the number of times Jonathan had to pay money to settle Dean's lawsuits."

Buck painted a detailed picture of a spoiled rich kid. "He fenagled his way into Jonathan's business and said he had a lucrative real estate deal. Jonathan took the bait." Buck leaned back and said, "Jonathan tried to make him a partner. I guess he thought he'd finally succeeded in getting through to the boy." Then Buck shook his head. "That kid took the money and spent it on a car—a car! A quarter of a million dollars, and he blew it on a car. Can you believe that?"

I could see why Buck didn't like him. "All we wanted to do was teach Dean a lesson. No one wanted him dead. I promise you that." Buck looked over his shoulder again. He didn't like having the officer stand where he couldn't see him. "Yes. We arranged to have his precious Bentley stolen. It was insured. He could get the money back and either pay Jonathan back or buy another. But he needed to see what happens when you brag and flash your money around for everyone to see. He had over three hundred thousand followers on those social media accounts, and he was telling the world he was made of money."

I started to understand Buck's predicament. He was hired to protect Jonathan Thomas, and over the twenty-plus years, they became friends. He saw what Dean was doing to his friend, and he'd had enough. Maybe what he was saying was true. Maybe they didn't plan on Dean's death. That would explain the sloppy and amateur staging of the crime scene. He continued.

"We went down there to see it happen—to make sure Tito showed up and took the car. If that idiot had waited only another minute or two—if he'd waited until Dean stood at the fence by the river, none of this would have happened." He sounded sincere.

"So," Captain Harris said. "If I understand you correctly, you and your men arranged for Tito Ruiz to steal the car, knowing insurance would pick up the bill?" Buck nodded. How clever. Now Captain Harris had him on insurance fraud as well.

"I acknowledge your affirmation by nodding, but please give your answer verbally."

"Yes."

The Captain nudged him further. "But, Tito was impatient. He started the car too early."

"Exactly!" Buck said as if he'd been redeemed. "He was supposed to wait until the boy got to the fence. But when Dean heard the engine and turned around, Tito put the thing in reverse and gunned it. He crashed through a orange construction divider and got the car stuck on top of it and that pile of scrap. We watched as he panicked. I never counted on Dean pulling a gun. I didn't even know the kid had one. Tito gunned him down. Dean dropped like a bag of potatoes. We had no choice at that point," Buck said matter-of-factly.

"I'm sorry," Captain Harris interrupted. "We who?"

"Oh, Chad, Zach, and me. Well, I wasn't in position to fire, but they did."

"Then what happened?" the captain asked.

"I thought Tito was dead. There was so much blood, but when I looked in the car, he was gone. Then I heard a car racing off. Someone had picked him up."

It all fit the timeline and the scene. Maybe he didn't plan to kill Dean—just to scare him and teach him a lesson. So why all the coverup?

Captain Harris was good. He was getting Buck to incriminate himself and his men, and he still hadn't asked for a lawyer. "Why didn't you follow Tito? He killed your boss's stepson."

"I tried. They were long gone when we got to our car. We'd

hidden it behind a semi-trailer. By the time we got to the road, we didn't know which way they went."

"Why, then, did you stage the scene?" Captain Harris asked.

"Those young bucks did that. I was out in the street looking for Tito."

"I thought you drove the car around," Captain Harris asked, feigning confusion.

"They picked me up in the car and said we were all clear. I didn't know what they did, but I knew someone would report the gunshots. There were so many of them." So, Chase was right. They did plan on stealing the car, but that was all. Unless Buck was lying to us too, but he had just admitted to the rest. And his story about when he got in Chad's car was shaky. It would have taken Chad and Zach a few minutes to set the scene like that.

Captain Harris flipped through some notes. "I have another question. Why did you have your men go to the hospital to finish Tito?"

Buck bristled. "I had nothing to do with that. Those idiots cooked up that lame-brained idea on their own. I tried telling them all Tito had on us was a phone number. He didn't know our names and had never met us." If that were true, he'd have no reason to follow up. No gang member is going to the police for help. They had to know that, too.

"What about the attack on Detective Tidwell—the one who was shot? Help me understand that logic." Captain Harris leaned back in the chair and folded his arms. He looked intently at Buck Pader. Buck leaned forward.

"I didn't know about that until I heard it on the news. I'd sent them there to find that soldier and see what he knew." He looked my way and said, "A little birdy told me you were looking for him as a witness. I had to know what he saw."

Captain Harris stood and stretched. "It's been a long day. You'll have to excuse me if I stretch out this old body. It's been through a lot." He rolled his head from shoulder to shoulder. I caught myself watching him, too. He stretched his arms and back. Then, after a few minutes pause that put us all at ease, he asked, "Does this little birdy have a name?"

"May—may I have a drink of water?"

Captain Harris winked at me and said, "Certainly. Officer Henderson would be glad to give you a bottle of water." Then, looking at the officer, he added, "It's behind you in the fridge."

The wink. Buck started to say a name that began with *may*. Was he talking about the mayor? Surely not.

"So, Mayor O'Reilly kept Mr. Thomas apprised of our progress, and he passed the information down to you." He didn't say it as a question. Captain Harris mentioned it casually, but I noticed a twinge as Buck drank the water. *Nice move, Captain.* I watched as a master bled information little by little. He'd gain Buck's confidence, acting as though he understood his position, and then setting him up once again to incriminate himself or his men.

While pretending to look through notes, Captain Harris said, "And it was Mr. Perez who gave you Denzel's name?"

"Yes." Buck didn't flinch, and Captain Harris didn't look up.

"And after you killed Javy Perez, you killed Chad Cole and Zach Clement, but they were your men?" Captain Harris looked lost and confused.

Before he realized it, Buck shouted, "I did not kill my men. I found them that way. That wild man did, and his friend wouldn't give him up, no matter what I did to him." It was then that Buck realized what he had done and said, "I want a lawyer." Buck tortured and killed Javy just to get Denzel. All on the chance he might have witnessed the shooting of Tito Ruiz.

Captain Harris rose and said, "I wondered when you would invoke that right, Mr. Pader." He turned to Officer Henderson and said, "We're done. Take him to a cell. We got all we needed."

After they left and the captain closed his door, I said, "That was incredible."

"Not really, Rhodes. Most men will hang themselves if you

give them enough rope. Besides, interviewing effectively comes with wisdom earned from years of mistakes. God knows I've made plenty." Then he pointed to me and added, "Make sure you learn from yours."

Chapter Forty-five

Thursday, April 10, 10:00 AM—Homicide

After a long night with interviews and reports, Spence and I agreed to come in at ten the next morning. I was glad. I got in a good run but was a little sore. I'd missed several days of my routine. That was the biggest downside of being a detective. Even though the shift was divided between day and night teams, you still had to work until you solved the case. That meant all kinds of crazy hours, going every time a clue presented itself. On patrol, we clocked in and clocked out. As an officer, working more hours meant overtime. For a detective, more hours just meant you had to eat and sleep when you could. For me, it meant my morning routine of jogging wasn't a routine anymore.

Spence and I met in the conference room and finalized the evidence and our detailed reports for the District Attorney's office. I told Spence how incredible it was to watch Captain Harris put Buck at ease during the interrogation. "It was like the legend of the frog in the pot. Buck didn't know he was cooked until it was too late." I thought momentarily and added, "How he relaxed Buck—it was almost like watching two old friends catch up with each other."

"I'll have to check out the video," Spence said as he sorted through numbered bags and checked them off the list. "And you'll have to watch Sergeant McNally's interview with Rusty...Rusty..."

"Rusty Gee. I bet that was exciting," I said. It would have been entertaining.

"Let's just say it didn't sound like two old friends catching up,"

Spence said, smiling broadly. "Sergeant McNally had him on his heels from the get-go, and he never let him gain his balance. I was on the other side of the window, and I was afraid."

"He has that effect on people." I added a file but stopped to ask, "So, Spence, do you think Jonathan Thomas knew his men were involved when he asked the mayor to expedite the case?"

"If what Buck is true, I don't think he knew initially. At some point, he had to, though. His security team was dropping like flies. What businessman would be ignorant of that?"

"I'm still not sure that I believe his story. It fits the fact and timeline, but it had to be more than just a car theft," I admitted. "Why else would he post two shooters behind the semi-trailer?"

"You think he was lying?"

"Yes, but Buck confessed everything else, even the torture and murder of Javy Perez. What would he gain by lying about a murder he didn't commit?" I thought of Chase Martin, whose body was lost somewhere at the bottom of the Cumberland River. He was so desperate for a job in security that he willingly conspired to grand theft auto that became a murder. I understood Buck's reason for going back to the homeless camps. He had to silence the only living witness. Of course, we'll never know if Lance Corporal Denzel Rushing even saw the murder. Even if he did, the chances were slim he knew what he was watching and could testify consistently to it.

One thing still puzzled me. Why was Chase there? What reason would he have to return? Denzel had nothing on him. We had witnesses placing Chase there with Dean, but they also testified Chase left on foot. Why did he take Susan as a hostage? Unless he told Susan, I'd never know. I wanted to know the answer, but I wasn't going to put Susan through that if I could help it. I had so many more questions than answers. What kind of detective wraps up a case that way?

"Hey, Abbey!"

"Spence, you don't have to yell. I'm right here."

"Maybe physically, but you weren't answering me. You just kept staring at the timeline in a daze."

"Sorry. It's been a long week. I'm exhausted in more ways than one."

"I get it," Spence said. "I asked if you thought Sam would come back to work?"

"Absolutely." I had no doubts. I knew Maggie well enough to know she would tire of having him around. For now, she loved the chance to care for her little brother. "Another week or so, and Maggie will push Sam out the door. He's been begging me for more details and tedious jobs he can do from home. He'll be running back with open arms."

"Oh."

"What do you mean, *Oh*, Spence? I thought you'd be cheering Sam on and be eager to get rid of me."

"Oh, yeah—of course. I can't wait to get back to my own cases and get you off my back."

We continued matching evidence to reports and details, making the transfer to the DA's office easy. "I won't tell Sam, but you're quick on your feet and much stronger than you look. I don't think Sam could have taken Buck down. Me either."

"Right. I've seen you hit the heavy bags. You would have knocked him out with the first blow."

"You flatter me." Then it struck me. "Oh, Spence. I never did thank you for saving my life back there. I appreciate it." Without his timely tackle, Buck or I—or both—would be dead. "Thanks."

"No problem, Abbey. We made a good team."

"Let's go over the list one more time before I give it to Deborah. Box number one contains evidence for Tito Ruiz. Box two is for Chad Cole. Box three is for Zach Clement. Four is Buck Pader. Five is Chase Martin, and box six…" I swallowed a lump in my throat. "That box is for Denzel Rushing."

"Check." Spence put tops on each of the boxes. We set them on a cart and rolled them to the front. Deborah took possession.

"Call the DA's office and let them know the evidence is ready for pickup."

"Yes, Detective Spencer," Deborah said.

"I still think it stinks that Jonathan Thomas gets away with everything. I know he was complicit in the theft. They would never have acted without his approval, especially when risking that kind of money."

"We have nothing to prove that theory, Abbey. Let it go."

"Everyone keeps telling me to stay in my lane and let things go. It's hard, Spence." I looked at the clock on my phone. "Oh, wow. How'd it get to be twelve-thirty?" I ran to my cubby and grabbed my billfold. On my way past Spence, I said, "I'm meeting Susan for lunch to let her know about Christy and the drug operation that got her killed."

"Good luck with that."

Chapter Forty-six

Thursday, April 10, 12:47AM—The Salad Bowl

"Sorry I'm late, Susan. Time got away from me." I took a seat opposite hers at the small table.

She looked at her watch. "Late? You were supposed to be here by twelve-forty-five. It's now forty-seven after. I'm leaving." She smiled, rose from her chair, and hugged me. "If I were waiting for Mark, I'd have another thirty minutes."

It was nice seeing her joke around and talk freely about Mark. "Well, for me, being on time is being late." Susan's outfit amused me. The plaid skirt, solid-colored shirt, and small white collar made her look like a preppy college schoolgirl. Somehow, she pulled it off. It was a good look for her demure frame. It also made her look younger than me, although she was ten years my senior.

"You military people—must be rough living by the clock. I don't think I could handle the army."

"It was rough, but it was also great. They taught me so much, especially about life in general. I do miss it from time to time."

"Are you ladies ready to order?" The waiter sat two glasses of water on the table. "My name is Mike, and I'll be your server today. Will you eat from the salad bar or order from the menu?"

Susan looked at me. "I'll have the Kale Caesar with grilled chicken and peaches on the side with a sweet tea," I said.

"Excellent choice. And you?" he asked, turning to Susan.

"I'll have the Mango Veggie Summer Salad," Susan said. "With the house dressing and a water to drink."

He took our menus and went into the kitchen. It was so nice to order something healthy and light. It was also good to be with Susan. We'd had a rough patch the last two weeks. I looked around. We were in a crowded restaurant with conversations going on every side. The perfect setting to talk about the other night. "Are you ready for the update?" I asked, seeing if Susan wanted to talk before we got our salads or after.

"Yes."

"We found her body." *That's it, Abbey, straight to the point.*

"Christy's?" I could see her eyes beginning to water. I nodded and waited to see if she wanted more detail or if that was enough for her. "Where was she?"

"In the river." I was determined to give it little by little, making her lead me as a guide as to how much she needed to know. "You know we don't have to do this for you to have closure. A synopsis will do."

She pressed forward. "Did she drown, or did someone hurt her?" Susan fiddled with her napkin, putting it in her lap and then setting it back on the table.

"We believe the tall man with the hatchet hit her in the head. Then she either fell in the river or was pushed." She lifted the napkin to her eyes and gently dabbed the tears. "I can stop, Susan."

"No, Abbey. I need to know. I was all she had. I need you to tell me everything, and then I need to know how to get her body for a funeral."

"Susan, don't feel obligated to—"

"Obligated?" She looked up for the first time since I started talking. "It's a common courtesy that every human deserves." She turned her eyes down to the table again. "Mark had so many people who cared. For nearly three months, people came by and checked on us. They brought us food, took the kids to activities, and even mowed my lawn. Christy had me, Abbey, no one else."

"Are you talking about a memorial service or just a burial?" I was confused. Who would the funeral be for? Christy wouldn't know. No one would know her, so attendance would be minimal if anyone came. Was it for Susan's sake? I didn't understand her need to do this, but I was determined to support my friend.

"I don't know. I just feel like she should have something."

The waiter returned and presented the salads. "Do you need anything else?"

"No, thank you," I said. Susan was unusually quiet. "Susan?"

"Yes."

"I hope this isn't rude, but is this about Christy... or Mark?"

She didn't say anything. I waited, simply for her reason. I didn't know what else to say.

"I'm not sure. I got involved with the homeless, thinking it would bring back memories of our meeting. Mark and I both volunteered at our college. We were collecting camping equipment at our BSU—"

"BSU? What's that?" I asked.

"Baptist Student Union," she said. "Like a church club on campus. Anyway, we were taking up a collection of camping equipment. A group of us volunteered to take the collected items to a large homeless site—kind of like the one by the river. Mark was one of the volunteers. Our leader teamed us up, wanting every girl to be with a boy for safety." She chuckled. "Mark was probably one hundred fifteen pounds soaking wet. We both laughed at the thought of him being my protector. The laughter grew into a long conversation leading to a date later that week."

I was beginning to understand. Her ministry at this camp sparked a memory of Mark, which brought both happiness and sadness. Meeting Christy gave Susan a new purpose that somehow tied her back to Mark. "That actually sounds nice."

"What do you mean, *actually*?" We both laughed. "Would it be tacky to have her cremated and pour the ashes in the river where she died?" She moved quickly back to Christy.

"I don't think that would be tacky at all." I put my hand over hers. "It may not be legal, but if it is, I'll do it with you, if that's okay." She sniffled and wiped another tear. Susan nodded. "Then it's settled. I'll let the coroner know you want to take possession as soon as he's through with the autopsy. You can find a funeral home that does cremation. I'm sure they'll know if we can do that or not."

"There's one the church uses all the time. They cremate bodies there, too."

I turned my attention to my salad, which I had not touched yet. I noticed Susan forgot to ask a blessing. Even though I didn't believe God sat up there and poured out a blessing on our food, it felt wrong to eat without one.

"So, Abbey, let's talk about Dallas."

"We have, Susan. There's nothing to talk about." I put a large chunk of chicken in my mouth, a visible sign that I was not talking about Dallas. She picked up on it immediately.

"Good. Now you can't talk back." She put that older sister attitude on and started telling me all the reasons Dallas and I would make a great couple. "He's really patient. Let's face it, Abbey, you need a patient man." I nearly choked on my chicken. "Come on; you know it's true." I couldn't help but smile, which was the worst thing I could have done. Susan took it as a sign of affirmation. She smiled and started to give me all the reasons Dallas would make a great date. "He's handsome, intelligent, a Christian—I should have led with that. That's the most important thing about a future husband."

"Husband?" I blurted it out so loudly that the restaurant immediately went silent. Everyone was staring at us. "Nothing to see here," I said. "Mind your own business." I could tell my firm disposition embarrassed Susan because she started apologizing to everyone. They eventually turned back to their own conversations. I whispered, "Husband? Susan, I'm not sure we're ever going to date. He's out of my league."

"So," she said, putting her finger in my face, "you have thought about it."

"Of course, I thought about it. I'm not dead." Poor choice of words. "He's like Mr. Perfect."

"I know, right? Well, you know no person is perfect, Abbey." She gave me a quick list of other reasons Dallas was as close to perfect as they came.

After listening to her exhaustive list, I said, "Maybe you should date him." She dropped her fork. It clanked against the plate, causing everyone to stop and look at the strange young women again. I saw something in Susan's face that hit me. "So," I said, putting my finger in her face. "You've thought about it."

"For a fleeting moment, yes."

"Then take him." I called her bluff. "You like him. He's in your league. You should have him."

"Abbey, he's not a pet that we can take possession of."

"Maybe not, but you'd like to. Wouldn't you?" I watched as she physically squirmed in front of me. "Susan, you like him." I waited. I was going to wait all day if I had to. She wasn't getting around this without an honest answer.

"I like the *idea* of him, Abbey. It's not the same thing. I'm a widow."

"So?"

"I'm not ready to even consider anyone after Mark. Dallas is the kind of guy I might eventually date, but that is a long way off. Besides, he's too young."

"Wow! You've really given this a lot of thought." Now, the idea of dating him was even more awkward. "If Dallas is the guy, he'll wait for you."

Susan put both elbows on the table and folded her hands. She gently rested her chin on them and gave me a funny look. "Professor Dallas Gatlin is interested in a certain homicide detective."

"I'll let Spence know." We both laughed so hard we didn't care if anyone was looking.

"Abbey Rhodes, you crack me up. Thanks. I really needed a good laugh."

"Me too." I looked at the time. "I'll get the bill, Susan."

"We're not done, Abbey. Please consider Dallas."

"Is this like an elementary school arrangement? Are you asking if I like him, so you can pass the note to his row?" I grabbed the check and put enough money down to cover the bill and a size-able tip.

"No. He's just confused. He can't figure you out."

"Susan, *I* can't figure me out yet, either. I've got to go back to work."

"Supper tomorrow night?" she said as I began to walk away.

"You got it."

"Promise me," She said, raising her voice above the sounds around us.

"I promise, Susan. I will be at your house tomorrow night for supper. Tell Hannah to get stretched out because I'm going to work on her dribbling and shooting." I waved and crossed the street to my car.

Chapter Forty-seven

Thursday, April 10, 5:32 PM—Home of Lieutenant Daniels

I had to seek unbiased advice if there was such a thing. The closest thing to it that I knew was Lieutenant Matthew Daniels. He didn't have a pony in this race. I invited myself to dinner since they had given me an open invitation anytime I wanted to come over. Unfortunately, my trips were much less frequent and almost always occurred when I needed advice. I'd reduced our friendship to counseling sessions. He didn't seem to mind.

His wife, Sherry, called us to the table and set down a nine-by-nine-inch pan of lasagna. Then, she brought a basket of garlic bread and a huge salad bowl. It smelled like heaven. I wondered who else was coming. It was enough food to feed six people. "Mrs. Daniels…"

"Ah-ah," she warned.

"Sorry. Sherry, it looks fantastic."

"Good, because I made enough for you to take some home with you. I understand you've been working overtime on this case and skipping meals."

They took each other's hand and extended the other to me. *Prayer time. Oh, well.* Lieutenant Daniels lowered his head and began to pray. He thanked God for his wife, his friend, and the food. He kept it simple—no hidden sermon for me.

"Abbey, how did the case go?"

"You two know better. No shop talk at the table," Sherry said sweetly but sternly.

"Yes, ma'am," her husband said with a smile.

After we each took several bites of our food, which was as delicious as it looked, I ventured out and asked, "Would it be okay, Sherry, if I asked for advice at the table?"

"Does it deal with work?" she asked.

"No. It's personal."

"Then of course, Abbey. Are you asking Matthew or both of us?"

"Anyone who has an opinion," I said. "There's a friend of Susan's." *Ugh! How do I say it without revealing too much more of my past?* "She says he's interested in me." *Too vague?*

"Interested how?" Sherry asked.

Thank you, Sherry. "He wants to ask me out on a date."

"Pardon me for being blunt and probably rude," Lt. Daniels said, "but are we adults or kids."

"Matthew!" She gave him a hateful look. "Go ahead, Dear."

"He hasn't asked because, as Susan puts it, I keep sending mixed signals."

"Well, do you like him?" he asked.

"Yes."

"Then send the right signal." He took another bite of his lasagna. I looked to Sherry. She seemed more sympathetic to my situation.

"What does that even mean, Matthew?" Looking at me, she asked, "Why are you hesitant? Your past? Lost your trust in men?"

"Yes, and yes." She got me. Thankfully, I didn't have to explain much more about that. "He's a professor of English and Bible at Belmont."

"How did the two of you meet?" she asked. She had her elbows on the edge of the table, and she was completely focused on me. Lieutenant Daniels was focused on the lasagna.

"He's been filling in at Susan's church, preaching for a month."

He about choked on his food. "You've been going to church for a month?" I nodded sheepishly. "You have it bad, Abbey."

"Eat your food, Matthew. Give the girl a break."

He had a big grin on his face. Sherry gave him another piece of bread. He understood.

"You obviously like him. He likes you. The problem, as I see it, is your past experiences and the fact that he's a preacher—at least for the moment." I nodded. She was on a roll. I didn't want to spoil it by saying something stupid. "Do you understand what Susan was saying about mixed signals?"

"Yes. I'm showing great interest in him even by attending church every Sunday. But then, when I meet him outside of the church, especially when I'm on duty…" I saw Lt. Daniels' look, so I immediately felt the need to clarify. "I met him at War Memorial Plaza while interviewing the leader of the homeless ministry he helped start. Anyway, I made a point to call him professor—even when he addresses me as Abbey." I was rambling.

"Oh." Sherry sighed. "That poor boy."

Now, I really felt bad. "I agree. He's too good for me. He deserves better."

"Oh, Abbey. That's not what I meant at all." She took a drink of her tea. "He's probably at home wondering what he did wrong."

"Nothing," I said. "He's done everything right."

"And yet you keep him at arms' length without explaining why." Sherry wiped her mouth with the napkin. "Abbey, what do you want to happen?"

I thought that was obvious. "I want him to like me for who I am."

"Then I think you should let him know."

"Me too, if my opinion matters at this table," he said with heavy sarcasm.

"But what if he finds out who I used to be? What I've done? That I'm damaged goods?"

"Abbey," Sherry said sweetly. "We're all damaged goods. If he's worth dating in the long run, you can sit him down and share whatever you think he needs to know. If he's not what you thought after a date or two, keep it to yourself and move on."

"You know my opinion, Abbey," he said. "You have to let the past stay in the past. You left that girl behind. Keep her there."

Easier said than done. "I'm afraid." It was hard to say, but it was the truth. "I'm afraid he won't like what he sees and stop dating me. Aaron…"

"He's not Aaron," Lt. Daniels said firmly. "Judge him for who he is, or you're guilty of doing what you're afraid he will do to you."

"So, you think I should give it a chance?" I wanted someone else to make the decision. I guess, then, I would have someone else to blame if anything went wrong.

"I think you have to take a chance sometime, Dear."

That was Sherry's answer. I needed a second. I looked at him. "We think he'd be a fool to let you go." That brought a smile to my face.

After dinner, I helped Sherry clean up. Lt. Daniels went in the den and watched the news. "Thanks, Sherry. I really needed help with this one. I want to go out with him, but I feel guilty and unworthy."

"That's love, Dear."

"Abbey, you need to come in here right now."

We rushed into the room. There he was, Jonathan Lee Thomas. He was sharing the news of his case—the death of his stepson, Dean Swain. He spoke fondly of a young man who, by all accounts, annoyed him greatly. He spoke plainly of his personal security team. Jonathan shared his dismay and shock at their actions. He said he fully supported Metro Nashville's Police Department and their tireless work over the course of the case.

He looked directly into the camera and said, "I owe a special debt of gratitude to Detective Abbey Rhodes. She refused to give up, even when Dean's murderer was apprehended. She followed the clues, which led her to my security team, and found each guilty man. Thanks to Detective Rhodes, they are all now behind bars."

"Is he serious?" Lt. Daniels asked. "He's putting a target on your back."

"No, Matthew, he's thanking Abbey for her great work."

I knew Lt. Daniels was right. Any criminal watching would be out for me now. "I'll be okay, Sherry." I didn't believe it myself.

"Detective Rhodes, if you're watching, I want to thank you from the bottom of my heart." Turning away from the podium, he paused and smiled at the camera.

"Did he just smile at you?" Lt. Daniels asked. "Was he complicit in the death of this stepson?"

"I would say yes."

"Then why isn't he charged?"

"We didn't have enough on him. I know. It stinks, but that's what we got. Everything we had on him was highly circumstantial. I dropped the ball; I know."

His demeanor shifted. "No, Abbey. You did a fantastic job. I'm sorry I put a negative spin on it. I should know better."

"What do you mean?" I asked.

He put his arm around my shoulder. "When I was a rookie, my captain gave me the best advice. I want to share it with you. He said, *Celebrate your victories while you can. You won't always get the chance.*"

"What does that even mean?"

"Look at what you did, not at what you didn't. You made a difference. Never forget that. If we do, they win."

I had to write it down. That was a saying worth keeping.

Chapter Forty-eight

Friday, April 11, 6:45 PM—Ripley House

I pulled into Susan's drive; a smile filled my face. Dallas was here. I took great patience in closing my car door as quietly as possible. I ducked below the window and pulled the door open. I let it close behind me, ensuring they couldn't hear the click. I could hear their voices coming from the kitchen. The supper smelled great—two wonderful meals in a row. I was going to gain weight if I kept this up. I snuck around the corner. Just before I hollered, "Surprise!" I caught them in an embrace. They were hugging—not a side hug, but a real one.

"How stupid of me," I said. I didn't mean to say it aloud. Or maybe I did. I don't know. They turned and said, "Abbey," in unison.

"I'm a fool." I turned and ran to my car.

Dallas ran after me, "It's not what you think."

"How original." I opened the car door, but he shut it. How dare he!

"Susan lost a friend, and I was consoling her."

"Whatever you want to call it," I said. "Now, move, or I'll move you."

He stepped to the side and put his hands in the air. "I can't do anything right," he said.

"You got that right." I snapped at him. It wasn't true. How could I be angry with them?

I told Susan they made a great couple. I practically pushed her into his arms. "You two deserve each other."

Susan burst through the front door and said, "Abbey Rhodes, don't be stupid."

"Excuse me."

"I'm not sure I will. Get your head out of your butt, Abbey."

"If you weren't my friend, I'd—"

"You'd what, Abbey? Shoot me? Do one of those spin kicks you do?" I was at a loss of words. I'd never seen Susan like this. "Dallas is here to eat dinner with us so I can get the two of you together." We both stopped and let Susan go on her rant. "You two act like backwards magnets sometimes and it—"

"Backward what?"

"You know, Abbey. It's when you turn your magnets upside down and try to push them together." She put her hands on her hips and rambled on in front of the whole neighborhood. She always cared what other people thought. Tonight, the moment her neighbor opened the door and stepped out, she snapped at her. "Go inside, Sarah. This doesn't concern you." Miraculously, her busy-body neighbor did what Susan said and went right back inside her house.

"Susan."

"Shut up, Abbey. I'm on a roll. If I stop, I may never say what I've been dying to say for weeks." She pushed a lock of bangs out of her face. "If the two of you would just take a breath and stop analyzing everything, you might realize you're perfect for each other. You each tell me how wonderful the other is, but you never say it to each other's face."

Dallas looked at me, tilted his head like a confused puppy, and smiled. I dropped my defenses and smiled back.

"He makes a move, and you snuff him out. She gives you an opening, and you miss it. You're two of the smartest people I know, but you're acting like blooming idiots!"

"Are you done?" I asked.

She looked up and noticed we were holding hands. "Oh."

"Speaking of missing signals, Susan. Tonight, you're blind as a bat." I gave her the best smile I could muster.

"Now, before I lose my nerve, do you mind going inside while we talk?" Dallas said. Susan turned and went inside. I noticed the blind in the den move ever-so-slightly. She was watching. "I really like you, Abbey. I can't say that I understand you, but I feel different when you're around."

"Different?"

"Like my pulse doubles, my vocabulary, which is excellent by the way, fails me, and I feel like a little boy looking across the playground at the prettiest girl in school."

I know he meant well, and that was probably the nicest thing anyone ever said to me, but he said the wrong thing. "Dallas."

"Did I say something wrong again?"

"For any other girl in the world, that was the perfect thing to say."

He lowered his head and kicked at a little rock between his feet. It was quite comical to see a man his height kicking pebbles. "But you're not any other girl in the world, are you Abbey?"

"No. I know this may sound egotistical, but it's the polar opposite. All my life, men have looked at my face and figure. They were attracted to me because of the way I looked." He started to say something, but I put my finger over his lips. It sent chills down my spine. I had to take a breath. "They liked me for what I was, not who I was."

"Oh, so I did say the wrong thing."

"Let me finish, please." He made a sweeping motion with his arm like a gentleman letting a lady pass by. "Thank you. I don't want to be anyone's object of affection." He looked puzzled. I figured he would. "I want to be his—your—subject of affection."

"That was beautiful. Are you sure you're not the professor?"

It made me smile, but I had to get to my point. "I want to be more than just a pretty face."

"You are."

I shot him a glance for interrupting, and he apologized. "You're a good man, Dallas, and any woman would kill to date you."

"Any woman but you?"

"Would you please stop interrupting and analyzing each and every word I say? Try to see the forest, not just the trees." He started to say something but stopped himself. He acted like he was turning a key on a lock binding his lips. He put the imaginary key in his pocket. "You have no idea of who I am or what I've done in my past. I'm not good enough for you, Dallas. And one day, sooner or later, you'll come to realize that. I know you preach on forgiveness and mercy, but it's one thing to preach it and another to give it. My father taught me that years ago."

"My turn."

"I'm not finished."

"No, but you can take a break. You have a desire—a need to be in charge, to be in control." This time, he put his finger on my lips. I felt the same surge of electricity surging through my body. "I'm not your father. Susan's told me about him. Secondly, as far as I'm concerned your past is the past. You want to bring it up, do so. I'll never push you to do it. I'm more concerned with your present and your future." Now, he was saying all the right things. I swallowed and tried not to cry.

"I have too much baggage. Don't waste your time with me."

He leaned in and hugged me. I didn't fight it. It felt good. "It's my time, and I will never consider being with you a waste of it. Can we start over and have supper with Susan? She's about to break her neck smashing her ear against the window."

"I'd love that." It was true. "May I ask one thing. I know it sounds awful, but here it goes. Why do you like me?"

"That's easy, and it's not just about your looks. You're smart, stubborn, fierce, great with kids, and a wonderful friend to a woman who desperately needs one. I could go on and on, but the point is I like you, Abbey Rhodes, and I'd love to spend a lot of time getting to know you better if you'll let me."

I nodded. I couldn't say anything. This was a beautiful moment, and I was determined that no one was going to ruin it for me.

My phone chimed with a text message. I didn't recognize the number. It chimed again and again—all in all, it chimed six times. It was a long message. The person called me by name, so they knew who I was. Whoever it was spent five paragraphs congratulating me on a case that was well solved. A final text rang through.

My Dear Abbey, I see you're still standing in the shadows of others. We can't have that; now can we? Let me be your Moriarty—your Lord Voldemort. You may be great now, but I can make you a legend.

I couldn't believe who signed the message.

Dallas leaned in over my shoulder. "Who's Skylar?"

Points to Ponder

1. How is Abbey's secret past affecting her present relationships? What does she fear? What else do you think Abbey is hiding?
2. I titled the book *The Least of These* to direct you to its themes. What are some possible themes? Use the text to support your answer.
3. Susan introduces Abbey to Dallas Gatlin. How might Dallas change the relationship between Abbey and Susan?
4. Dallas gives a new interpretation of the Bible story with the woman caught in adultery. How is it different from Abbey's father's views? How might this new interpretation offer freedom for Abbey?
5. Holding grudges hurts the victim more than the one who caused the hurt. How does the novel reveal that message? Do you believe it is true?
6. I believe every life has value, but not everyone agrees with that statement. How is that conflict shown through the lives of Denzel, Dean, Stacey, and Susan?
7. God is still working on Abbey, leading her toward reconciliation with Him and her past. Where is this shown in the book? How are Sam, Susan, and Dallas integral to Abbey's growth?
8. What is your opinion of Dallas? Is he a good match for Abbey? What is your prediction for their future?
9. What part of the book affected you most? Why?
10. What do you think Skylar's return will mean for Abbey?

A Message from the Author

Thank you for investing in the first two books of the *Abbey Rhodes Mystery* series. I wrote these stories for you. Without an audience, I lose purpose. When you read the books, my tales come to life, and I feel as though we have connected in some way. After all, connecting with you and sharing Abbey's struggles and successes are my goals. I hope we continue this journey together and more readers join us along the way. That happens best by word of mouth. Please, tell others you know about the series and encourage them to read them.

As you can see from the end of book two, *The Least of These*, Abbey's story continues. I hope and pray you invest in Abbey and follow her further journeys toward reconciliation and growth. In the meantime, I have two favors to ask of you:

1. post an honest review of the previous books wherever you purchased them;
2. Go to my website and sign up for my newsletter (www. mitchellskarnesauthor.com) to stay to date on all things Abbey Rhodes. While you're there, send me a note and tell me what you think of Abbey's journey so far, or ask a question that's plaguing you. I'd love to hear from you.

As a thank you for investing in the *Abbey Rhodes Mystery* series so far, please turn the page for a sneak peek at book three, *The Cleansing*.

The Cleansing

"It can't be Skylar?" I said with a mix of doubt and terror. *How did she get a phone? How did she get my number? What did she mean? Focus!* "She's still in NCDC."

"Who is she, Abbey? What's NCDC?" Dallas asked.

I stared at the text, waiting for the punchline—for someone to say, "Just kidding." It never came. This was no cruel joke. This was my nightmare coming true. Dallas pressed me again.

"NCDC is Nashville's Correctional Development Center for females. Skylar is a teenage inmate who thinks she and I have some sort of connection."

I looked up from the phone and lost myself in Dallas's eyes, those rich brown eyes. They were a brief respite from the terrifying prospect of Skylar having access to technology. Then, the gravity of that thought pulled me back to reality.

"She was instrumental in the death of two people. One was her own mother."

"Did you put her away?"

I nodded.

"Do you think she's out for revenge?"

I shrugged my shoulders. Was She? Did she still think we had some sort of attachment?

"Why is she texting you, Abbey?"

He continued to press me for answers I didn't have.

"Surely those facilities don't let the women have phones."

He began pacing back and forth. I could tell his mind was racing too. He stopped, put his hands on my shoulders.

"And how in the world did she get your number?"

It was a great question. I knew he wasn't criticizing me, but his tone put me on the defensive. I'm sure he didn't mean to consciously, but he was acting like it was my fault—like I invited her to text me anytime she wanted. I tried to explain that I never encouraged a relationship with the girl. But that wasn't exactly true. At first, I felt sorry for her plight and somehow projected my own abusive past onto her. Her rape tapped the intense pain from my past. But we were very different people. What was she now, seventeen? Eighteen?

"Abbey, how did she get your number?" he asked again.

"I don't know!" I shouted.

About the Author

Mitchell S. Karnes is a husband, father of seven, and grandfather of nine. Mitchell uses his experience and insights as a minister, counselor, and educator to write and speak on challenging issues and concerns with an ever-growing audience. He has published six novels, three short stories, a one-act play, and numerous Bible study lessons.

Through two separate battles against Non-Hodgkin's Lymphoma, God has given Mitchell a new perspective on life that challenges him to create stories not only to entertain audiences but call them to action. Mitchell's mission is to reach and reconcile those who have been disillusioned with God and His church and inspire the church to live out the love of Christ Jesus in a broken and hurting world.

Connect with Mitchell online at:
mitchellskarnesauthor.com

Also available from

WordCrafts Press

A Mystery on Church Street
by Gail Kittleson

Angela's Treasures
by Marian Rizzo

Canelands
by Gerry Harlan Brown

Oh to Grace
by Abby Rosser

The Endurants
by KL Palmer

WordCrafts.net

www.ingramcontent.com/pod-product-compliance
Lightning Source LLC
LaVergne TN
LVHW090806030725
815177LV00001B/4